Seeking Exile

S. Mia McCroskey

ISBN: 0996304002

ISBN-13: 978-0-9963040-0-9

DEDICATION

To my mother, Dorothy Susan McCroskey, who said: "Smart people are never bored, they find something to do." So I did.

CONTENTS

ACKNOWLEDGMENTS

I am forever grateful to Herb Shick, my first sailing instructor at the California Sailing Academy in Marina del Rey, California. Herb took me beyond the classroom basics and nurtured my growing enthusiasm for harnessing the wind. I also thank Arthur Karpf, who, after my own cross country move to New York, provided years of boat maintenance advice and guidance. He also took me on as racing crew, giving me the opportunity to experience what it's like to crew a winning sailboat. Finally I am grateful to the dozens of sailing buddies from the Academy Sailing Club, St. Barts Sailing, and The Sailing Club: the three clubs that have provided me with the sailing adventures from which this story is drawn.

ONE: SEVERANCE

"Beth, as you know we've been mandated by senior management to make another round of budget cuts. I regret to inform you that because of this, your position is being eliminated. You have an appointment with Personnel in fifteen minutes. They will review the exit procedure with you," Marc Sexton stood up and extended his hand across his desk.

If I sit perfectly still it will all just vanish. I'll be at my own desk with the production schedule in front of me.

Beth stared for way too long at Marc Sexton's hand. Just as it started to droop she gave a slight shake of her head and stood up.

Not happening. Not happening. Not. Hap. Pening.

"Beth, I want you to know that it has been a pleasure working with you. If there's ever anything I can do ..." his voice trailed off as she shook his hand, her eyes riveted on it to avoid his face.

"So I should go right to Personnel?" she asked, her voice embarrassingly weak. She wanted to look him in the eye. She wanted to make him work for this, not simply accept his dismissal and slink away.

"Yes, that would be appropriate," he replied succinctly. She released his hand and turned away, hoping he couldn't see her tail tucked in between her legs.

Beth stabbed the button for the fourteenth floor, grateful that she was alone in the elevator, knowing that her face was flushed with controlled emotion. *Dammit! Why can't I react the way I imagine? Quiet dignity – that's all I wanted. How hard would it have been to look him in the eye and make him squirm in the face of MY strength?*

In Personnel Miss Huff made her dismissal seem like a golden opportunity. She presented Beth with an envelope full of brochures about unemployment and outplacement services and forms for the dispersal of her 401K account and continuation of medical benefits. Beth felt as if she were expected to skip out of the building freed of the burden of her company ID, corporate credit card, and regular paycheck, blowing kisses to the security guards in the lobby as she went.

Beth was intimately familiar with the management speak used to tart up waves of layoffs to compensate for the enormous advances that Trident Publishing was paying to superstar authors. She had ceased caring about the dismal state of book publishing at least a year ago, just after the last reorganization. And as she carried her box of personal belongings down the subway steps she realized that she had ceased caring about her little piece of it – the timely preparation of jacket, catalog, and promotional copy for the several hundred mid-list books – a few months after that. She shoved herself and her box onto the rush-hour crowded train, ignoring a few glares as well as several pitying looks from other passengers. *Gee, do they know that I've been fired? Does the repurposed copier paper box give it away? Or do I have "REJECT" stamped on my forehead?*

"To be fair, he probably meant it when he said he regretted having to do it," she told her sister Trish over the phone that evening. She heard Trish snort in derision as she took another gulp of beer from her third bottle.

"That's what they always say, Beth. It's, like, in some handbook somewhere," Trish said. "If he regrets it it's because that's one less person reporting to him. It takes him down as a manager."

"When did you become so cynical?" Beth asked.

"After the second time I was laid off. Give it time, kiddo."

"I've lost my nerve, Trish. I've always gotten out before the axe fell before – remember my first job?"

After three years in her first job out of college Beth had realized that the light at the end of the tunnel was an oncoming bankruptcy. She had sought and secured another job, and given notice just a week before the company went bust. The oncoming train had plowed through all of her former co-workers, leaving them without paychecks for that final week of work.

"That whole thing was such a disaster," Trish agreed. "But it's not a question of nerve, it's reading the signs correctly. Maybe you just don't understand the New York subtext."

An image of a busy Manhattan street crowded with New Yorkers, all sporting word balloons over their heads distracted Beth.

"Supertext," she muttered absently, watching the imagined word balloons bobbing along over the heads of the imagined crowd.

"What?"

"Nothing. I'm just worn out, Trish. I think I need a beer."

"Yes, you deserve one. But just one – you know alcohol is a depressant. It won't help, in the long run."

Beth arched a single eyebrow as she looked at the row of empty bottles on the coffee table in front of her. "Thanks for the lecture," she grumbled, and then winced at herself. On the other end of the line she could hear her sister scowling at her. "Sorry," she added.

Trish sighed audibly. "It's okay kiddo. I'm going to call you in the morning. What are you doing this evening? Is there someone you can hang out with?"

Beth shrugged, then arched her back to reach beneath herself and fish the TV remote out from between the sofa cushions. "Sure. I'll call Eva," she lied, aiming the remote at the TV in anticipation.

"Good. I love you, Beth. Everything is going to be just fine."

"Thanks Trish," Beth simultaneously turned off the phone and turned on the TV.

Pedantic as her older sister could be, Beth loved Trish and appreciated the insights she sometimes offered. As her eyes followed the flickering wheel spinning on the television, Beth contemplated her sister's suggestion. After five years in New York, she did still feel like an alien most of the time. Although she'd been pleased and excited to be offered a place in publishing in New York City, she'd come here with a chip of California firmly stuck to her shoulder. And she was still clinging to the sliver of it that remained. New Yorkers were so – so – driven. *Yes, put a positive spin on it. Just because you mean "crazy," you don't have to be derogatory.* Back in Los Angeles the signs that the one-hundred-person publishing company was failing had been as plain as the burnt brown lawn in front of the building.

Only the CEO had maintained the self-delusional myth that investors were about to knock on the door – begging her to stay with offers of stock options and a marketing junket to Japan. She'd sat in his office and imagined getting stranded in Tokyo, her employers suddenly unable to cover the cost of her return flight. If she'd believed he'd really send her she might have accepted just for the adventure. Or at least she liked to think so. But instead she'd just smiled and refused his worthless stock options. She'd run directly to the bank with her severance check, which promptly bounced. Fortunately, the bank clerk had taken pity on her and arranged to find the money to cover it in one of the company's other accounts. Hers was the last check any employee was able to cash, and it had helped finance her move east. Trident Publishing had provided a stipend, but it had proven inadequate for relocating and putting down the deposit on her New York apartment.

And from the start, she reflected now, she had never really understood what her sister called the "New York subtext." Because in New York when a company was on the skids the signs were much more subtle. The office supply cabinet was not restocked, the coffee supply in the break area ran out a few days before being replenished. The maintenance service was not called when the photocopier jammed. But everyone from the CEO on down acted like it was business as usual right up until layoffs happened. She had thought that LA was the land of appearances, but she had quickly learned that for all New York's vaunted claims of deep substance and culture, looks were everything here, too.

Beth allowed herself to wallow in self-pity for the next week, right up until an hour before her first appointment with the outplacement service. This was one of the many advantages of being laid off: her former employer was footing the bill for several sessions with a placement consulting firm. Together, according to the brochure, they would re-craft her resume and sharpen her interview skills. And they would evaluate her strengths to help her shape the course of her future. Beth imagined a pair of hands attempting to shape a glop of vanilla pudding that just kept running back into the bowl.

TWO: CITY ISLAND

"You sure don't know how to sell yourself, do you?"

The brassy-haired, chain-smoking headhunter eyed Beth from across her office. They were fifteen minutes into the interview and she had yet to sit down.

"I guess not," Beth said, aghast at the woman's blatant criticism.

She had sent her re-crafted resume in response to an advertisement in the New York Times, and been called to this interview with Magda Brooks, Executive Recruiter. When she'd told Mr. Fitch, her outplacement counselor, he'd blanched, then recovered himself and jumped ahead in his curriculum to spend a frantic half-hour coaching her for the interview. But the damage had been done – he didn't think she was ready for a live interview with a headhunter. And the headhunter obviously didn't think she was ready for an interview with her client.

"Look, they want someone who knows how to market concepts and programs to their employees. Can you do that?" Her tone suggested that if Beth couldn't sell herself, she couldn't possibly sell anything else.

"I have six years experience preparing marketing materials for all kinds of books. Every one of them was a new concept that I had to grasp and then describe in terms that would first appeal to the bookstore buyers, and then to the buying public. I can sell ideas, Ms Brooks."

Beth sucked in a breath after delivering her speech, her eyes flicking over to meet the headhunter's and then dodging away.

"Eye contact!" Ms Brooks snapped, dropping down into the chair behind her desk.

"Pardon?" Beth looked Ms Brooks in the eye.

"You would be more convincing if you would look me in the eye."

"I see," Beth resisted the urge to drop her gaze to her lap. And then she noticed that Ms Brooks's eyes were the color of split pea soup and she couldn't look away.

Ms Brooks scribbled something on a large self-stick note and held it out to her.

Go ahead, paste it on my forehead. Beth took the note and read it. It was a man's name, a company name, and an address, date, and time.

"Here's your shot at it," the recruiter said. "Do some homework on them, and do your best. I'll call you when I hear something."

"Thank you Ms Brooks." Sensing that the interview was over, Beth rose and slipped out of the office, forcing herself to glance one last time at those pea-soup eyes.

The second interview – the real interview, Beth preferred to think – went remarkably well. Beth tried not to be awed by the enormity of the mid-town corporate headquarters, but she couldn't help it. For all its pride and high-minded ideals, publishing was a poor business. Certainly the small company in California had had none of the trappings of corporate America, but even Trident Publishing was a modest enterprise. The very walls of this top tier financial institution radiated respectability, establishment, and wealth. She was escorted over thick, bouncy carpets and met with three managers in lushly decorated offices. She shook many hands, sipped water from a logo-emblazoned mug, and chatted knowledgeably about marketing trends and techniques.

When her telephone rang the following afternoon and Ms Brooks curtly informed her of the offer they had made all she could do was grin. The money was better than her old job and she could not help feeling eager to bounce along those rich halls every day.

"This is your desk. The phone number is on the phone. Support should have set up the PC for you, but if you have any trouble dial extension thirty-three. There's a staff meeting at ten in the conference room. It's over in the corner – see the door?"

Beth looked from the end of Tom Archer's pointing finger across the heads of other workers at a door in the far corner of the windowless work area.

Beneath her feet the thin grayish carpet tiles were almost as hard as cement. A dozen desks were arranged at angles to one-another so that no worker was directly facing another. In addition to the conference room, there were six more doors in the perimeter walls, half of them standing ajar to reveal offices lit by external windows. The decorator who'd worked on the offices where she'd been interviewed had sent his least able assistant to this space. The framed prints on the walls in between the office doors looked like they'd been bought at a hotel bankruptcy sale.

Beth overcame her disappointment by visualizing her paycheck. By the end of the day she was able to convince herself that the lackluster environment was offset by the substance of the job. She had been assigned to three projects and handed several thick manuals to review in order to learn the company's systems.

It was easy to bury herself in the new job for the next few weeks. There was a lot to learn and a lot of people to get to know. Beth came home each night completely drained and spent her weekends catching up on the personal chores that she neglected during the week.

"You really bounced back, Beth!" Trish declared on the phone at the end of her first week. "I knew you would. You can probably stick with this company for the rest of your career, if you work smart."

Beth shuddered at the notion, but she knew her sister meant well. Finding a corporate home with pension and health insurance was Trish's idea of career success. Beth appreciated the benefits of such a future, but just the same it seemed stifling. When she imagined herself in ten years she did not see grey carpet tiles and bad prints, or even the dense carpet and fine décor of the managers' offices. She wasn't quite sure what she saw, but she knew it wasn't a comfortable corporate job.

On the Friday afternoon at the end of her fourth week as she dragged two catalogs and three credit card offers out of her mailbox a white number ten envelope dropped to the floor. The stylish logo of her apartment building's management company formed the return address. Upstairs in her living room she slipped a finger under the sealed flap, slicing the back of the top knuckle as she opened it. She pulled the single folded sheet out and stuck her injured finger in her mouth while she read the letter.

Lease renewal. Monthly increase – a hundred and ten dollars!

She groaned, plopping onto the sofa still wearing her coat. The increase in her salary had been largely whittled away by taxes and other deductions. Now she saw the last of it and more trickling through her fingers. She had planned on saving. She had planned on using her vacation time, when it accrued, for travel.

She needed to find a cheaper apartment. In New York City, in a hot market – or so her co-workers told her when she related her dilemma to them on Monday.

"Get a roommate," Sandy the assistant suggested. She lived with two other girls and a guy in a two bedroom fifth floor walkup in the East Village. Beth was not willing to share her one-bedroom with anyone who had not made a serious personal commitment.

"Try Hell's Kitchen," Jeff the gay graphic designer put in.

"Oh come on Jeff, I know the neighborhood is getting better, but Beth's a single woman," Carla the matronly copywriter chided. Beth hated to admit that Carla was right, but she would never consider living in a neighborhood where the drug dealers on the corners outnumbered the hookers, and they collectively outnumbered the non-using, non-john residents.

"Here's something," Frank the straight designer with the acerbic sense of humor said, tugging a notice off of the break room bulletin board. "Thirty-six foot sailboat for rent or sale. Live-aboard option. Located on City Island. Where's that?"

"The Bronx," someone replied.

"Ugh," someone else said.

"I grew up in The Bronx," Carla said, silencing any further open criticism. "City Island is cool."

"Let's see," Beth said, taking the notice from Frank. He frowned at her and she realized that he'd intended it as a joke. For a moment she considered reading the notice and laughing, just to assure him that she understood his intention. But then she pictured City Island.

For several weeks two summers ago she and Peter, her now ex-boyfriend, had taken the subway and a bus out to City Island for sailing lessons. She had enjoyed every moment of it – from the long ride that made it seem like an adventure, to sailing on open water within sight of the Manhattan skyline, to mastering the jargon and equipment. She had discovered a previously untapped talent: an understanding of wind and water and the dynamics of making a sailboat move. Peter, however, had mostly been frustrated by it, and when he'd lost interest she had allowed herself to stop seeking sailing opportunities.

But Peter was out of her life now, and she needed a new place to live.

City Island would not be an easy commute, but neither was her apartment in suburban Queens. The notice did not specify a monthly rental price and Beth had no idea what the going rate might be. As the lunch crowd dispersed she tucked the notice in her pocket and in the rush of day-to-day business that afternoon she forgot about it.

At the end of the week she was going through her bag looking for an earring that she'd dropped into it late Thursday afternoon when she found the notice. During the course of the week she had checked the rental listings in several newspapers and done an Internet search. The results had been grim. To find an apartment that was cheaper than hers she would have to move out of New York entirely, and the prospect of uprooting herself and moving to New Jersey after relocating from California was just too hard to swallow.

As she re-read the notice about the boat on City Island her hand moved to the telephone. Before she knew it she was dialing the number.

THREE: DOUBLE TROUBLE

"It's not fancy," Mrs. Thomson, the boat's owner, explained. "I never wanted it, but my ex-husband did, so my lawyer made certain that I got it in the settlement. Would you like to see it? I suppose you should before agreeing to take it."

"Yes, I suppose I should," Beth heard herself saying.

"If you tell me when you want to go by I'll tell the marina manager," Mrs. Thomson said, "He's there Saturday morning if you want to go tomorrow. He'll give you the key."

Beth had agreed to this plan before she had time to fully assess it. But as she hung up the telephone she realized that she had little else to do on Saturday. A ride out to City Island would be nostalgic.

Sometimes she missed Peter terribly – he had been clever and romantic, sometimes, and she had truly enjoyed his company. But he had also been remarkably self-centered, and that was what had eventually driven her away.

As she watched the neighborhoods of The Bronx go by outside of the elevated subway on Saturday morning she resolved to enjoy the visit to the island for the things that it had meant to her, not because she had always traveled there with Peter. At the end of the subway line she transferred to the city bus that went through Pelham Bay Park and along City Island Avenue. Half way along she glanced at the directions she had jotted down and pulled the cord to request the next stop. A few minutes later the bus growled away leaving her standing on a quiet corner. There was a small market cattycorner to where she had gotten off and two restaurants in the previous block on the avenue. The rest of the buildings were a mix of one-story office and storefronts and single-family wood frame houses. This was further out the long, narrow island than the marina where she and Peter had learned to sail, but it looked much the same.

Double-checking the addresses she walked along the side street, eventually seeing the entrance to a marina at the end. Before she reached it the neighborhood had transitioned from quaint cottages to an industrial marine zone, with a vacant lot serving as parking for two boats up on wooden blocks and a travelift – a hoist on wheels that lifted boats from the water and moved them to parking on dry land.

She realized that the marina must use the lot for winter storage, although in mid-June most of the boats were in the water.

Inside the marina's wide-open gates she located a small, business-like office. A lone, middle-aged man sat at a computer behind a desk placed at an angle to the front door. As she turned and shut the door she saw the familiar interface of a popular email program on his screen. He saw her and touched a button on the monitor and the display went dark.

"Can I help you?" he asked, his tone acknowledging that she was an outsider.

"I'm looking for a boat. The owner said she'd call and tell you to give me the key."

"Trouble," he replied enigmatically. He rose as he spoke, going to a file cabinet against the wall behind him.

"I'm sorry?" Beth wasn't sure what he meant.

"That's the boat," he replied, fishing a set of keys from a folder inside the cabinet. "*Double Trouble.*"

"Oh. Mrs. Thomson didn't say."

"But she's the only owner who's called and told me to give a visitor the keys."

"I see. Well, that must be the right boat then. Can you tell me how to find her?"

"Mrs. Thomson?"

"*Double Trouble.*"

"Oh. Right. It's on the right dock, about half way down on the left. There are mostly powerboats along there, so she ought to stand out."

"Thank you," Beth accepted the offered keys.

"My name's Sid. If I'm out when you come back just drop them through the mail slot."

"Will do, Sid. I'm Beth. Beth Anderson."

"Nice to meet you Beth. Are you looking for a boat?"

"Not really. I'm looking for a place to live. Mrs. Thompson advertised the possibility of renting it."

Sid sucked in his cheeks and nodded slightly. "Another liveaboard. She should have let me know."

"Is it a problem?" It had never occurred to Beth that there might be rules about living aboard boats.

"No. But I like to know about it when I assign slips. You'll let me know what you decide. Have a good look at that boat, then," he said.

"Is it a good boat?"

"It's a good make, well cared for up until she took over. Since then it's been sitting, so there will be some issues. You can have it surveyed if you want." Something in the way he said it made her think he thought she should.

"Thanks. I'll let you know what I decide and we can talk more."

She glanced at the corroded metal slot in the office door as she stepped out.

She had dug her topsiders out of the back of her closet just so that she wouldn't look like a complete landlubber. The leather uppers and rubber soles had hardened through disuse and even during the short walks she'd taken so far they had given her a blister on her heel. Trying hard not to grimace at the discomfort she crunched over lose stone chippings that concealed a world of environmentally damaging paint and fuel spills and descended a splintery wooden ramp down to the floating docks where the boats were secured.

As promised, about half way down the right dock in a gap in the row of hunching powerboats she looked down at the deck of a sailboat. It was dwarfed by the tall, wide boats all around it – so much so that Beth felt pity for it.

Shaking the notion from her head, she walked out the finger dock and stopped alongside a latch in the white lifeline that encircled the deck at about knee height. The latch mechanism was obvious, but something made her pause.

Am I really considering this? She asked herself, letting her hand rest on the top of a stainless steel stanchion as she looked around. At first she thought the dock was awfully deserted for a Saturday afternoon, but gradually she recognized signs of habitation. Water spurting from a fitting near the waterline on the powerboat on the left meant that its engine was running. Just over the low drone of that machine she could hear music – bright pop with a lot of guitar – coming from a boat across the way. A light breeze rustled flags attached to boats and on flagpoles all around her and not far away a seagull squawked angrily. The air was alive with the odor of salt, diesel fumes, and the tang of decaying sea life.

Yes. I really am. She hastily unfastened the latches on both top and bottom lifelines and stepped aboard *Double Trouble.*

The deck and cockpit showed signs of neglect – a line of bird droppings just below the bare boom, a torn canvas cover on the compass and wheel, decayed plastic covers over instruments mounted in the bulkhead. Dead leaves and other debris had collected in the corners of the cockpit foot well. And yet, each of the multitude of lines was coiled neatly, and the fiberglass seemed to be in good condition beneath the dirt.

The key ring Sid had given her included two keys: one large and one small. Looking around she realized that the small one fit several small locks on the compartments in the cockpit. The large one worked in the padlock securing the companionway, which she now unlocked. She set the lock and keys aside and slid the hatch back, which allowed her to lift the three wooden boards out of grooves framing the companionway to reveal the interior of the boat.

It was dim down there, and she hadn't thought to bring a flashlight. There was also the faint odor of mildew and something else that was even less pleasant. She stepped carefully down the steps and alighted on the cabin floor.

I should have asked if there was power, she chastised herself. I'm not going to be able to make a decision in the dark.

Just then, to her left a small space heater sitting on a counter clicked on. She followed the cord to an ordinary outlet on the wall – *bulkhead* – next to a panel of switches. *If there's power for that, there must be for lights,* she decided, and reached up to find the switch on a fixture on the ceiling. Nothing.

Master switch, she thought, looking again at the panel. Sure enough, when she flipped one marked DC Main and another marked Cabin Lights, the fixture came to life. Feeling victorious for having puzzled it out, Beth worked her way around the boat switching on lights.

The interior showed the same signs of good care overlaid by recent neglect. There were a lot of wooden surfaces all stained and varnished in a warm maple shade. The rest of the surfaces – the ceiling and walls mainly – were a creamy off-white shade of fiberglass. Although Beth had previously sailed only on small day sailors, she had an instant appreciation for the economy of space on *Double Trouble*. Every inch was put to use, with enclosed cabinets and open shelves tucked against every wall, and glass racks behind the fold-up dining table, and drawers that had to be lifted slightly to pull out so that they didn't slide out on their own in rough seas. The little heater, she quickly realized, was there to ward off the inevitable damp, but it seemed to be fighting a losing battle against the mildew. She found it when she looked into the cabinets in the heads and the drawers under the berth in the forward cabin.

She lifted the floor panel in the middle of the main cabin and saw a few inches of water in the bilge below. There was also a white floating switch that should turn on the pump if the water rose much more. Beth knew that it was normal for a boat – particularly one that was a few years old -- to have a little water in the bilge, so she replaced the cover and stood in the middle of the cabin wondering what else she should look at.

She suddenly felt woefully inadequate. She didn't know a thing about taking care of a boat. Resisting the urge to give up on this mad scheme, she tried to think about how she would evaluate an apartment. *Check all the faucets, flush all the toilets.*

She stepped into the galley and turned the cold-water handle on the faucet. Nothing happened. Water pressure. How do you get pressure on a boat at sea level?

She turned back to the panel of switches and smiled as she flipped the one labeled Fresh Water. Somewhere within the cabinetry an electric motor hummed to life. She tried the faucet again and got a trickle of water. Encouraged, she shut it off and returned to one of the two small head compartments. The toilet looked normal enough, although it lacked a tank. Next to it there was a pump with a small lever below the main pump handle and labels for "flush" and "dry bowl."

Beth lifted the lid and looked into the bowl, which was stained grey about an inch above the narrow round opening in the bottom. She tentatively tried pumping the handle, noting that the lever was on the "dry bowl" setting.

The pump wheezed and groaned and the small amount of water standing in the bottom of the bowl gurgled. Emboldened, she switched the lever and tried again. After a couple pumps brownish water swirled into the bowl from under the rim just like in a regular toilet. It quickly filled the bowl half way so she flipped the lever back to dry bowl before pumping more. She felt inordinately proud as the bowl emptied.

She repeated the procedure on the other head and jumped back when water spurted at her from around the base of the pump. She calmed down quickly when she realized that it was just seawater, not raw sewage. But even so it would have to be fixed. This head was *en suite* with the forward cabin that she imagined sleeping in.

And at that moment Beth realized that she wanted *Double Trouble*.

FOUR: COMMUNITY

"I don't know, Beth, it's awfully small," Eva Hamilton said, looking over the top of the box she was holding at the companionway opening. Down in the cabin Beth took the box and carried it over to set it on the port settee, which was already piled with boxes.

"It's just because I haven't unpacked," she said, knowing that she only sounded as convincing as she felt, which was not very. "When I get everything put away it will be just fine – I've downsized, and put the rest of my stuff in storage. How much room do I need, anyway?"

Eva smiled noncommittally as she climbed down the steps and looked around. When Beth had called Mrs. Thomson back to discuss renting *Double Trouble* to live aboard, the owner had informed her that she had decided that she wanted to sell, not rent. Beth's disappointed silence on the other end of the line must have surprised her, because she quickly went on to suggest that she could be flexible. Beth could begin making payments, until she secured a loan to buy the boat outright. Mrs. Thomson would give her seventy-five percent credit on whatever she'd paid so far. The deal reminded Beth of the lease-to-buy arrangement her parents had made for her flute in high school. Except that Mrs. Thomson's asking price for *Trouble* was considerably more than her flute. Beth had spent the better part of a day researching loan rates and storage facilities, and stayed after hours at the office plugging numbers into a spreadsheet on her office computer. She had concluded, with some anxiety, that she could swing it. Assuming a bank agreed with her, and *Trouble* passed a marine survey.

She'd called the marina office for a heart-to-heart talk with Sid about *Double Trouble*'s prospects. He wasn't nearly as negative as she'd feared he would be. Rather, he gave her the names of a couple marine surveyors and told her about the boat's repair history since taking up residence in his marina. She scribbled three pages of notes with double underlining on things that sounded important, although she really had no idea. She decided that she should move aboard and get to know the boat before deciding whether to go ahead. If she changed her mind she'd be out the rent for however many months she stayed, but that would be the same in an apartment, and Mrs. Thomson was not demanding a security deposit.

She had insisted that Mrs. Thomson have the boat professionally cleaned and have the head repaired, to which the owner agreed. So the cabin that Eva looked around at was considerably different from the one that Beth had first entered. The woodwork gleamed, the fiberglass bulkheads were shiny, and the whole boat smelled of lemony disinfectant. But even so Beth could see Eve grimacing at the modest space.

"What about electricity?" she asked, eying a brass oil lamp hanging over where the table folded down. Beth had found the lamp tucked away in a storage locker and brought it out.

"The boat is plugged in to the power on the dock," she explained, flipping the appropriate switches to turn on all of the lights.

"Oh," Eve seemed to soften a little. "And plumbing?"

"One hundred fifty gallon water tank."

"How do you refill it?"

"With a hose." Beth had no idea how long it would take her to use a hundred fifty gallons of water, but she refused to imagine herself wrestling a hose across an icy dock. In fact, she had not discussed her winter options with Mrs. Thomson because she doubted the woman had a clue. She needed to talk to Sid.

"You're a brave woman, Beth," Eva said. "Now what were you saying about a cheap seafood place around here?"

"Hello aboard *Double Trouble*, anyone home?" The call of a friendly woman's voice was accompanied by a light rapping on the hull. Beth shut off the sewing machine and went to stick her head out through the companionway.

"Hello?" she replied.

"Good morning dear, I'm Susan Goldberg, from *Second Million*," the visitor standing on the finger pier pointed up the dock toward one of the hulking powerboats, Beth wasn't sure which one. She had seen that name painted on the back of one of them in dollar green, however.

"Good morning," she replied to the buxom, middle aged woman with bottle-red curls. She was carrying a shopping bag. "Nice to meet you. I'm Beth Anderson. I moved aboard last week."

"Yes dear, we know," Susan Goldberg said in a tone that conveyed that she was the self-appointed queen of the marina. "It's good to see someone taking care of *Trouble* again. We all miss Bill."

Beth easily heard the unspoken message – that Mrs. Bill was not missed.

"Has anyone invited you to Sunday brunch yet?" Susan went on.

"No – I haven't been around that much," Beth replied, instantly annoyed with herself for assuming the responsibility for the lack of an invite. In fact, she had not been around because she had to leave before seven thirty in the morning to catch the express bus. She had missed the return express every night that week and ended up taking the much slower subway and city bus. If her budget could possibly afford it, she would buy a cheap car and drive to a more efficient transportation hub. But in any case she had only been around the marina in the late evenings and at night, and she wasn't the type to hang around the docks hoping to make friends.

In fact, she'd undertaken several projects on behalf of *Trouble*. Susan Goldberg had interrupted one that was turning out to be more work than she'd expected. She was making covers to conceal the worn brown and cream tweed upholstered settee cushions using Eva's borrowed sewing machine.

"It's a potluck, every Sunday up on the patio – the wooden deck with the coke and ice machines. Everyone comes by with their own coffee or whatever and brings something to share. My specialty is corn muffins," Susan leaned closer across the lifelines and lowered her voice, "I advise you to avoid Aaron Stein's latkes."

"I will, thank you," Beth replied. "Would you like to come aboard? I'm just in the middle of some projects, so it's a bit messy, but –."

"Oh, no – I don't want to impose. I'll drop by again when you've gotten settled. But I wanted to give you this," she raised the shopping bag and set it on the deck.

Beth dutifully climbed out into the cockpit to retrieve the bag. It contained a supply of goodies that included preserves, quick cookie mix, some gourmet spices, and an assortment of fresh fruit.

"It's just a little welcome basket, without the wicker," Susan explained. "The market up the street isn't strong on luxuries, but this should tide you over until some makes a run to Trader Joes."

"This is so thoughtful," Beth replied, truly touched. She'd never been welcomed like this when she moved to a new apartment in Los Angeles or New York. "What time is brunch tomorrow?"

"Around eleven thirty," Susan replied. "You'll come then?"

"Sure. I look forward to meeting everyone."

"That's wonderful. I'll spread the word to expect you. And I'll let you get back to your projects now. Have a good day," Susan waved as she set off down the dock.

"Bye," Beth called after her, then took the shopping bag back down the companionway. She set it in the cluttered galley and went back to the sewing machine. She had set herself a goal of finishing the sewing today so that she could return the machine to Eve tonight.

Second Million, she repeated to herself as she worked. *But not second wife, I'd guess. Unless she's the one who's made the money.* Suddenly she was curious to meet more of the marina inhabitants.

Brunch felt to Beth more like the weekly convening of the marina ladies social club, Susan Goldberg, chairwoman. Susan sat in state on a white plastic chair pulled up to one end of the wooden picnic table on the deck. Women Beth had not met, but had seen around, sat on either side of her on the benches. A couple of men were standing over by the soft drink machine holding coffee mugs and talking. Another was taking a bag of ice out of the ice machine next to it. Herb Goldberg was hovering behind Susan holding a carafe with a trickle of steam rising from it.

Beth mounted the two steps onto the deck, her arrival catching Susan Goldberg's eye.

"Here she is: our newest neighbor. Beth, come meet everyone."

Smiling and nodding a greeting around the deck at everyone, Beth stepped over to the table and set down the plate of muffins she'd carried up from *Double Trouble* on the end of the table. They were from the mix that Susan had given her the day before.

The man who'd retrieved the bag of ice nodded at her as he carried it past her down the steps and toward the docks.

"Blueberry?" one of the men by the soda machine asked.

"Yes."

"My favorite. May I?"

"Of course!"

He set down his coffee mug and took one of the muffins.

"I'm Beth Anderson."

"You're on *Double Trouble*," he nodded, his thick fingers peeling the paper away from the muffin. Beth took in his deeply tanned skin and furz of greying beard stubble that suggested a moratorium on weekend shaving. He wore a plaid flannel shirt in muted colors over a white t-shirt and blue jeans that, based on the paint stains, had been around for several seasons. "I'm Phil Eaton. This is my wife Anna," he nodded at the woman sitting on Susan Goldberg's right. They were both in their late thirties, Beth estimated, both tanned and physically fit, and both dressed in well worn, inexpensive clothes.

"Hi. Nice to meet you," Beth said to her, then turned back to Phil, "Yes. I'm renting her, thinking about buying."

Herb Goldberg had come around the table with his carafe and a chipped ceramic mug. He poured coffee into it and handed it to Beth.

"Thank you," she said, raising it to take a careful sip. It was strong and black and the flavor nearly matched the delicious aroma.

"You going to race her like Bill did?" the other man asked.

"No, I'm just trying to get used to living on a boat."

"Give the girl a chance to get settled, Alan," Susan said. "She's still getting her sealegs."

"Why did you decide to move onto a boat then?" Alan asked, apparently uninterested in his neighbor's advice.

"I learned to sail a couple years ago, but didn't keep it up. I decided to get back into it." Beth tried out the answer that she had developed for her co-workers. They had accepted it, since none of them were boaters and therefore had no idea whether her rationale made any sense. Alan was not so easily placated.

"A lot of easier ways to get back into it!" he laughed. "Half the racers on the island are always looking for crew. Half of them will take anyone who can walk down a dock without falling in the water."

"Racing isn't the same as cruising Alan," Susan said. "Beth seems more like a cruiser to me."

Beth was grateful for Susan's interjection: it allowed her to calm her bristling nerves at Alan's confrontational manner.

"Really I just needed a cheaper place to live, and *Double Trouble* was available, and I thought I'd give it a try. I may be back on shore before the end of summer."

"I hope not!" Susan declared and, to Beth's surprise, Alan nodded along with all the others.

"You're going to love living on the water Beth," Anna said. "We all do."

All told the marina housed the three live-aboard couples and two single men, plus, Beth was pleased to learn, Sid the manager. As the brunch went on a few more crews arrived by car and proceeded down the docks to various sailboats, one person or another stopping to get a bag of ice. Beth realized as the boats departed the marina one by one that they were going out to race.

The party was enlarged by three or four other sailors who kept their boats in the marina but did not live aboard. The introductions swirled and Beth struggled to permanently attach names to faces. By one o'clock the crowd had dwindled to Susan and Margaret, Alan's wife, who were intently discussing something. Beth took her empty plate and waved a farewell, feeling drained from all the new faces. A strong sense of comfort swept over her as she climbed back aboard *Double Trouble*. She paused, standing on the lazarette in the cockpit with one hand on the boom. It was a feeling she had not experienced in longer than she could remember: she felt at home.

A week later Susan Goldberg and her husband Herb invited Beth to join them along with a couple other friends on a fireworks cruise on the fourth of July. Beth had been so busy with the move and work on the boat she hadn't made any other plans, so she accepted. They set out mid-afternoon, motoring their fifty-foot cruiser into the East River past LaGuardia airport and Riker's Island, the city prison. They passed through the junction of the East River and the Harlem river at a treacherous patch of water called Hell Gate and then motored on a swift current past the United Nations and mid-town Manhattan, the lower east side, under the Williamsburg, Manhattan, and Brooklyn Bridges, and finally out into New York Harbor. Beth was mesmerized by the site of the city from the water – an experience she'd only had once or twice before on the Staten Island Ferry. And this was totally different – they could go wherever they wanted in *Second Million*. Herb, who was a jovial little man completely at the beckon call of Susan, eagerly steered them along just a few yards off of the Battery so they could wave at the "landlubbers" lining Battery Park. They went on up the Hudson River for a while, taking in the sights of Manhattan's west side and the Palisades on the New Jersey side. As evening approached they returned to the harbor and Herb showed Beth how he anchored the big cruiser in the calm waters in between the Statue of Liberty and Ellis Island. From the flying bridge he lowered the anchor by pressing a button, then used the engine to back away from it until it dug into the muddy bottom. Beth appreciated his taking an interest in teaching her, but since *Double Trouble* lacked a flying bridge with anchor windlass controls the lesson was not that effective.

Susan presided over the galley while Herb uncovered a large propane grill mounted on the stern rail. They cooked up steaks and potato salad, corn, and a big tossed salad while their friend Tom mixed up drinks at their well-stocked bar. Beth and the third guest, Sylvia, were left to enjoy the late afternoon sun and the view of passing boat traffic.

Tom was a divorcee in his mid-forties with a prissy goatee and oddly hippyish, round, dark-lensed sunglasses that Beth had not yet seen him remove, even inside the boat. Although the glasses were a little off-putting, his ready laugh and kind smile balanced the effect to a degree.

Sylvia was the same age as Susan – she had told Beth so when she cornered her for what she described as a "get-acquainted" chat shortly after their departure. She had been widowed five years before, and with her children both grown she had needed to find new outlets. She'd returned to the Synagogue where she'd met her husband and this time met Susan and Herb. They had taken her in as an adopted sister.

Beth's protestant upbringing made her reluctant to share even such a mild personal detail with a stranger. As she listened to Sylvia's condensed biography her dread that the woman would expect her to reciprocate grew and grew. As soon as she could she excused herself as politely as possible.

They ate the Goldberg's meal seated around a folding table and chairs on the spacious aft deck, their conversation occasionally interrupted by boats passing very close by, airplanes flying banners overhead, and the wakes of the many ferries and excursion boats crisscrossing the deeper water.

The Harbor was alive with traffic, and Beth appreciated being settled at anchor to watch it. She couldn't imagine sailing out there, dodging the huge yellow Staten Island ferries as well as the occasional huge barge being pushed or pulled by a tug and the multitude of smaller craft weaving in and out of all the rest. She expressed this to her companions and Herb Goldberg patted her shoulder encouragingly.

"Now you've got *Trouble,* you need to get some more experience under your deck shoes," he said, grinning toothily at his nautical word play. "Thomas, do you have room in your crew for a novice?"

"Sure!" Tom smiled across the table at Beth. "*Huckleberry* can always take an extra body."

An intense rush of apprehension manifested itself in a wave of nausea. Beth set her fork down and took a deep breath.

"There you go, Beth – a few races with Tom and this kind of traffic won't make you blink," Herb went on, oblivious to her reaction.

"That would be great," she said with as much enthusiasm as she could manage.

"Now Herb," Susan said, "It sounds like you're pressuring Beth. She may not want to race."

"But it's the best experience, honey," Herb countered. "Right Tom?"

"Absolutely. Even if you never race your own boat, you'll learn to get the most efficient performance from her."

Tom's sincerity along with the logic of his and Herb's arguments calmed Beth's fear.

"When do you race?" she asked him.

"Almost every weekend. We've got the Manhasset Bay series next weekend. And we go out every Thursday night. You're definitely welcome to come along on those, they're pretty low-key."

"I'm not sure I could get home from work early enough," Beth replied – she was actually disappointed since the "low-key" races sounded like a better way to start.

"Can you leave at five?" Tom asked.

"Yes, probably. The express bus reaches my stop about quarter after, but it doesn't get to the Island until six thirty."

"Are you in mid-town? I can pick you up."

"Oh! Well, yes, that would work."

"It's settled then. You'll join us on Thursday."

They stayed at anchor to watch the fireworks over the Manhattan skyline from folding chairs up on the bow. Beth felt a surprising sense of awe celebrating Independence Day under the protection of the Statue of Liberty in the company of new friends. For the first time in a month she felt that she had made the right decision moving aboard *Trouble*.

When the fireworks ended they watched some of the smaller boats that had settled around them haul up their anchors and gun their big outboard engines. Three sailboats closer to Ellis Island showed no sign of departing and Tom observed that they were probably going to wait until the morning tide change to make the passage through Hell Gate, if that's where they were going.

When things had calmed down a bit Herb raised the anchor and pointed *Second Million* toward the East River. By the time he slowed the engines to navigate the anchorage outside of their marina Beth was stretched out on a settee in the main salon dozing. Tom and Sylvia were sitting on the aft deck sipping single-malt scotch and talking animatedly.

Susan had finished tidying the galley and turned on a small television to watch the late news and Jay Leno. Cued by the change in the engine sound she switched off the TV and went out to help with the dock lines. Beth automatically roused herself and followed, wanting to be helpful. But she quickly realized that Susan and Herb had their routine down, so she ended up standing with Tom and Sylvia watching as Herb backed the boat into the slip and Susan stepped off and secured the lines.

Herb invited them all to have another drink before leaving, but Tom and Sylvia declined so Beth also made her excuses and made her way down the dock to her own boat. The next morning – Sunday – she arrived at the weekly brunch to find that Herb and Susan were talking about how nice their excursion had been, and how pleasant they had found Beth. She felt her hackles rise as she realized it had all been a test – sort of an initiation – and that she had passed. But as Sid and several of the other marina regulars greeted her with open smiles she decided that it wasn't worth being angry. All social groups had their boundaries and their ways of admitting newcomers.

FIVE: RACING

"Ready about? Hard alee," Tom spun the wheel of *Huckleberry*, his forty-two foot racing sailboat almost before his crew had confirmed readiness. Beth scrambled across the cabin top deck and slid down the rough gel coat on the far side, sticking her feet out over the rail just as the boat settled in on the opposite tack. In the cockpit Fred grunted as he use the sheet winch to grind in the last few inches of the jib sheet and Hal cleated it. Then they both climbed up to the high side and settled in along the rail with her.

Andrew, the foredeck man, crouched to her right, ready to move around should something need adjusting. After four tacks Beth was beginning to sense the rhythm of the boat and crew as they worked together. Her goal was to stay out of their way.

As planned, Tom had picked her up in mid-town at a corner that was along his driving route. She envied the financial resources that allowed him to both own a car and drive it into the city to work – the parking alone had to be several hundred dollars a month. As he threaded his way through rush-hour traffic, cheating the jams on the expressway by using exit lanes and then cutting back in at the last moment, he explained that he had ridden the subway for a couple decades so he'd paid his dues. Now he avoided the underground transit system even while acknowledging that it was more efficient.

He phoned ahead and ordered two pizzas that they picked up before pulling into the marina. Fred, Hal, and Andrew had already been aboard preparing *Huckleberry* to sail. They stopped long enough to gobble down the pizzas, and then without a word of command stowed the empty boxes and began undoing the dock lines. Tom started the engine and they were away.

Their remarkable teamwork continued as Tom drove the boat northeast toward the race course. The crew raised the main and began observing and reporting wind and sea conditions. Beth felt like an outsider listening to them discuss strategy, predicting the likely course for the race, and joking with one another. She took a position standing in the companionway on the ladder, her body mostly inside the boat's sparse cabin. But as they approached the racecourse Tom had instructed her to take a spot on the rail – the cockpit crew would need to trim the main from where she was.

She quickly suppressed the impulse to feel hurt – she was obviously not capable of trimming the mainsail and she knew it – and climbed out into the wind on the rail.

Her heart was in her mouth as Tom maneuvered *Huckleberry* amid the rest of the fleet during the pre-start. She could hardly focus on Andrew's explanation of what was going on as she hovered between exhilaration and sheer panic. There must be a hundred boats all circling, all avoiding one another by what looked like inches. But Tom said it was just fifty when she asked, and their division was only twelve, so the rest didn't matter. It seemed to her that any boat that they might hit, or be hit by, mattered, but she kept her thought to herself.

She watched another division of fourteen smaller boats all surge toward the invisible starting line, every sail trimmed in tight, every bow throwing up a small wake as it sliced through the swells. Just as a horn sounded on the anchored powerboat that was acting as race "committee" all of the boats adjusted course to angle across the starting line. Moments later two tacked, changing course away from the rest. When another one followed suit Hal and Fred both laughed and explained that the skipper of the third boat was known to always follow the first two, who consistently won. But the third boat never even placed, so his strategy was obviously flawed.

The crowd of milling boats had thinned considerably by the time *Huckleberry* prepared to start. Tom had timed their speed during the pre-race in order to put the boat on the starting line just as the horn sounded. Beth pulled her legs up as a neighboring boat skimmed along beside them just a few feet away. Glancing over her shoulder she saw another boat just as close on their other side. And then the horn sounded and Fred was grinding the winch for the main sail and Hal was doing the same on the jib to tighten both sails as Tom adjusted their course as close to sailing upwind as possible.

They had stayed on that course for a full ten minutes, *Huckleberry* surging through the water, keeping up with some of their competitors, passing others, and falling behind the fastest entries. From the crew's talk Beth learned that they usually placed fourth or fifth, but sometimes managed to get a second or third when the most competitive boats were not out.

"Ready about," Tom ordered once more. "Hard alee."

Beth scrambled across the cabin again, noting that they were changing course to avoid the lighthouse she remembered from her sailing lessons. The instructor had told them about the myth surrounding the structure – that during the revolutionary war the British had gained control of the lighthouse and brought colonial prisoners to it for execution. Legend had it that they'd tied the unfortunate men to the rocks at low tide and left them to their fates. The next prisoners would be treated to the sight of the crab-consumed corpses. The lighthouse was appropriately named Execution Rocks.

Soon they were approaching a clanging green buoy with a flashing light on top just off of an island. Ahead of them one boat after another rounded the buoy and adjusted its sails to run downwind. As they approached the buoy someone on a boat coming in on the other tack shouted "starboard!"

"Damn!" Tom swore quietly.

"They have the right of way," Fred explained to Beth, who had actually understood the meaning of the call from the other boat. "Tom's going to have to bear off and give them room at the mark. That does it for us tonight."

"We can make up the time, can't we?"

"Maybe, but we usually don't manage it on the downwind leg. A couple boat-lengths now will do us in."

"But heck, we have fun anyway," Hal put in.

As Fred had predicted, Tom turned the bow away from the mark, aiming for a moment at the stern of the other boat. Then the other boat passed by and rounded the buoy. A few seconds later Tom called for another tack and they executed a turn around the buoy as well. Up on the bow Andrew had prepared a light weight aluminum pole and as soon as they were on their new course he attached one end to the corner of the jib and the other to the mast. The pole held the forward sail far out on one side of the boat while the main stood out on the other. *Wing-on-*

wing Beth remembered the sail configuration was called.

All around them the other boats were using the same technique to catch every breath of the breeze from behind. The downwind leg went on for nearly twenty minutes, with Andrew and Fred moving around the deck making small adjustments to the sails and lines while Tom occasionally noted their speed and heading. Beth soon realized that every member of the crew knew exactly where the next buoy was, knew how fast they were going, knew where their competitors were amid the fleet of boats all around, and knew their position in the standings – all without having to stop and think about it. She doubted that she would ever become such a natural sailor.

"Next time we're putting you to work," Tom said as he settled his bag on his shoulder and turned to walk along side Beth toward *Trouble.*

"You don't mind if I come again?" she asked, still feeling as if she'd been ballast.

"Of course not – I hope you will. It's nice to have a pretty face to look at," he said this last loud enough for Hal to hear as he caught up with them.

"Yeah," Hal replied, "and he didn't yell at us tonight either, so please come again."

Two days later Beth was back aboard *Huckleberry* shifting from one side to the other over and over again as they competed in the Manhasset Bay regatta. They sailed two races on Saturday, placing third and fourth, respectively. Beth shuffled down the dock to *Trouble* late in the afternoon totally drained but also exhilarated. She had been far less frightened by the crowds of boats, and she'd even handled the jib sheet a couple times when Fred was needed on the bow.

She went back for more on Sunday, and was treated to the post-race party at Manhasset Yacht Club where sailors from a wide spectrum of backgrounds consumed several kegs of beer and pounds of burgers and hot dogs. Hal and Andrew had to drag her away from a rowdy group telling outrageous stories to get aboard the boat for the trip home.

Her many projects aboard *Trouble* had suffered from a weekend of neglect, but it had been worth every minute.

SIX: FREEDOM

Grrrrrrooooom.

Beth glanced around the dock as *Trouble*'s diesel engine thundered to life. She wasn't sure why she felt as if she should be surreptitious about starting the engine on her own boat; maybe it was because this was the first time.

For the last two months she had kept *Trouble* connected to shore power with the oversized yellow power cord, too timid to sit in the cockpit and turn the key that transformed the boat from a floating apartment to a vehicle that could carry her to new worlds.

Sitting there behind the wheel, listening to the engine hum, she felt a wave of fear. *I really could go. I could just untie the lines and drive out of this slip.* She held the wheel and craned her neck to look back over her shoulder toward the open channel and the boats in the opposite slips. *And then what? I'm not even sure how to set the sails.*

Suddenly she felt like a child on a grocery store hobbyhorse. She left the engine running and went up on deck to study the lines that operated the sails.

"Thinking of going out?" the voice from the dock was high and clear enough to carry over the rumbling engine. Foolishly embarrassed, she stepped down to the side deck nearer the speaker. It was Doug, owner of a small sailboat berthed out at the end of the dock. Tall and blond and about three times her age, he had a friendly smile and a charismatic presence that made him welcome on every boat in the marina. More than once in the past weeks he'd found her working on something on *Trouble* and offered very useful advice.

"Maybe," she replied. "But I'm not sure I can do it."

"On your own? Have you single-handed before?"

"No."

"Then you might want some company the first time. You said you took lessons, right?"

"Yes, with a boyfriend a couple summers ago."

"Puttering around on little J-boats or the Solings?"

"Pretty much."

Doug nodded, then looked over *Trouble*'s decks. "The theory of sailing is the same on any boat, but the equipment and larger scale make this much different. Haven't you been racing with Tom?"

"Yes. And I know what you mean – everything's bigger and harder to do on *Huckleberry*. But *Trouble* isn't as big. I think I can handle her."

Doug grinned at her sudden expression of confidence. "Well if you'd like some company for your maiden voyage, I'd be happy to help."

"I – I'd really appreciate that, actually," Beth stammered, surprised at his offer. Doug was friendly, but he also struck her as a bit of a loner. "Maybe this Saturday?"

"Name the time and I'll bring the wine."

Beth chuckled. "Ten? Just for an hour or so?"

"Ten it is, and we'll have a picnic, with my wine, when we get back. You're buying lunch."

"It's a deal. Thanks Doug."

"Better shut that thing down now, or we'll run out of fuel when we need it," he nodded toward the stern, then waved as he strode on down the dock on his long legs.

"Will you come? Please? It will be perfectly safe, and I'd like a familiar face around," Beth opened and shut the hinged lid of the refrigerator, having forgotten what she was looking for. She held the phone to her ear with her free hand, listening to Eva express hesitation about joining her with Doug on Saturday.

"I'm sure it's safe, Beth. I'm just afraid I'll get seasick. I did once, on the ferry? It was gross."

"You felt like you were going to die, I remember," Beth struggled not to sound impatient. "Sailing is different, the boat moves with the water, doesn't fight it like the ferry does."

She was lying through her teeth, but apparently it sounded convincing.

"Okay. Okay. I'll come. Tell me what to bring."

If Doug was surprised to find Eva aboard *Trouble* on Saturday morning he didn't mention it. Going over *Trouble*'s lines with him while Eva's watched from the cockpit Beth questioned her motivation for inviting her friend. Was it really for the familiar face, or did she fear that Doug had an ulterior motive? *Don't flatter yourself*, she scoffed, focusing on his analysis of the main halyard.

"You'll need to replace it soon. It'll hold for a while – the rest of the season – but you should get a new one spliced over the winter."

"Okay," she nodded, noting the wear that he had pointed out. He glanced down at her, then looked at the other lines attached to the mast.

"The spinnaker halyard looks new," he said, obviously trying to encourage her.

"Yes, Mrs. Thomas said it was," she replied. "And so is the sail. Let's get moving, Doug, and maybe someday I'll be ready to try using it."

"The good news is there's a great breeze for sailing," Doug said as he uncleated the stern line. Beth stood behind the wheel looking at the channel behind *Trouble*. This was it. She had to back the boat out of the slip, turning at the same time, and point the bow out into the open water. "The bad news is, it's coming at you broadside so you'll have to compensate for it as you pull out."

"Okay," Beth said, realizing that she once again sounded very tentative. "It seems like I should give it some power to get some speed, right?"

"Right. Remember she's not a powerboat – she won't accelerate very fast. But you also don't have any brakes."

"Right." Beth looked down at the simple engine controls again. A horizontal lever controlled the transmission. A vertical one controlled the throttle. She became intensely aware of Eve sitting in the cockpit watching her. Her friend, she suspected, was rapidly loosing faith in her.

"Here goes," she said, pushing the transmission lever into reverse and pushing the throttle forward. Doug guided the boat for a few feet, then stepped on board. Beth turned the wheel a little and felt the stern shift to the left – port – as it cleared the back of the slip.

"Watch the bow," Doug suggested, walking forward on the side deck. Beth looked way forward and saw that the bowsprit where the anchors were mounted was passing dangerously close to the neighboring powerboat. She yanked the wheel the other direction. Now *Trouble* was shooting backwards across the channel toward the boats on the opposite side. She pulled back on the throttle and the boat slowed a little. Up forward Doug pushed the bow away from the powerboat until it was clear.

"Okay, turn it now," he called back. "And give it a little gas, you're losing speed."

Frustrated, Beth spun the wheel back the other way and pushed forward on the throttle again. Trouble swung obligingly out in the channel and she throttled back, pulling the transmission into neutral, and then into forward. At the last moment before the bow swung back toward the neighboring powerboat she remembered to spin the wheel the other way, swinging her into the middle of the channel.

She heard a faint sigh from Eve – it sounded like relief – and felt herself make a similar noise. Doug hopped down into the cockpit carrying the two inflated rubber fenders that he had removed from the lifelines.

"Not bad for a first attempt," he proclaimed cheerfully.

As they reached the open water past the moored boats beyond the marina Beth grew increasingly grateful for Doug's supportive presence. It was obvious that he knew everything that she should do long before she did, but he held his tongue and gave every appearance of a relaxed, happy sailor.

Confidence growing, she pushed the throttle forward and felt *Trouble* respond with a little surge of speed. They were out in Pelham Bay now, the narrow stretch of water between City Island and the nearby Bronx shoreline. Three enormous barges loaded with gravel were moored out there, but otherwise the water was clear. The breeze ruffled Beth's hair and she looked up into it. To the south east a dozen or more sailboats moved lazily across the western end of Long Island Sound, some coming from the East River, some going that way toward Manhattan.

"This is a good place to raise the sails," Doug commented too casually. "Plenty of open water and the breeze isn't too strong."

"Right," Beth nodded, looking down at the compass on the binnacle, then at the engine gauges. *Quit stalling.*

"Okay," she said. "I think I should do it, though. Would you take the wheel?"

"You got it," Doug said, moving to the back of the cockpit.

Beth was a lot less worried about handing over the helm of her boat to Doug than she was about trying to raise the sails herself. She walked up to the mast holding onto various handholds, her balance uneven as the boat moved through the low swells. Once again she became aware of Eve watching her, but as she glanced back at the helm she saw Doug's eyes move from the engine gauges to the wind and depth gauges and then out across the water. At least he wasn't staring at her.

Taking a deep breath she reached out to remove the webbing ties that secured the mainsail to the boom. She worked her way back, the freed folds of the sail flapping, and dropped the bright blue ties down into the cockpit onto Eve's lap.

"Hang onto those, will you?" she asked, not waiting for an answer. She climbed back into the cockpit and leaned over the deck to open the lever-operated cleat that held the end of the main halyard. After wrapping several turns around a big winch she inserted a stainless steel handle into the notched hole in the top and began to turn it.

She leaned back as she turned the winch, watching the Dacron sail unfold as it rose slowly up the mast. It seemed like it was taking forever. She'd been able to raise the sail on the small sailboats she'd learned on with a few fast tugs. But her racing experience on *Huckleberry* reassured her that it really was this hard to haul up this much sail.

"Did you ease the mainsheet?" Doug asked in an off hand tone that she was sure meant it was an important question.

"Right," she said, scanning the lines arrayed in front of her. She had been looking at these lines for two months, noting which one was which, operating the cleats, and spinning the winches. But now it took several seconds for her to recognize the mainsheet – the line that controlled the angle of the sail once it was all the way up. In in order to get the sail all the way up she had to remove the tension on the sheet. She popped open the cleat and the let a couple feet of the line pass through it. Over her head the boom began to wiggle and dance, lines snapping around frantically. She returned to the winch and put her shoulders into grinding it a few more turns.

"Looks good," Doug commented, eyes at the top of the mast. Beth snapped the cleat shut and took the handle out of the winch. "Can I fall off?" he asked from behind her.

"Um, yes. No, wait," Beth closed the cleat on the main sheet as well, looked up at the sail again, and then looked over her shoulder at Doug. He grinned, sharing her flash of pride, and turned the wheel slightly to port. *Trouble* hesitated for a moment, and then the sail filled and the boat leaned over and surged forward.

"Wow!" Eve exclaimed, clasping the sail ties tight as she braced herself with her feet. "Is it okay?"

"Perfect!" Beth laughed, still grinning at Doug.

"How about the jib?" he asked.

"Okay," she said, swallowing hard as she turned to look at the bow. *This is the easy one*, she reminded herself.

"Eve, see that line wrapped around the winch right behind you?" Doug asked. Eve turned awkwardly, obviously trying not to slide off of her seat.

"Yes," she replied, eying the winch suspiciously.

"Please unwrap it. Just let it lay loose."

Eve slowly unwound the line from the winch, clearly expecting something dramatic to happen. But nothing did, and after a moment she straightened and looked expectantly at Doug.

"That's the 'lazy sheet,'" Beth explained, kneeling on the bench across from Eve and fitting the winch handle into the winch. "We only use one jib sheet at a time."

She started to turn the winch and then stopped, looking forward at the sail rolled around the forestay. Something wasn't right.

Then it hit her. There was another line preventing the sail from unrolling. She needed to uncleat it. *Where is it?*

"I can get the furling line," Doug said. She looked at him and saw his hand on a small line that was cleated at the side of the cockpit within his reach.

"Okay, great. Let me know when you're ready," she replied, once again grateful for his kindness.

"Any time," he replied.

Beth began turning the winch again, and this time the sail unrolled as Doug paid out his line. Beth ground away at the winch until the sail was trimmed in tight.

"Here Beth, take this," Doug said, moving aside to make room for her behind the wheel. "Your boat, your first sail," he explained.

Beth took his place behind the wheel and gradually turned it away from the wind until *Trouble* heeled a little more and seemed to gallop forward as the breeze filled her sails. Doug planted himself beside Eve and shot her a reassuring smile.

"Feel good?" he asked Beth.

"Perfect," she nodded, looking around them and realizing that during the sail raising process they had covered the length of Pelham Bay and entered Long Island Sound. And then she realized that at some point Doug must have shut off the engine, because all she could hear was the wind and the swish of *Trouble*'s hull moving through the water.

"Perfect," she repeated.

SEVEN: ORI

Beth invited Doug on a short sail again the following weekend, and the weekend after that. He was good company – self-assured without being arrogant and supportive without being condescending. On each sail he took different roles so that she could try everything, and each time they returned to the marina he patiently helped her practice docking several times.

At the same time she continued racing with Tom on *Huckleberry*, and with each outing the crowds of boats were less frightening and the tactics became clearer. She was also learning the local waters, both from the racers and from Doug. After their sails they would spread charts out on the cockpit table and have their picnic lunch while he pointed out the features and helped her connect what she had seen out on the water with how it was represented on paper.

The mid-year reviews at work came at the end of July, and although Beth had only been there for three months, she still had a one-on-one meeting with her supervisor Tom. Working for small companies at the beginning of her career she had not received this sort of formal performance appraisal so it made her uncomfortable. But Tom was uniformly encouraging, noting specific things she had done right and identifying things she could do better. She left the meeting feeling good about her work and herself.

"Beth? Are you on board?" Susan Goldberg's voice carried over the water running in the galley sink. Beth shut it off and took a couple steps up the companionway ladder to look outside. She had caught the early bus home and was hoping to get a coat of varnish on the exterior woodwork before it got dark, but she'd had to wash the coffee pot and her mug first to clear the sink for brush cleaning later.

"Good evening Susan."

"Beth dear, Herb and I are going to the supermarket. Do you need anything – or you're welcome to come along if you'd like."

"Thanks Susan. I really need to do some brightwork. But I do have a list – if you don't mind." She had learned to keep a list of grocery items that couldn't be found at the stores within walking distance. Every couple of weeks someone with a car offered to pick things up or take her along.

"Hand it over my dear," Susan said, extending her hand over the lifeline. Beth grinned and backed down into the galley to get her list and a twenty-dollar bill.

"That out to cover it," she said as she handed both to her neighbor.

"I'm sure it will," Susan replied without looking at either piece of paper. She would, Beth knew, put everything together and pay no attention to the cost. But Beth would not dream of taking advantage of Susan's generosity, even if she and Herb were on their second million. She watched her neighbor sashay on down the dock, then chuckled to herself when she saw Herb come trotting along after her, his hands buried in his trouser pockets as if he was searching for his keys. She still had not figured out which of them was the million-dollar earner. Stereotypes suggested that it must be Herb, but Susan seemed like the ambitious one.

Beth was still trying to accept the realization that the marina community was the most supportive she had ever known. The Southern California suburb she grew up in had been populated by the usual characters – the gregarious young couple with little kids, the old woman with cats, the lawn-proud husband who shot dirty looks at the kids on skateboards. She and her sister had been friends with the neighborhood kids, and her parents had been friendly with the adult neighbors. Looking back on it now she knew that it had been a group of families living in close proximity, but it hadn't been a community. Since setting out on her own, she'd had cordial relationships with neighbors in various apartment buildings, but she had never considered them friends – she rarely entered their apartments or invited them in to hers.

The community of boaters shared something deeper than mere hallways and doormen. From live-aboard to daysailor to the guy who owned the houseboat at the top of the dock that didn't have an engine, they all had the sea in common. They all shared the constant struggle to keep bilges dry and iceboxes cool, decks leak-free and wood varnished. They advised one another, teased, shared tools, and lent a hand. On any given evening you could find someone to share a beer in a cockpit or upper deck. And you could also count on privacy – nobody ever set foot on anyone else's boat without being invited.

It had taken Beth a long time to accept that her new neighbors were genuine, that an offer to pick up groceries was just that, no strings attached. But Doug's informal sailing lessons and Tom's adding her to his race crew and Herb's occasional navigation lessons over red wine aboard *Second Million* had all been offered freely. She was, she had finally come to understand, a member of the club – the community of boaters. It felt good, and just a little bit frightening since she wasn't sure what might be expected of her.

And as the summer progressed she was growing concerned about the coming winter. She'd come home on the first of August to find a letter from the marina in her mail slot in the office. A surreptitious glance told her that each of the live aboards' mail slots had one. It was, the letter announced, time to reserve space for the winter. She could keep *Double Trouble* in the water, or have her hauled out to the big gravel-covered parking area for the duration. In the water was cheaper, but Beth wasn't sure what the impact of a winter of snow and ice would be.

When she asked Susan the older woman had just laughed and assured her that there was no way she'd live on board any boat in the winter. She and Herb would be moving back to their apartment in New Rochelle in November. This was the first Beth had heard of their land-based home, but it did not surprise her.

Doug said he always had his boat hauled and covered for the winter – he wouldn't be using it, so best to protect it. He seemed to imply that Beth's circumstances were different – assuming she intended to stay on board.

After numerous discrete inquiries, Beth learned that the hermit-like houseboater who she'd only said hello to in passing, Margaret and Alan, and the people from the powerboat on the other dock would all be staying on board their boats in the water for the winter. Sid in the office had explained that the occupied boats – including his own houseboat – would be moved to the slips closest to the shore. Phil and Anna and another single liveaboard were planning to stay on their boats up in the parking lot.

Beth had tacked the notice from the marina on the small bulletin board where she kept her short grocery list and her lengthy "to do" list, putting off the decision for as long as she could. The cost difference aside, she could not decide which would be worse – having to climb up and down a ladder to get in and out of her "home" all winter, or navigating the icy docks and deck. As a California girl at heart, neither option was overly attractive.

"That's what I'm trying to decide. I'm leaning toward staying in the water, but I'm afraid it could be a big mistake," Beth painted another swath of glistening varnish onto the cockpit trim, then looked up at her audience.

Ori – short for Oregon – and her thirty-six foot sailboat *Dream Catcher* had appeared in the slip next door the previous afternoon. The powerboat that lived there had been taken by her owners on a two-week cruise. Ori had introduced herself as a "transient cruiser," which Beth had come to know meant she was on a long-term voyage. She was stopping over on City Island for an engine tune-up and some sail repair.

It was obvious to Beth from the way she walked up the dock and greeted everyone that Ori was a long-time member of the boating community. And the realization was fascinating – the community was portable, its members were on every dock all over the country, probably the world. The idea was incredibly seductive. Every waterfront where boaters gathered was an extension of her home.

"But either way, you're staying here?" Ori asked. She was stretched along the near side bench in her own boat's cockpit sipping occasionally from a bottle of Corona with a sliver of lime shoved down the neck. She had offered one, but Beth had declined – at least until she got this stretch of wood varnished.

"Well, yes," Beth squinted at a stray brush hair that had become embedded in the varnish. "I have a job to get to, and I don't think there's a cheaper option – not closer to transportation anyway."

"Woah, commitment!" Ori groaned. Beth looked over at her and she shrugged. "Well, come on girl, there's a lot of world out there that this little sloop can take you to."

"But this little sloop won't take me anywhere if I don't earn a living to pay off the loan," Beth replied, immediately hating how practical she sounded. She was relieved to see Ori nod.

"I see your point," the cruiser said. Her words were kind, but her voice betrayed her true feelings – pity for the tied-down New Yorker.

"So where will you be over the winter?" Beth asked, looking for a diversion and the chance to live vicariously.

"I haven't decided whether to head out to Bermuda or go down the coast to Florida. But I will definitely be in the islands by January. Maybe earlier."

Beth had learned the "the islands" was shorthand for the Caribbean. She dipped her brush into the varnish and applied a careful stroke to the edge of the wood trim. A small drip ran down the adjacent fiberglass and she mopped it up with a rag kept on hand for the purpose.

"That sounds great," she said. She had never been to the Caribbean, although she had been to Hawaii as a child when her father won a sales competition and took the whole family. *Ori isn't interested in that. Why am I trying to impress her?*

"You need to pay off this hulk and run away," Ori observed, taking a long swig of beer. Beth snorted a laugh, thinking of the years of payments still left on her loan, on top of the insurance and the rental on her storage unit.

"I mean it," Ori said. "You think moving aboard a sailboat is an adventure? Try sailing it."

Beth felt her hackles rise and rocked back onto her heels to stare at the other woman. Ori caught her look and winced.

"Sorry – that was way too harsh. It's none of my business."

"Well, that's true," Beth said slowly. "But you mean well – I think. And I am tempted. But I just can't sail away without making some plans. It's not in my nature."

"Fair enough," Ori replied quickly, and Beth realized that she had managed to stand up for herself without offending. It felt good.

"Listen, I'm about done here. The pizza at the place up around the corner is pretty good. Do you want to go get a pie?"

"New York style pizza? You bet!"

EIGHT: GROWTH

"You'll never know if you don't – ugh! -- try it," Ori declared as she ground the last few inches of jib sheet in with the winch. "She sails beautifully, and everything is cockpit rigged."

Dream Catcher's engine was up in the shop. Beth had come home from work and caught Ori staring longingly out across the boats at the open water. She said that she'd had a rough day at work and invited Ori out for a head-clearing sail. She had not had to ask twice.

Now Ori put the winch handle away and lounged back on the cockpit bench, her expression envious as she looked around at *Trouble*. Beth had learned enough about her boat to realize that *Trouble* was well designed and easy to handle, and not that old. *Dream Catcher* was at least a decade older and designed along very different lines. Ori had described her as a "sailor's sailboat," meaning the rigging and equipment was very traditional and lacked some of the conveniences that *Trouble* had. She was obviously very fond of her boat, but Beth could see as she helped sail *Trouble* that she did appreciate the newer boat.

Beth reached behind herself and manipulated a pump fitted to the backstay, tightening the tension on the wire. The knot meter told her that *Trouble*'s speed had just increased by two tenths of a knot.

"Who are you racing against?" Ori grinned.

Beth shrugged sheepishly. The other sailor was right – her experience racing with Tom was seeping into her supposedly relaxed cruising. Maybe Ori's proposal was a good idea: to sail together out to Oyster Bay over Labor Day weekend. But Ori's plan was for them to each take their own boat so Beth would have to sail solo. Her assurance that *Trouble* was made to be sailed by one person was encouraging, but Beth was still nervous about it. It wasn't so much the sailing – she knew that she could steer the boat and handle the sails by herself. The problem was around the edges – undocking and docking without anyone else to handle the lines, and anchoring the boat on her own.

"I've only anchored a couple times," she said, *and one of them was during sailing class on the Soling,* she didn't add out loud.

"Piece of cake," Ori shrugged, reaching for the open beer in the cup holder on the binnacle. "How about if I anchor first, and then if you have a really hard time we can just raft *Trouble* up to *Dream Catcher.*

"And not anchor her?"

"You could put out the hook once we're secure, if it comes to it."

A little wind gust heeled *Trouble* a little more and Beth felt a rush of excitement as she adjusted to it.

"Okay. Let's do it," she said before she could stop herself.

"See you back home," Beth called as she steered *Double Trouble* in an arc away from *Dream Catcher* and toward the entrance to Oyster Bay. It had been a marvelous weekend in every way. Beth had studied her charts, entered coordinates into her global positioning system, and sailed *Trouble* the twenty miles to Oyster Bay. Despite her concerns, she had successfully stopped the boat in place and gone up to the bow to drop the anchor. And then she'd hurried back to the cockpit to reverse the engine and dig it into the bottom. She knew she was lucky that the breeze was steady and light in the protected anchorage. She'd only felt a little outdone when Ori came in and anchored Dream Catcher so that the two boats ended up right next to one another. Then, as planned, they'd tossed lines to one another and secured the two boats side-by-side – "rafted up" for the night.

Ori had turned on the stereo loud to share Jimmy Buffett with the rest of the anchorage, then fired up a gas grill mounted on *Dream Catcher's* stern rail. She cooked up steaks while Beth tossed together a salad and steamed vegetables in her galley. They had eaten in *Dream Catcher's* cockpit and lay stargazing on the two benches late into the night.

Ori had been determined to show Beth all of the good things about the cruising life in one weekend. On Sunday morning she'd launched the dinghy that was suspended on davits at the back of her boat and they'd puttered with its little outboard engine to the town dock and then to a little diner for breakfast. They'd wandered the village for the rest of the morning and finally taken the dinghy back for lunch on board. In the early afternoon Beth switched on the radio to the weather channel. The weather forecast had sounded a bit ominous – isolated thunderstorms building into the afternoon and moving west to east with winds gusting to forty knots. But it was a familiar forecast: variations on it were almost a daily occurrence during July and August on Long Island Sound. But Ori had shaken her head and switched off the radio.

"I think I'll sit it out and hope for a better report tomorrow," she announced.

"I have to get back today," Beth replied, realizing as she spoke that Ori had not been trying to talk her into staying.

"Right – commitments," Ori said in such a way that Beth could not take it unkindly.

"Yeah, the loan payment," she nodded. "I guess I'll just make a run for it and dodge the storms."

She had visualized someone trying to run in between raindrops as she climbed back over the lifelines to *Trouble*'s cockpit and started the engine. She'd once read of a study done in England that proved that you got less wet if you ran in the rain. *Or was it that you get just as wet?*

In any case, she'd taken a few minutes to make sure everything was secure below, then Ori had helped her cast off the lines tying the two boats together. She'd reversed the anchoring process fairly easily, although the anchor chain brought up several pounds of disgusting muck when she heaved it onto the bowsprit. She couldn't take the time to haul up a few buckets of water to wash it away – not with nobody at the helm to steer *Trouble* away from the other anchored boats.

She'd secured the anchor and hurried back to the cockpit to regain control, then waved at Ori and pointed her boat toward the mouth of the bay.

A half hour later she had the mainsail up and the jib unrolled and *Trouble* was heeled far over as she plunged across the Sound toward the Connecticut shore. The weather report had been right about the wind direction – it was blowing hard from the west. Fortunately, City Island lay to the south-west, so once she sailed across the Sound she could turn and sail almost directly toward home. For the time being she settled in and enjoyed sailing.

About an hour later her GPS confirmed her guess that the land ahead was the Greenwich Islands. She had created a waypoint in the device at place where she should turn, because she still was not confident in her judgment and local knowledge. As *Trouble* came close to the invisible point in the water the GPS beeped and she prepared to tack. The boat responded quickly as she turned the wheel and released the jib sheet. Dropping the line, she moved to the other side of the cockpit, still behind the wheel, and hauled in on the other sheet. This was the tricky part: she had to finish trimming the jib while steering at the same time. She had devised a simple solution yesterday – she put *Trouble* on the course she wanted to steer, then turned the knob on the binnacle that locked the wheel. It wouldn't hold in really heavy weather, but it had worked well enough on the sail out, and it did again while she ground the winch to bring in the sail inch by inch. She gave up sooner than she wanted to, but the boat was heeling more than it had been on the other tack.

Glancing at the wheel, which seemed to be holding, she dropped down the companionway ladder and switched on the radio. But the forecast was on a five minute loop, and she couldn't afford to stand there waiting for the pertinent part, so she turned it up as loud as it went and went back out to the wheel. *This is why they all have portable radios* she thought as she strained her ears. She had thought the racers and others who kept hand-held VHF radios in the cockpit were just gadget freaks.

As she listened to the electronic voice describing weather conditions out in the ocean beyond Long Island she scanned her surroundings looking for other boats. Under sail *Trouble* had the right of way over power boats, but not necessarily over other sailboats, and not over the big barges and commercial fishing boats that also sailed these waters.

Her jaw dropped and she forced herself to suck in a deep breath when she looked at the southwestern horizon.

". . . increased probability of thunderstorms with concentrated squalls. Winds gusting to 80 miles per hour . . ."

Over her head the sky was blue, but down near the Westchester county line -- less than half way home – the sky was completely black. She looked around at the other boats in the area. Three powerboats were charging toward the darkness as if oblivious – and if they were on autopilot they might very well be. A sailboat with only the main sail up was motoring toward her coming from the bad weather, but two more under full sail were moving at various angles across the Sound. A fleet of small boats was clustered near shore behind her. *But they're racing, they'll probably stay out until it hits.*

She was temporarily unsure of what to do. Keep on sailing and risk damaging her boat, injuring herself, or worse? Or drop the sails too soon and look like a coward?

Trouble heaved over and water sloshed along the deck on the low side. Beth gripped the wheel and steered slightly into the heavy gust of wind, knowing that the boat could be sailed this way and that she was not in any danger – yet. And as quickly as it had come, the gust ended and *Trouble* righted, her sails flapping for a moment until Beth got her back on her original course.

Without further hesitation, she turned on the engine and freed the line to roll up the jib. She had to turn into the wind and lock the wheel to use both hands, there was so much pressure on the madly flapping sail. But her good maintenance over the summer paid off: the roller up on the bow was lubricated and the line was sound. The sail finally rolled up tight and she cleated the furling line as well as both jib sheets so that they would not flap around. The next part was going to be much harder, and her hands were already shaking.

NINE: TRANSFORMATION

The temperature had dropped about twenty degrees as *Trouble* and the dark squall line converged. Beth looked around again to confirm that she was in clear water, then she lifted the cover on the starboard side bench and leaned way into the deep compartment below, straining to wrap her fingers around the strap of an orange lifejacket. She dragged it out and let the cover slam, then pulled the lifejacket over her head and secured the buckle. It was hardly much insulation but it made her feel immediately better.

For a few minutes she sat holding the wheel, listening to the mainsail and boom rattling furiously, the reefing lines whipping around above her head. *Trouble* was pointed straight into the wind, the engine at a low forward idle. Beth looked to the left and the right, then down at the churning water, and finally at her GPS display. The boat was not moving – at least not over the ground. The boat's speed was just enough to counter the current. The squall line was much closer now and the sky over her head was darkened by streams of high-level clouds.

Get to it now. It's only going to get worse.

She tightened the lock on the wheel moved to the front of the cockpit.

Tighten the sheet.

She listened to her own orders and used the winch to tighten the main sheet as much as she could. This reduced the flapping and banging, but didn't silence it. There was only one way to do that.

She made sure the main sheet was cleated, then took the line off of the winch and wrapped the main halyard around it instead. With a couple wraps around the winch for leverage she lifted the handle of the cleat and felt tension on the line. Peering up at the sail she began to pay out the halyard. The sail dropped, falling in loose folds onto the boom, and then sliding off to hand on either side flapping in the wind. When the sail was half way down she realized that she had to get it under control.

Sail ties.

She had tossed them below when she raised the sail a couple hours ago. Cursing at herself, she climbed down the ladder, gathered the scattered ties from the floor, and climbed back out. She had done her share of snickering at the anal habits of sailors – everything in its proper place, everything tied down. But now she was getting a hard lesson in seamanship and the things she'd found amusing didn't seem funny at all.

The boom was waggling around more now than ever, and as she emerged into the cockpit she tugged on the sheet again, taking up slack that had been created by the sail being dropped.

Do it now.

She swallowed hard and climbed up to the side deck. Suddenly the bobbing, rocking motion of the boat as she flogged against the increasing wind was very frightening. She grabbed a hold of the wooden railings mounted on the cabin top and worked her way forward, climbing up onto the cabin when she reached the mast. The wind had carried the sail part way back up the mast and the halyard was flapping wildly around the spreaders and shrouds. If she didn't secure it, it could become hopelessly snarled on the upper rigging. Feeling that her balance was far from up to the task, she wrapped her left arm around the mast and used her right hand to drag the sail down. It was much harder than she expected with the wind flapping the sail back and forth and the halyard resisting because she'd left the other end wrapped around the winch.

She had no choice but to keep at it – the darkness was nearly upon her and she did not have time to return to the cockpit and free the line. As soon as she could reach the metal plate at the top of the sail she threaded a sail tie through the fitting that connected it to the halyard and tied the tie around the boom. *Trouble* bucked and slammed into a swell as she started working her way back along the boom. She glanced over her shoulder and saw that the squall had brought waves – not really big, but bigger than she was used to. The wind was stronger now than she had ever experienced. As she turned her head it roared deafeningly in her ears. She hugged the boom, bundling up the sail and wrapping each tie around it with shaking fingers.

She was on the third one, standing on the cabin not far from the cockpit when the first splash of rain struck her back. It felt like icy needles. She hastily secured the sail tie and dropped to her butt, swinging her legs down into the cockpit as another splatter of rain sounded like hail on the deck.

With her center of balance closer to sea level she felt much better. She hastily slid the companionway hatch shut – *should have done that before I went up there* – and started for the wheel.

Without warning *Trouble* heeled over on her side again, throwing Beth painfully against the low side bench. She caught herself on the lifelines, her face far too close to the water. And then to add insult to injury *Trouble* bounced on a big swell that splashed up into her face as it passed beneath the hull. More deeply shaken than ever, she half turned and grabbed the binnacle to pull herself up. The wind had caught *Trouble*'s bow and turned her. She was sailing without sails into the middle of a vicious squall.

As Beth scrambled in behind the wheel the next phase of the storm revealed itself: a loud rumble preceded a bright flash by a few seconds. Beth realized that she'd been hearing thunder for a long time, but hadn't consciously identified it.

Another flash, this one in conjunction with a loud crack. And another – she watched the jagged line of electricity reach from the heavens to the water a few hundred feet away.

She looked at *Trouble*'s stainless steel wheel, and up at her fifty-foot mast, and scanned the surrounding waters and sky. It looked slightly clearer to the south. Fortunately, that was at an angle away from the center of the storm. She reached down and pressed on the throttle and then turned the wheel to the left. *Trouble* stayed heeled over, but she responded to the helm and turned. Now the wind streamed over the side and drummed on the side of Beth's face. With it came raindrops as hard as rocks. She turned her head away from them, and then pressed her right hand to the side of her face to try to cover her ear and eye as well as keep her hair under control.

She was shivering so hard now her teeth were rattling. She clenched her jaw and tried to ignore the spears of deadly electricity jabbing at the sea around her. Beth couldn't believe her boat could heel over so far without any sails up, but she was, and she was still moving along, plunging through the swells that were hitting her now nearly broadside.

Every now and then one of them splashed up, adding salty water to the stinging rain pelting Beth's right side.

As *Trouble* heaved over still further the numbers on the digital wind speed gauge flicked from 78 to 79 and from 79 to 81. Beth's jaw ground harder and she reminded herself that the more violent the storm, the quicker it would pass. At least that's what the race crew had said one night when they'd skirted the edge of a squall.

And then, gradually, the numbers on the wind speed gauge began to go down. *Trouble* straightened up and Beth unclenched her jaw. She even managed to smile at herself when the wind speed hovering around 30 seemed like a light breeze.

Above her the sky was a carpet of dark grey, but not the frightening black of the squall. Looking back over her shoulder she could still see it lumbering along just to the north, bright flashes marking the edges of the violent center.

They had traveled more than half way across the Sound, so now her course for home was nearly due west. Now that the storm had passed she could turn the bow in that direction.

Residual swells slammed against the bow, but it was more comfortable than having them slam against the hull broadsides. The rain had stopped, and the temperature had climbed back up a few degrees. Beth dragged her fingers through her soaked hair and reached down to lock the wheel. She felt restless, although she couldn't think of anything that she should do – other than get home as fast as she could.

I should sail.

She looked at the bundled main sail and felt herself shiver again. *No. Not today. It's not like falling off a horse. I don't have to get right back on.*

And whether she believed that or not, she allowed herself to take the easy way out. The engine, which had performed flawlessly throughout the storm, was purring away. The sea ahead was wide open, all other boats having apparently run for cover. And the sky was actually clearing.

She climbed down the cockpit ladder and pulled off the sodden lifejacket and her t-shirt and shorts. She left them on the floor at the base of the ladder and went to her berth to get a pair of blue jeans and a sweatshirt.

Warmer and deliciously dry, she pulled on her foul weather jacket and returned to the cockpit. The world seemed changed once again: a beam of sunshine made *Trouble*'s wet decks sparkle, and the wicked breeze had dropped to nearly nothing. The only remaining hint of the previous weather was the endless parade of rolling swells through which *Trouble* plunged. And the still ominous dark line to the northeast.

TEN: DESCENT

Thirty minutes later Beth had changed back into dry shorts and a t-shirt and hung the wet ones on one of the lifelines with clothespins. She felt justified in using the motor rather than re-raising the sails since the post-storm breeze was less than ten knots: not enough to move *Trouble* faster than a snail – or counter the current.

Two hours later as she passed Execution Rocks lighthouse she moved around the deck checking her dock lines, pausing to wave at a familiar looking sailboat going the other way. It was one of the Thursday night racers, she realized. Someone who wouldn't know her or *Trouble*. But the skipper waved back anyway and Beth felt herself smile fondly – not at the other sailor, but at the camaraderie of sailors, and at herself for getting her boat through the storm.

"Had a rough one?" Doug called as he cleated her bow line to the dock. He had seen her coming in and came over to help her tie up. She put the engine in neutral and climbed out of the cockpit with the stern line, stepping onto the dock to cleat it, and then walking to the mid-ships cleat to pick up the spring line, which she'd left attached to the dock.

"That storm was something," she confirmed as she climbed back aboard to wrap the spring line around the winch, which was, she had learned, as good as a cleat for holding lines fast.

"Tree limbs are down all over the island and over in the park," he said, walking out the finger dock to stand near her cockpit. "I came over to check on my boat after it passed. I left the family partying in my backyard."

Beth remembered that he'd had relatives coming for the weekend – his sister and her children and grandchildren, she thought. So far as she could tell, Doug was divorced but with no kids of his own.

"Is she okay?" she asked, absently coiling a line while she spoke.

"Sure. I should have known – I always leave everything ship shape. But you never know when some bozo," Beth knew he was referring to the owner of the powerboat berthed next to his boat, "didn't put on a spring line or something."

"That's for sure."

Doug watched her secure the coiled line and pick up another one – the main sheet this time – to begin coiling.

"You look like you could use a drink, and some dry land," he said, taking Beth by surprise. In fact she was still feeling a bit shaky and a few hours on shore before bed time would feel darned good. When she didn't immediately answer Doug went on, "Come on back over to my place – there's plenty of food and drink. I'll drive you back here later."

"That's really nice of you Doug."

"Yes it is. But you're a nice girl. Come on – grab your purse or whatever and get off this boat."

Beth stood on the dock waving as Ori backed *Dream Catcher* out of her slip and turned to point the boat out toward open water.

"Safe sailing!" she called to her friend. The other woman raised her left arm to wave, her right holding onto the wheel.

"I'll write you – you'll come cruising yet," she called back, then stooped to reach for the engine control mounted near her feet. *Dream Catcher* accelerated and was soon weaving her way among the boats moored beyond the docks. Beth watched her until she melded with water and far shore, lost in the early morning haze.

Her mother had always chastised her for forming friendships with people who she knew would not be staying around. She seemed to have a habit of it as a child, and her mother had regarded it as a dumb strategy, rarely offering sympathy at her daughter's loss when a friend moved away. Even so, she had obviously never broken the habit. She was decidedly glum as she picked up her tote bag and headed up the dock toward the street and the bus stop. She really didn't expect to hear from Ori – she knew how these friendships deteriorated. And over the past few weeks during Ori's extended stay in the marina she had allowed her connection with Eve and other friends to slip. Now she was back in the same position her mother had always warned her against.

Later that morning, sitting at her desk with a muffin, coffee, and the text of an employee notice about the annual United Way campaign on her desk, she stopped to consider the pros and cons of her friendship with Ori. Yes, it was most likely over, a definite "con." But Ori had taught her more than any of her non-sailing, stable friends. And not just about sailing. She would never have sailed *Trouble* by herself to Oyster Bay, and she would never ever have been out in a storm, if it weren't for Ori. While people might consider the second point a negative, Beth knew better. The storm experience had revealed things about herself that she had not understood. She was brave. Even when terrified, she didn't panic. So many times she'd watched Tom handle *Huckleberry* in tight situations during races and wondered how he could not be afraid. Now she realized that he might well be, but he didn't panic, and he didn't show his fear to his crew. It was ironic that Ori's refusal to risk getting caught in a storm had pushed Beth toward this new self-knowledge. Or perhaps, she reflected, Ori had known exactly what she was doing.

In any case, although she was sorry to have lost Ori, she felt that what she'd gained through their brief friendship was worth it.

"I'm sorry to keep you Beth, I know it's late in the day," Beth's supervisor Tom fidgeted with a pen as he spoke.

"No problem," Beth lied – she was going to miss the express bus.

"Beth, we have really enjoyed working with you for the last seven months."

Oh hell.

"But as you know, we've been mandated by senior management to restructure the department."

Not again. It's not fair.

"This is very hard. But we're going to have to eliminate your position."

Eliminated. I'm eliminated.

"I'm very sorry, Beth. If I could, I wouldn't change a thing. But things are difficult right now."

Beth nodded slowly, the reality sinking in quickly as she mentally calculated her monthly expenses and compared them to her bank balance.

"I'm disappointed," she said. "I thought things were going well."

"It has been Beth. Honestly. But the reorganization is beyond my control."

"So what do I do?" she asked, disinterested in hearing his excuses. She didn't believe that he'd had no hand in the decision, but it didn't really matter. She did believe that if he'd had problems with her work he would have said so, however, and for some reason that lessened the sting just a little.

A half hour later she was on the sidewalk with a box of her belongings that was lighter than the last time and a surprisingly generous severance check in her handbag. Tom, it seemed, had been sincere. The man in personnel had assured her that her supervisor had dug in his heels about it giving her a package that was rather generous – especially after such a short stay at the company. It was enough to pay off the loan on *Trouble*.

"Oh geez Beth. You aren't joking are you?" Trish groaned that evening on the phone. Beth had realized as she dialed the phone that she'd been neglecting her sister as well as her friends all summer, and now she was calling with terrible news. She felt lousy – about her job and about being irresponsible toward her family and friends and about having to sit on the subway with the box all the way to Pelham Bay, and then on the city bus the rest of the way home. The sympathetic stares from the other riders had almost been enough to push her to tears.

"I'm not joking," she said, pressing her cold beer bottle to her forehead.

"Honey, you'll have to sell the boat – right? I'm so sorry, I know you've been enjoying it."

"Maybe. Maybe not. I could pay off the loan," she replied, knowing she sounded defensive.

"Beth, is that practical?"

"It's my biggest monthly expense."

"But you need the severance pay for a deposit on an apartment – where are you going to live this winter? I know I haven't lived on the east coast, but I can imagine that a boat is not the best place to spend winter."

"People do it," Beth replied weakly. Trish's arguments were sounding pretty reasonable, but they were not what she wanted right now. She wanted sympathy and moral support, not rational advice. There was silence on the line for a moment, as if Trish was trying to think of a more convincing argument.

"Well then, I'm sure there are ways to make it comfortable," she said to Beth's utter surprise. "I suppose since it's a small space it won't cost so much to heat."

"Yes," Beth said, chuckling, "They say that if you keep the interior above freezing it keeps ice from forming around the hull. Of course, the tapered shape of the hull prevents the ice from damaging it if it does form – the boat just rides upward as the ice closes in until it's sitting on top."

She was kidding, although the principle she was describing was true. It was very unlikely that the water around *Trouble* would freeze solid given the tides, wave action, and warmth of the boat. But she had read about arctic expeditions where what she described happened.

"Wow, that's kind of scary," Trish replied, swallowing her story whole. Sometimes it was painfully obvious that she hadn't ever lived outside of balmy Southern California.

"I'm kidding Trish," Beth snorted. "It doesn't get that cold here – maybe it'll freeze for a day or two, but otherwise I'll be fine."

"Okay, okay, don't tease me like that. So what about income? What about a job?"

"I was thinking of going to some temp agencies," Beth replied truthfully.

"Why not an employment agency, a headhunter?" Trish countered, as usual thinking of stability and permanence.

"Maybe," Beth hedged. "I need to analyze my monthly cash flow and figure out what I really need."

"It sounds like you're considering aiming for poverty level."

"I'm aiming at living the life I want. And I think that it includes some freedom for a change. I've been tied to desks and the nine-to-five since college. Temping I can have a day off now and then."

She was sure Trish wanted to counter that it would be an unpaid day off, but thankfully her sister refrained. Perhaps she knew that Beth was well aware of the negatives of her plan. If so, Beth was doubly grateful to her for not pointing them out.

ELEVEN: INCOME

Beth called on three temporary employment agencies over the next week, filling out forms and providing her resume. One, she learned, specialized in bookkeepers and other back-office help, so she withdrew her application. Another was predominantly retail. She had a tiny bit of retail experience, and with the holidays approaching there would be lots of short-term openings, so she kept her fingers crossed. The third agency was more general, and the associate she met with commented on her language and communications skills. She thought she had something with one of the major financial institutions. But when Beth called back the next day the opportunity had vanished and the placement agent seemed uncomfortable about it. Surfing the agency's website at the library a while later Beth noticed that they listed her former company as one of their clients.

"They can't do that," Eve said. "They told you they eliminated your job." She licked at the salt on her margarita and took a sip.

"Strictly speaking, they said they reorganized the department. But that's what I took it to mean," Beth replied, stirring her slushy green drink with the plastic sword that skewered a bit of lime.

"But you saw your job listed on their website?"

"Yup. They've got it listed as a short-term position – that's why they have the agency looking, I guess."

"But they didn't give you a reason for firing you – a performance reason."

"No. None. I really believed that he would have told me if there was something wrong."

"They did you a favor, if they did have a problem – telling you they eliminated your position is a layoff. They could have told you it was 'for cause' and you wouldn't be able to get unemployment."

"I wasn't working there long enough to get it."

"But you were at the job before that long enough. You mean you haven't filed?"

"Well, no. I --."

"You should. You've paid into it all these years."

"It's so embarrassing."

"Bullshit. You paid it in, you should get it back when you need it. Lord knows there won't be any money left in Social Security when you're old enough for it."

"Have you ever collected unemployment?"

"Yes. I know the system is a pain to deal with – they can be really demeaning. But if you can get past that, it's worth it."

Beth sighed and took a sip of her margarita. Eve had insisted that she come out drinking, and had insisted on buying the first round. After discovering the situation with her old job Beth had been eager to comply.

She had no idea what had happened that had made them let her go only to replace her with a temp. And if it weren't for the nagging curiosity – the sense that she had made some fatal error of which she was completely oblivious, but that her employers thought was so obvious it didn't bear mentioning – she would forget it and move on. She'd liked the job and the people, but she had never regarded it as her perfect career. Crafting internal corporate communications had been challenging a few years ago, but over the last few months – since her split with Peter, really, she had grown more and more cynical about being a part of the corporate mouthpiece. Since moving to *Trouble* she had definitely focused more of her attention on the boat and sailing, but she didn't think her job performance had sunk that low. But now, with autumn in full color and winter ominously near she could tell that marina life was going to change. Soon it would be a cold, empty place, with none of the boaters around except the handful of liveaboards scurrying across the parking lot to the relative warmth of their boats. No afternoon beers, no Sunday brunches. It was like her friendship with Ori in a way – just when she was totally happy with it, it came to an end.

Two days after Beth and Eve's Mexican food consolation dinner, the retail oriented agency called with an assignment at a major chain electronics store.

"The assignment is through the holidays, but you'll have to work the Thanksgiving sales," the agent warned her. Beth accepted. It was mid-September, and the prospect of steady work for the rest of the year seemed like a mixed blessing. The income was a positive, of course. But as she thought through the logistics of getting to the store, the notion of going to a job almost every day was deeply disappointing. She had, she realized, been looking forward to a period of freedom, even if it would be in poverty. But Trish was on her about coming to California for Christmas, and the only way she might be able to swing that was if she earned some extra money now. The fact that the job might require her to be in New York immediately before and after Christmas was a scheduling problem she'd address later.

She soon realized that she had underestimated the logistical problems when she took the job. The store was in downtown Manhattan. Her shift most days started at eight a.m. to restock the shelves and price items before the store opened. She worked until two with a half hour lunch break around eleven. The earliest express bus reached mid-town at eight a.m., too late for her to get downtown on time. That meant she had to take the city bus to the subway – a much longer ride – starting around six. The homeward trip was equally inconvenient, unless she hung around the city until the first evening express at quarter of five.

She arrived bleary eyed at the bus stop the first morning and was astonished to see a line of others already waiting. The bus to the subway was standing-room-only. Fortunately, it was just a fifteen-minute ride. The only advantage to getting on the subway at the first station was that she could always get a seat, although she often felt compelled to run up the steps to the elevated platform to beat out the middle aged matrons.

But then, at one hundred twenty-fifth street she faced a daily dilemma: stay on the local train, which made about thirty-eight stops before it finally reached her destination, or switch to the express that made a half dozen stops but was bursting at the seams already when it pulled into the station. If she got to the transfer station by seven fifteen she stayed on the local. Any later and she couldn't risk it. The crowded express was the only way to ensure that she clocked in on time.

Clocking in – now that was demeaning. It had been years since she'd worked on a time clock and she'd forgotten how some supervisors could be. At M&P they seemed to train them to hover over the mechanical clock during the minutes before the start of the shift. Clock in early and you got docked twice the extra time. Clock in late and you got reprimanded and had to work doubly late. Beth suspected that these policies were in violation of some sort of labor laws, but as a temporary worker it wasn't worth it to her to protest. But it did make her think about the people who made a career of this. It made her days writing flyers about the corporate Holiday party seem like a dream job.

"That's a great little laptop," Alex, one of the full-timers, had come up to look over her shoulder as she played with a sleek, white computer with a brilliantly sharp monitor. She had always been drawn to Macintosh computers, but her jobs had always required that she use Microsoft Windows and other PC applications.

"Hi," she said to the curly headed young man. He was about a decade younger than her – a real gadget freak. "I didn't know you worked in this department – I thought you were behind the PDA counter."

"I'm filling in. But I like it up here. The Apple customers are always interesting."

"Graphics nerds," she suggested, knowing that every graphics department she'd ever worked with had been populated by die-hard Apple fanatics. Although their enthusiasm had rubbed off on her, she didn't want to admit an association with them.

"Yeah, and film students, and photographers. Musicians. Students. It's cool."

"And so is this," she agreed, scanning through the collection of songs in the iBook's music software. She double clicked on an old Oingo Boingo tune and it began to play through the attached speakers.

"Are you thinking of buying one?" Alex asked.

"I'd love to have one. But it would cut into my cash reserves," she said, shaking her head wistfully.

"You don't have a computer at home?"

"No. I've always had them at work. But since I've made some changes – taken this job – I'm going through Internet withdrawal."

"Not to mention email," he sympathized.

"I go to the library."

"That can't be easy," he said, glancing around the nearly empty department. "I don't know how your cash reserves are, but if it would help, I'd buy it using my employee discount," he said quietly.

Beth's eyes widened. The thought had crossed her mind, but she would never have asked. Still, she wasn't sure if a computer was a necessary item or a splurge. But whenever she considered it, she remembered Ori's laptop mounted in *Dream Catcher*'s navigation station. She had hooked it up to the phone line and used it to check the weather patterns on her planned route. She'd used it for email, and for her ship's log. She'd explained that when she sailed long distances along the coast she subscribed to a wireless service. The weather data alone had saved her from some rough passages, she'd explained.

Don't be silly, you're not going cruising.

"Can we calculate what it would cost?" she asked Alex.

Four days later she handed him just over a thousand dollars, in cash as he'd asked, and took possession of a powerful little laptop with a big hard drive, a wireless network card just in case she found herself within range of a network, Alex had explained, and internal modem, CD/DVD-burner, and tons of memory. He'd thrown in a sleek case, a package of blank DVDs, and gotten her his discount on some critical add-on software.

So I spent all of my earnings on a new toy, she admitted to herself as she watched the computer dial up the Internet from the comfort of *Trouble*'s main salon. Most of the liveaboards had switched to cellular phones, but since the landline had been installed along the dock to *Trouble*'s slip she had simply re-activated it when she moved aboard. She had to remember to unplug it when she went sailing, but otherwise it was reliable and cheap. But that made her one of the four New Yorkers without a cellular phone.

That changed in her third week at M&P. The price on a discontinued model of basic phone was cut by two thirds. Basic service was just thirty dollars a month. Noting that the service area included the entire east coast, she laid down her credit card and signed up.

TWELVE: CONVICTION

"You're on a spending spree, Beth!" Eve said, looking around *Trouble*'s salon. After working a month Beth had pocketed about a week and a half's pay and spent the rest. But she could defend each item in terms of its value to the boat: the laptop, the phone, the new digital camera, the hand-held VHF radio and GPS, all were standard equipment on well-found boats.

"Everything, except the camera, is really a safety item," she said.

Eve opened her mouth to counter this but stopped, considering each item. "You've got me there," she shrugged. "And if you want you can say the camera is too – you can photograph any damage for your insurance claim when you crash because you're surfing the net when you should be steering the boat."

She laughed while Beth groaned.

"What about your old job – did you ever follow up on why they had posted it?" Eve asked. Beth's groan became a cringe. She had hoped Eve would not bring it up.

"I called Tom – my old supervisor," she said. "He told me that the reorganization had been delayed. He was all apologetic about letting me go and then needing someone."

"So you told him you saw the posting?"

"Sure. And I joked that I was thinking of applying."

"Wow – what did he say to that?"

"A nervous laugh. I could tell he absolutely did not want to take me seriously."

"Like, he absolutely could not hire you back?"

"Something like that."

"And you still have no idea what you might have done –," Beth shot her a scowl. "I mean, what their problem was?"

"Not a clue. But I don't want to pursue it any more. I've moved on – I have this great job in retail."

"You're marking time in retail until something else comes along."

"Something like that."

Dear Beth, the letter began. Beth gulped her wine and forced herself to read on. The letter was a few weeks old as it had been forwarded from her old apartment. She'd forced herself to look at all the other mail before pouring a glass of wine and opening it. *I've missed you the last few months. I hope you are well. I know that the choices we both made led us to end things, but I can't help it. I have to tell you what I think.*

"Why?" Beth asked out loud. "I don't see any need to tell you what I think."

I know you think that I was finding new interests in order to distance myself from you. But I wasn't. I cared very much for you and I wanted us to be together. I offered you the chance – I invited you cycling. But you refused. I suggested we try rock climbing, but you wouldn't. And it's great, Beth – you'd love it.

Beth rolled her eyes. They'd been in a sporting goods store with a practice wall when Peter had suggested it. She had assumed that he just wanted to try it at the store, so she'd told him to go for it and she'd watch. He had, and he'd enjoyed it, and she thought that was the end of it. She'd had no idea that he'd pursued it, or that he harbored this ill will toward her over it.

It was you who kept changing things, Beth. You made new friends. "I went for drinks with my co-workers every couple weeks." *You quit bowling.* "It was the same night as *Survivor* and I didn't feel like watching it on tape. I made a choice." *You never wanted to go running.* "That's right. I never wanted to, but I did, for a while, to please you."

The rest of the letter went on in the same vein – whining and accusatory, concluding with an assertion that their break-up had not been mutual, but her responsibility alone. It left her feeling emotionally abused and depressed. She refilled her wine glass and climbed out into the cockpit for a change of scenery. Herb Goldberg walked by on the dock, smiling and waving as he passed. She waved back and repositioned herself to look west toward the setting sun.

"Is he right?"

She took another sip of wine.

"Does he have any right?"

A pair of seagulls flapped by calling to one another in course, raucous voices.

No.

"Bethy? Do you want to come for a drink?" Susan Goldberg called from the dock. Her eyeglasses reflected the yellowish light from the footlights that lined the dock. They had just switched on as the sun was setting. Beth turned and held up her wine.

"I have one, thanks," she called back.

Susan eyed her for a moment and then replied, "Bring it along then."

She made a beckoning gesture with her hand and turned to clatter back toward *Second Million* in her hard-soled shoes.

Beth shrugged in surrender and climbed out of the cockpit to follow. Sometimes she thought Susan Goldberg was telepathic – at least about people feeling low. She made it her job to cheer them up.

But Beth's slump after Peter's letter continued despite Susan's efforts. She'd run out of new things to buy – at least that she could justify as necessary boating equipment. A flat plasma TV would be much less bulky than her old fourteen-inch Sony, but it was hardly essential no matter how attractive the sales display was. So she put the money in the bank and looked into their on-line banking services.

And then Tom invited her to race on *Huckleberry* during a late fall regatta, but she could only do one day since she had to work the other. It was cold, wet, and windy, but she enjoyed every frightening minute of it. She got home from work the second day just in time to go to the yacht club for the awards party. Tom's crew as well as other racers she'd gotten to know over the summer welcomed her and the buoyant feeling it gave her helped her understand her depression. Peter's letter, the long commute, Ori's departure, and the encroaching winter had eroded the edges of the new life she was creating for herself. But it was still here – she was still here, and if she was the center of her life, it was up to her to fight the erosion.

That night she made herself re-read Peter's letter, and the whiney tone came through even more clearly than before. He accused her of moving on, and by God she had. *He's the one stuck in a rut! What happens when he runs out of new sports to try?*

The next day she found a water-stained letter postmarked Miami, Florida, in her box in the marina office. True to her word, Ori had written when she reached Florida. The letter was rather quaint – a written, mailed missive in an age of email and instant messaging. But Ori knew that Beth relied on the library with its twenty-minute time limit and nickel-a-page charge for printouts, so she had promised a traditional letter.

Getting here was more than half the fun, the letter began. *I'm sure you tracked Hurricane Ernst last week. I did too – from a secure slip in Jacksonville.* Beth felt a surge of irresponsibility – she had heard something about a hurricane hitting Florida, but she'd paid very little attention. And now she learned that her friend had been caught in it. *It just spit some heavy winds at us, and a lot of rain, but it was a tense couple of days. I had every line out securing* Dream Catcher *to the dock. And I had to strip off the sails. And that was only the most recent adventure. Off the coast of North Carolina the transmission belt snapped. I drifted for three days in no wind, then it picked up like the devil had spotted me. I had to sail into a very shallow anchorage and drop the hook so that I could take the dinghy ashore. I beached the dinghy and hiked to a road, then hitch-hiked to a town about five miles away. Naturally the only auto parts shop was closed.*

I was going to walk back and hitch another ride the next morning, but the guy who gave me the ride insisted that I stay with him. I said no, but then he mentioned that his wife would be angry with him for not asking me. So I said yes.

Beth tried to imagine what she would have done in such a situation. She had never hitch hiked – the horror stories of abduction, robbery, and worse were enough to make her find other means of transportation. She could well imagine Ori hitching a ride. And she could also picture her declining the man's offer. She was sure that even after he mentioned his wife Ori was cautions.

I still didn't trust him – until we got to his house and I met the wife. She was drop-dead gorgeous, and so nice! I think he lives to please her. I certainly had nothing to worry about with her occupying his attention.

Beth laughed, imaging Ori's flashing blue eyes as she laughed and her close-cropped jet-black hair. She wasn't a beauty, but she had an inner light and a ready smile that made her very attractive. But it was typical of her that she didn't think she could compete with a gorgeous woman.

So next morning I got a transmission belt, and an extra, and Joe – that was his name – drove me back to the spot on the road closest to my dinghy. Then he insisted on hiking to it with me, because there are snakes in the area. I'm glad I didn't know that going in. I guess I came in on a high tide and it was low when we got back, because the dinghy was high and dry and Dream Catcher *was sitting on the bottom and listing to one side.*

Joe helped me drag the dinghy out, but there was nothing I could do about Dream Catcher *except curse the out-of-date charts until the tide returned and floated my boat.*

Beth wondered how long Ori had waited to use that old cliché.

Ori went on to describe each stage of her voyage, including details that suggested she expected Beth to follow her path – notes on channels that were not well marked, and a new marina not in the cruising guides where she got very good service. The letter read like a combination adventure novel and travel guide. When she finished it, Beth immediately started back at the beginning.

Quit dawdling, Beth. Quit that dumb job and hit the open water. You know you want to. I don't know what to tell you about the loan. Borrow money from your sister? It's a terrible thing to live under the burden of our possessions. Escape now before it's too late.

Beth re-read Ori's conclusion with a fond smile. She had never found out how her friend supported herself. Clearly she didn't subscribe to any traditional system of fiscal responsibility. Beth knew that people like that were either dirt poor or very wealthy. She'd known both types, but she hadn't been able slot Ori into either category.

"You know you want to," she read out loud from the letter. "You're right, Ori. I do. And I think I'm ready."

THIRTEEN: GIFTS

"This is it," Beth looked at the small pile of boxes tucked into the corner of Eve's mother's garage. "Thank you again for letting me store them here, Mrs. Johnson. It makes a big difference in my budget."

"Of course dear," Mrs. Johnson replied, her thick Brooklyn-accent distorting the O and U sounds. "With just the one car, and since Eve's brother finally took all of his things away, I have the room to spare," the older woman leaned closer, glancing at Eve as if trying to keep a secret from her. "I think what you're doing is very brave – I wish I'd had the guts to do something like it when I was young."

"Well, it's never too late," Beth said in an equally conspiratorial tone, "Do you want to join me?"

They both burst out laughing and Eve groaned.

"Come on," she said. "I'm treating for lunch in the village. Lord knows neither of you can afford it!"

That wasn't true – Mrs. Johnson lived on a comfortable pension, but neither she nor Beth elected to argue with Eve's generosity.

After lunch Eve borrowed her mother's car to drive Beth back to City Island. She parked in the gravel covered lot between two boats already hauled and covered for the winter and walked with Beth down the dock to *Trouble*'s slip.

"Last chance," she said weakly, looking at the boat as if it were a hearse.

"No, not really," Beth replied. "I can turn back at any time."

Eve forced a weak smile then dashed at her eyes with the back of her hand. "Not if you're out in the water and a storm hits, or your engine dies and there's no wind. Or you're eaten by a whale –."

At that Beth burst out laughing. Her friend, she realized, had been researching sea disasters. Eve grimaced, realizing how foolish she sounded.

"Please be careful," she said simply, taking Beth's hand. "Call when you get to the Virgin Islands. I'll come join you then."

"Oh sure, you'll come for the warm part."

Eve shrugged, admitting that Beth was right. Then she pulled her into a tight hug that went on and on until Beth finally groaned and broke it off.

"I promise to be careful. I promise to avoid all whales. And I promise to call you when I get to the Caribbean. Hell, I'll probably call you long before that."

"Okay." Eve took a step back, giving Beth tacit permission to board her boat. She took it, stepping up on the deck and then into the cockpit. When she looked back at the dock Eve waved, blew her a kiss, then turned and strode away as fast as she could. Beth stood watching her until she disappeared behind the boats in the parking lot, and then she reached out to open the combination padlock on the companionway and open the door to her home.

The following afternoon she waved at the Statue of Liberty smiling down on her as she sailed past on the outgoing tide. She looked back over her shoulder at the Manhattan skyline and felt a pang of regret. *Am I running away from New York? If I couldn't make it here, will I make it anywhere?*

She rolled her eyes at her own pathetic notion and turned around to face the Verrazano Narrows and the open sea beyond.

But just two hours later she dropped the anchor in the protected shallows behind Sandy Hook, New Jersey. The first day of her cruise had been short, but she was happy to celebrate it anyway. She took an anchor bearing – a note of landmarks that she could check later to see if the boat had moved – and went below to break out the party.

When Eve had given her the small bottle of Veuve Cliquot and told her to save it for a special occasion, she probably had not meant the end of her first day. But this first, small step had been the hardest for Beth, so she felt it was exactly the right occasion to honor with good champagne.

The cork made a satisfying pop and the wine bubbled cheerfully into her plastic wine glass. She switched on the stereo and turned up the volume, filling the cabin and cockpit with Vivaldi. She set the bottle on the top step and returned to the cockpit with her glass in one hand and a folded piece of paper in the other. Ori's letter seemed like the perfect way to bolster her nerve for the next step.

"Beth, I can't believe this. This is so irresponsible! It's not like you. At least, not like the old you. What the hell has happened to you lately?" Beth held her cell phone away from her ear and listened to her sister's tinny voice coming through the cheap speaker. It was nearly an exact replay of the tirade she'd endured when she told Trish that she was cutting loose and going cruising. This time Trish had called her to discuss Christmas, and Beth had been forced to explain to her sister that she was not going to fly to California – that she couldn't afford it, and she wasn't sure where she would be by then so she couldn't even book the flight. As she let Trish wear herself out she realized that her sister had not really accepted what her decision to cruise meant. Until now.

"What am I going to tell mom and dad? You are so selfish. Do you know that? First you move three thousand miles away and leave it to me to take care of them. Now you're not even coming for Christmas. Dad's having a hard time remembering you – did you know that?"

"What?" Beth gasped. "What do you mean? Is he all right?"

"He's getting old Beth. There are signs – he forgets things."

"Why are you telling me this now?" Beth lost control and yelled. The line went dead. For a moment Beth thought that Trish was just too stunned to speak. Then she looked at the phone and realized that she had lost her connection.

"Dammit!" she cursed. *Trouble* was gliding along the calm waters of the Chesapeake Bay on a heading for Annapolis, Maryland. And she had glided right out of the cellular service zone. There was nothing Beth could do until she got back into a service area, so she carried the phone below and plugged it into the twelve volt outlet to charge it. She stood in the companionway for a moment watching the boat steer itself, smiling in appreciation of the favors that her friends had done for her during her hasty preparation for departure.

Once she'd decided to do it, she knew that she had to do it immediately or survive the winter on City Island. In another few weeks it would be too dangerously cold to start the journey – if she were caught in a nor'easter here in northern waters she could easily lose everything.

She'd mentioned her plan to the Goldbergs when they came to the marina to winterize *Second Million*. Winterizing their boat meant removing the house plants and food from the galley. They paid the marina staff to pump antifreeze into the fresh water system, lay-up the engine, and haul and cover the boat.

Susan had seemed less surprised than Herb. But Beth soon realized why: He understood the impact of what she was proposing. To Susan it was no different than their excursion to New York Harbor for the fireworks. The following afternoon Beth had found Herb in *Trouble*'s cockpit when she got home from work. Once she got over her astonishment at this unprecedented violation of privacy, she asked him what he was doing hunched over behind the wheel.

"Auto helm," he grunted.

"Otto who?" she asked, frowning.

Herb straightened up and she saw that he was holding an electric screwdriver and there was a cordless drill on the bench beside him.

"Auto helm – self steering mechanism," he said. "I'm just checking your set up so I can order the right one."

"Herb, I --."

"Hush. You can't be behind the wheel all the time. I know how you do it now – locking down the wheel while you run forward to do things. That's fine out there," he gestured out toward the Sound. "But you can't always count on steady breezes and flat water. And even when you don't have chores to do on the sails, you can't be steering all day."

"But Herb --."

He raised his free hand palm out in a silencing gesture. "It's a *bon voyage* gift. Don't be ungrateful."

"But it's too much!"

"Beth, this winter I'm planning on trading *Second Million* up for a new boat – probably call her *Third Million*. An auto helm for you is a drop in the bucket."

"I don't know what to say," Beth dropped down on to the bench.

"Never mind sweetie. I'm just a do-gooder at heart. But don't tell any of my employees. And don't tell Susan about *Third Million* – it's a surprise."

The boat or the million? Beth wanted to ask. But she held her tongue, busying herself instead with unlocking the boat and preparing a thank-you cocktail for her guest.

Aside from the gift of the auto helm, that exchange with Herb Goldberg had satisfied some of her curiosity about him. It was he who had earned the millions, not Susan. And he had a somewhat different reputation with the employees of his clothing distribution firm.

Herb's gift had been the first of many. Tom had dropped by with a thick roll of charts covering most of the eastern seaboard. Doug had brought her a box full of non-breakable galley supplies – plastic storage containers, the plastic wine glasses, plates, mugs, and a set of worn stainless steel pans.

"If it's not stainless, get rid of it," he'd instructed her, looking at her pots and pans. She had collected them over the years from friends and relatives, and the occasional new purchase. Over the summer she had whittled it down to just what she needed on board. But Doug seemed to think it was all junk. "It'll rust," he explained, pulling out her scarred non-stick fry pan and turning it over. There was rust around the connection between the pan and the handle. "See?"

Beth had followed his orders, discarding some of her old pans and packing the rest up in the boxes that she'd moved to Mrs. Johnson's garage. She had taken greater pleasure in packing up almost all of her business clothes. She kept one all-purpose dress and one pant suit on board, along with boating clothes from yacht-club tidy to bottom-scrubbing grungy. The space that this freed up made room for another gift – this one from the marina staff.

"This has been lying around the office for a year. We figure that it this point it's unclaimed goods," Sid had explained as he dropped the sailbag into *Trouble*'s cockpit. "Out at sea, you can never have too many spare jibs. This one's from an Island Packet just like *Trouble* that was here last year. There's something else, too," he waved to someone on the dock and she heard the rumble of a cart rolling over the boards. Sid went to meet it and heaved out a white plastic rectangular box.

"You shouldn't do a long cruise without a life raft," he said. "We're going to mount it on your stern rail so it's out of the way.

"Good heavens, Sid, those are expensive!" Beth said. She had attended a Safety at Sea seminar back in June.

"It's a demo model that Chris got from the store," Sid said rather vaguely.

Beth frowned, not sure whether he was implying that it was stolen, and wondering if it had been inspected recently. It would do little good if she pulled the cord and it didn't inflate.

But she didn't have time to express her concerns before Sid returned to the cart.

"This last thing's not a gift – it's an offer. This is a four-horse-power outboard: good enough for a small dinghy. I used to use it, and I overhauled it last year. But then I got a bigger one. I'll sell you this one for thirty bucks – if you want it."

"I don't have a dinghy," Beth pointed out, looking at the small engine that he had lifted out of the cart. "If I did, I'd want the engine."

"You can't go cruising without a dinghy," Sid declared, sounding a lot like Ori.

"I know. It's a problem. I just haven't had time to work on it."

"Okay, here's the deal then – if I can find you a dinghy, cheap, you buy this engine."

"Deal," Beth grinned.

"Fine, then we'll just mount this on the stern rail too – as long as Chris is at it."

Two days later she'd come home to find a man in her cockpit installing the auto helm, Herb looking on enthusiastically, and a grey rubber inflated dinghy in the slip next to *Trouble*'s bow.

"Afternoon Bethy. This is Al. He's going to get your auto helm connected. I'm glad you're here – he needs to get inside," Herb blurted all at once as she stepped on board. Al raised his head and nodded, then went back to his work.

"And Sid brought that dink over," Herb pointed toward the little boat. "It's seen better days, I think. But I guess the price is right."

"What is the price?" Beth asked Sid a few minutes later, after opening *Trouble*'s companionway for Al and wandering around the docks to find him.

"I got it at a tag sail. A hundred dollars."

Beth swallowed hard. She was in hoarding mode after her spending spree, and a hundred dollars seemed like a fortune. But she quickly considered the alternative – being unable to get ashore when she anchored. She imagined Ori's predicament with the alternator belt – and having to pay for water taxis when they were available. Having to pay for slips instead of much cheaper moorings. She could go through a hundred dollars in one marina stay. She had stopped at a cash machine on the way home, so she pulled out her wallet and counted out five twenties.

"I'll come by later and show you how to mount the engine – make sure it fits and stuff," Sid smiled.

FOURTEEN: GUILT

"What do you mean, Dad forgets things?" Beth said as calmly as she could. She had reached Annapolis and taken a mooring in Spa creek for a nominal daily charge. Although it was late October and the leaves were a brilliant orange, the temperature was much warmer than back in Long Island Sound. Beth felt like she really had run away, and having to conclude this conversation with her sister only added to a growing, if misplaced, sense of guilt for shirking her responsibilities.

"Oh Beth, I'm so sorry to have sprung that on you like that. It was mean. And I was about to apologize when the line went dead. Is everything all right?"

"Yes – I just sailed out of the service area. But I'm in Annapolis now – there are plenty of cellular users around here."

"That is so cool!"

Beth was astonished. Trish had had nothing good to say about her plans from the moment she'd shared them. *Now she thinks sailing to Annapolis is cool?*

"It's a neat little town," she agreed, although she had only seen the waterfront from the water. But the Maryland capital dome rose pristine white on the top of the hill in the center of town. She was looking forward to exploring the brick streets tomorrow. "But tell me about Dad."

Trish sighed, and it sounded like there was a catch in her voice when she spoke.

"Well, late – lately he's been leaving the house and wandering the neighborhood. The Bentleys down the street have brought him home a couple times. I talked with them when we last drove out for a visit and they were very kind about it, but I could tell they were concerned. They said he was standing in the middle of the street watching birds on the telephone pole one time."

"Good lord, Trish. Has he seen a doctor?"

"No, not yet."

"Why not?"

"You know how they are – if it isn't pneumonia, they're not ill."

"Trish, do you think it could be Alzheimer's?"

"I don't know Beth. It could be, but I don't know enough about it to even guess."

"There are drugs now to slow it down," Beth glanced at her computer, thinking that she could go on line and do some research. Then she remembered that she didn't have a phone line out here on the water.

"Are there? I didn't think there was a cure, if that's what it is."

"I didn't say it was a cure. But it helps them hold on longer. That's all I remember reading. It was in *Time* Magazine not long ago. Trish, you have got to get him to see a doctor. It might not be Alzheimer's. We need to find out."

Trish was silent for a moment and Beth could practically read her thoughts: *You want to know, but I have to do the work.* Beth had not forgotten the news she'd delivered that had precipitated this discussion – she wasn't going to fly west for Christmas. She wasn't going to go help her sister manage their parents.

But it was just a doctor's appointment. Hell, she could make the phone calls, set it up, from here. Trish just needed to be sure he actually got there. Beth listened to her internal monologue and knew that no amount of long distance participation would be equal to being there. So she held her tongue.

"You're right," Trish finally said, although Beth thought it had cost her a great deal to say it. "I'll speak to Mom. If anyone can get him to the doctor it's her. But I'll go out there for the appointment too."

"Thank you Trish. I can't tell you how much I appreciate your taking this step."

"It's okay Beth. I'm the one living close. I should take care of it."

There was an edge now that Beth couldn't identify. Is she still mad at me for not coming? Sure. But is it more? Does she regret that she stayed close? I can't be held responsible for that.

"You'll call and tell me what the plan is?"

"Of course. When we have it set up."

"I love you Trish. Tell Mom and Dad for me too."

"You could call them."

"I will call them."

Beth was woefully lax in her duty to her parents. She knew it, and sometimes, like now, it preyed upon her conscious. But she'd always been that way – so independent and focused that she didn't notice when weeks went by without contact with her family. Trish frequently called her on it – chiding her about being remote, the black sheep.

Of course Beth had called and talked to her parents about buying *Trouble*, and then again about going cruising. But they were in a very different world in their suburban house in Southern California. She could tell when she described her plans that her mother was making one of her good natured shrugs and mouthing to her father on the extension across the room: "I have no idea what she's talking about."

She called them late that evening, around dinner time in their time zone. She didn't mention Trish's concerns, but as she chatted with her father she listened closely for signs of confusion. There were none. He discussed all of their usual topics – politics, the weather, the condition of his garden, a lunar eclipse that was to occur next month. Her mother asked about how she was cooking on the boat – clearly unable to visualize a sailboat galley. Beth promised to take photographs and email them to Trish to bring to them, and she could tell the concept of email was alien to her mother too. They ended with warm wishes and "I love you's." And Beth crawled into her berth feeling utterly drained. *From the long sail.*

The rumble of an engine near her ear awakened her and she opened her eyes to see the grey square of the hatch over her bunk. And then she remembered where she was, and her sense of accomplishment made her throw her legs over the side of the bunk and get up.

She ambled out to the galley, lit the stove, and put on water to warm. There would be no hot water in the ship's tanks – it required electricity from the engine or shore to heat – it would run the batteries right down if she left it on without an external power source. While the pot of washing water warmed she put together the stainless steel percolator that Doug had given her and put the coffee on another burner to perk.

Only then did she poke her head up through the companionway, sliding the hatch open but leaving the washboards in place, to look around.

The creek was misty with only the closest boats clearly visible. But still she could see that there was movement all around. Crew on the decks of sailboats dropping moorings and preparing sails, other boats already motoring out toward the drawbridge and the Chesapeake Bay.

She ran her fingers through her tangled hair and watched the parade, realizing that it must be a regatta. And that her hair needed washing. In fact, it really needed cutting.

She sat in the cockpit forcing a wide-toothed comb through her salt-saturated hair between sips of coffee. The creek anchorage emptied out very quickly, and with the forest of masts gone she had a clear view of the drawbridge and the shore on either side. And of a low motorboat puttering across the creek with several people seated on benches along either side. A canopy over the top bore a sign that said "Water Taxi – VHF 16/69."

Not only do they sail in late October, but the water taxi is still running. This is a great town.

An hour later the taxi came along side *Trouble* and she climbed aboard with a small backpack. She had the boat to herself for the ride to the town dock, so she asked the driver about the racing fleet. He told her it was the annual fall regatta with at least a hundred boats in six or seven divisions. The party, he made sure to mention, would be at the tavern up on West Street late that afternoon.

She thanked him for the info as she paid the two dollar fare, and then shouldered her bag and strode up the dock taking in the sights. Inside the large waterfront hotel she scanned the rack of local brochures and found one that contained a stylized street map of town. She used it to tour the streets and admire the well-kept federal style architecture. Despite the nip in the air the brick-clad town had a warm, small town feel that made it hard for Beth to believe it was the state capital, not to mention the home of the U.S. Naval Academy. She wandered past two separate gates into the Academy, both watched over by uniformed guards. The gleaming statehouse dome watched over the entire town and was visible from nearly every corner.

Early in her walk she came across a barbershop. Back in Manhattan she'd had a favorite stylist at a salon in the village, and she'd paid New York City rates for her haircuts. But her budget wouldn't support that kind of expense anymore. The barber didn't bat an eye at her request for an appointment for a wash and cut, and he penciled her in for early afternoon. Half way through her walk she spotted a familiar round green sign inside a storefront. She ordered a basic coffee and a cinnamon scone, set up an account to use the wireless network, and set up her laptop.

She checked her email and sent a message to Alex from M&P thanking him for insisting that she include the wireless network connection in her computer. Then she researched Alzheimer's disease, focusing on early symptoms and treatments. The news was better than she expected and more frightening than she'd feared. She emailed links to a dozen pages to Trish, hoping that her sister would understand that she was trying to help, not dictating action.

The barber was surprised when she asked him to crop her hair. But when she explained that she was living on a sailboat dependent on a limited water supply he nodded understanding and picked up his clippers.

All her life Beth had despaired of her hair – at first because it didn't fall in glossy straight sheets like some of her friends'. Later because it was impossible to have an active life without developing frizzy split ends. Most recently she'd felt betrayed by it as she spotted more and more grey hairs amid the brown. But this wasn't the time to begin coloring it, and she hoped that if it was short she could keep it from getting to frizzy.

She had never had short hair, so when the barber set aside his blow dryer and handed her a mirror she took a deep breath and braced herself. Looking into the mirror she saw a distinctly heart-shaped face with strong cheekbones and too-thick eyebrows framed by a halo of feathered brown waves. She shook her head and the lightness was amazingly freeing. Delighted, she gave the barber a generous tip and asked him where she might find a grocery store.

He directed her to a warehouse across from the town dock that housed a number of food stalls. She'd had more of a supermarket in mind, but the cheeses and fresh breads and shellfish looked better than anything she'd ever seen at the A&P. She realized as she carried her food and backpack back to the town dock that she would probably have to learn to provision in all sorts of shops in the future. The Annapolis dock market was going to seem very normal by the time she was done. Whenever that would be.

The water taxi driver gave her a second look when she boarded and told him her destination.

"Nice haircut!" he said with a grin.

"Thanks. I needed to get control," she replied.

"Been cruising long?"

Beth felt herself inflate with pride. *That's right: I'm cruising.*

"About a week," she admitted.

"Where'd you start?"

"New York."

"Where you headed?"

"South."

"Nowhere in particular?"

"The islands. Not sure which one," she shrugged.

He nodded sagely and spun the wheel to place the taxi along side *Trouble.*"

"This is a good boat you've got here," he said. "She'll take you anywhere you ask her, I think. But do you plan to go it alone the whole way?"

He was holding onto the stanchion next to the opening in *Trouble*'s lifelines. Beth put her pack and the bag of food up on the deck and then stepped up on the gunwale of the taxi.

"So far I do. But who knows what will happen?"

"A word of unsolicited advice?" he held her gaze with his sharp grey eyes. She nodded. "A woman alone in the islands will be a target, no matter how capable you are. If you don't want to carry a weapon – and I'm not saying you should – you should probably have company."

"Sounds like the voice of experience."

"Charter skipper, seven years. Best job in the world until the lousy sailors and the rum and the lazy heat melt your brain. But I've seen a lot down there, and I know that the men on a lot of the islands don't have very progressive attitudes toward women. You'll have a lot more fun if you don't have to worry about putting them off all the time."

Beth nodded thoughtfully. "I guess I'll have to give that some thought," she replied.

"Just my opinion, miss," he added.

Beth pulled herself up onto *Trouble*'s side deck and turned to thank him.

"You going back ashore later?" he asked.

"Yes – I think I'll crash the racers' party."

He grinned and nodded. "Just give me a holler," he said, then waved as his radio crackled to life with another call.

FIFTEEN: GRACE

The tavern across from the State House was a rambling brick building with several dining rooms and an outdoor patio. The beer seemed to flow from the taps directly down the gullets of several hundred raucous, damp racers. Beth threaded her way through the crowd picking up the familiar buzz of sailors coming down from an exciting day on the water. She realized that she had subconsciously noticed the strong breeze all morning while she was exploring, and then listened to it whistling in the rigging while she cleaned up for the party. Out on the Bay it had given the racers quite a ride. Through snippets of conversation she gathered that all of the divisions had gotten in three races – almost unheard of on Long Island Sound – and there had been some close calls around the windward mark. But it seemed as if some of the best crews were not at the party. She kept hearing references to "the middies," and sometimes "the damned middies," but it was obvious whoever they were they were not around to defend themselves.

She was sitting at the end of one of the bars on the outskirts of a group when she realized to whom they were all referring. A framed photograph behind the bar showed a crew of brawny male sailors and two fit but petite women lined up on the bow of a dark hulled sailboat. A caption beneath it identified them as the USNA J-109 team. *Midshipmen. "Middies." Duh.* And the midshipmen were not allowed to come over to the tavern to a drunken party on Saturday afternoon.

"You crew?" the bartender was standing across from her wiping a glass with a white towel.

"Nope, crashing the party," she replied honestly. The free beer and food were long gone and she'd paid for her first beer, so she didn't have any qualms about crashing. The bartender didn't seem to care.

"Looking for a sailor?" he asked.

"No, not really. I am a sailor, so I thought I'd come hang out with my kindred spirits."

"So why didn't you race today?"

"I'm just passing through. I came in last night. My boat's down in Spa Creek."

"You *are* a sailor," he smiled, filling the glass with beer from the tap.

She nodded, inclining her head in confirmation. He set the fresh glass in front of her, winked, and moved off down the bar.

Beth swiveled on her stool and watched the drunken sailors some more while she sipped her fresh beer. A few minutes later he was back.

"You want to race tomorrow?" he asked.

"How do you know I can race at all?" she replied flirtatiously.

"Something about the way you hold that beer glass," he replied. "Are you interested?"

"Um," she thought about her plans for the near future and couldn't come up with a reason not to stop over an extra day. "Why not?"

He nodded, then waved at someone at the other end of the bar. A moment later a man about Beth's age pressed through the crowd and came up beside her.

"Hi," he extended his hand to her. "I'm Jeff Allen. I'm short a crew for tomorrow on my Farr 520. Chuck said you're a sailor. Ever done any racing?"

"A little, in Long Island Sound last summer."

"Rail meat?"

"Mostly," she grinned. "But I've handled the mainsheet, and the traveler. On a 42."

"What's ten feet among friends?" he grinned back. "Are you local? We're all in a Holiday Inn outside of town."

"I'm not local – my boat's in the creek."

Jeff's brows rose slightly and he glanced across the bar at Chuck, who was unselfconsciously listening in. "You cruised down from Long Island Sound," he said, not a question. Beth nodded. "You've got crew around here somewhere?"

"Nope, just me. But I'd be happy to spend a day going fast."

He smiled. "Okay. Well, *Grace* is in the creek too. Maybe we can have the taxi pick you up on our way out."

"That would be great. I'll just monitor his channel. You can tell him to stop at *Double Trouble* – he should remember her."

"*Double Trouble?*" Jeff grinned. "Should I be regretting this invitation? Do you live up to your boat's reputation?"

"What reputation?" Beth asked blankly.

He paused, unsure if she was serious. "The name?"

"Oh that! I just inherited that. I'm no trouble at all."

"Too bad."

Beth was up at dawn, her sleep marred by nerves about her skill aboard a racing sailboat as big as Herb Goldberg's *Second Million*. She'd come back after dark last night, so she hadn't been able to try to identify *Grace* among the crowd of boats in the creek. She would have asked the water taxi driver, but it wasn't the same guy. So as soon as the hatch above her bunk lightened this morning she was poking her head out the cockpit to scan the fleet.

There. She pointed her binoculars at a long, black hull down near the bridge. From this angle she could only see part of the stern, but she was sure the first letters of the name painted there were "Gr." The boat was enormous, the boom almost as long as all of *Trouble*. The mast seemed to scratch the clouds. Beth gulped, then climbed back into the salon as if she were hiding from the big, scary boat.

She was nearly bouncing off the walls of the salon with tension and caffeine from the strong coffee she'd made when she heard a voice on the radio request a stop at *Double Trouble*. She did a last check to be sure the power and gas were off then climbed out and locked the companionway. She was fully equipped with her foul weather gear, rigging knife, and gloves. Jeff had assured her that there would be plenty to drink and lunch on board.

The taxi came along side a few minutes later and Jeff introduced her to his regular crew who looked to Beth like a gang of thugs. Their biceps looked like hams, their necks were thick with ropey muscles. She felt a huge hand wrap around her own upper arm as she climbed into the boat – a crew with a shaggy light brown haircut and sweet blue eyes. She smiled her thanks at him and the taxi driver – her friend from yesterday – shot her a knowing look as she sat down. She shrugged innocently. He was chuckling as he turned to face forward and drive them all to *Grace*.

If she'd been asked before that day whether she knew what racing sailboats was all about she'd have said "sure!" But by the end of three grueling races during which she developed eleven new bruises, two blisters, and a cut on her left hand, she realized that she knew nothing. She thanked Jeff several times for his patience with her, for he had never raised his voice even when she made an error that had cost them a first place. He assured her that for a substitute she'd done very well, and he appreciated her willingness to come along – he couldn't have raced with fewer crew the second day than he had on the first, and one of his guys had sprained his wrist the first day. She'd heard several variations on how the accident had happened from the rest of the crew, all of them insisting that the injured man had been the heroic victim.

She was tempted to just climb aboard *Trouble* and collapse on her bunk, but Jeff urged her to come to the final party at the restaurant on the town dock. Grace would be taking a trophy in her division, he assured her. She had helped earn it and she deserved to enjoy it.

So she washed up and changed and got back on the taxi amid some other boat's rowdy crew. And once she was there she was glad she'd come. Jeff's crew spotted her and dragged her to the table they'd appropriated, treating her like something between a mascot and a little sister, although most of them were younger than her.

Terry of the sweet blue eyes set a glass of beer in front of her, its contents sloshing onto the already sodden table. During the day she had found herself next to him on the rail a few times and she'd found that he was more talkative than most of the others. He was also closer to her in age, and she guessed that maturity helped with communications skills. He and Jeff were business partners, and Beth got the impression that they were successful enough to spend more time playing than working. Their conversations during the day had been continually interrupted by maneuvers, so Beth was delighted when he returned to a line of questions that they'd not been able to finish.

"So you cruised down from New York, and you're headed where?" he asked.

"The islands," she replied. "I guess I have to come up with a more specific plan than that eventually, but so far that's working."

When Terry smiled the corners of his eyes crinkled appealingly. His lips, Beth noticed, were chapped from exposure and his skin had the rugged look of someone who spent a lot of time outdoors. There was a fine network of veins on both of his cheeks. His complexion would probably not age well, but Beth liked it.

"It should hold up at least until you get to Florida – assuming you're going intracoastal that far," he said. "Are you thinking of the Bahamas from there? Or Puerto Rico? The Virgins?"

"I guess the Virgin Islands have been at the back of my mind all along," she confirmed. "I'm thinking that the USVI might be a good place to get my first taste of island life – it's still the US, but it feels like the Caribbean."

"You aren't thinking of a straight shot from Florida to St. Thomas, are you?"

"I --," she paused, realizing that she hadn't really thought it out at all. Her plan, she realized, was to hook up with Ori and rely on her planning. But she'd never discussed this plan with her friend. Ori had probably left Florida for the islands by now. "I guess I need to really make some plans," she admitted, watching Terry's smile fade to an equally appealing serious expression. *Concern. He's concerned about me. At least for the moment.*

"You should consider Puerto Rico as a stop-over," he said. "It's also US, and a lot safer than Jamaica or the Dominican Republic or Haiti. But even so, a woman alone is taking a risk – even in the US."

"You're not the first person to tell me that," she said.

"And I won't be the last. Are you heading south right away?"

"I'll leave in a day or two and make my way down the Bay to Norfolk," she replied. "I hope to get to southern Florida in at least a couple weeks, so I may sail through the night here in the Bay. After that, once I'm in the warmer climate, the pressure is off. But I hope to be in the Caribbean by December."

"Is this some personal mission – to sail this alone?"

"No," she smiled at the notion.

"I can free up my schedule, if you want crew."

Alarm bells clanged in Beth's head, but she remembered how she'd reacted to Doug's first offer to day sail with her. That had worked out fine. *But I don't need a babysitter.*

She forced a smile. "Maybe I *am* trying to prove something," she shrugged.

He shook his head slowly, studying her. "I'd hate to see you get into trouble out there. Even if you're a competent sailor, what you're doing is taking a lot of risks. Maybe you should reduce some of them. Take my card," he pulled out his wallet and extracted a creamy ivory business card printed with his name and contact information. No business name was listed and she realized that it was a calling card – delightfully anachronistic. His eyes met hers as she took it from him. "I'm not making a play here, if that's what you're thinking. I just like to sail, and it seems like you could use some company. But it's up to you."

"Right – of course!" she nodded too quickly. Of course he's not suggesting anything else. Why would a rich man with time on his hands be interested in anything else?

He studied her again and she felt as if he could see right through her jolly grin to the flicker of hurt that his assertion had sparked. She took a gulp of beer and turned her attention to a friendly argument among some of the other crew. But he kept studying her and she got the impression that he wanted to say something else. *Please don't apologize. Just drop it.*

A moment later one of the regatta organizers stepped up to a rostrum and cleared his throat into the microphone to get everyone's attention. The awards presentation began and Jeff gestured for Terry to join him at the other side of the table.

Grace took second in her division, which inspired the crew to another few rounds of drinks. Like preppie hockey players they emptied a pitcher of beer into the silver bowl trophy and dumped about half of it over Jeff before passing it around to drink from it. Beth thought Jeff was remarkably good-natured about it as he sat there dripping sticky, cheap beer. As the hour approached nine p.m., when the last water taxi was scheduled to depart, Beth began saying her goodbyes. She soon realized that all of the crew members were too drunk to understand that she was leaving, so she moved around the table to Jeff and leaned close to be heard over the increasingly loud party.

"Thanks again, Jeff. I had a great day. Congratulations on taking second."

"You're leaving already?"

She realized that Jeff was also rather tipsy, although he concealed it well.

"I have to catch the water taxi to my boat. How are you getting back to the hotel?"

"Taxi," Jeff nodded. "With wheels."

"Good. Maybe we'll find ourselves in the same harbor again some time."

"I'd like that Beth. And I suspect it will happen," he replied enigmatically. She pursed her lips, and then decided to chalk it up to the beer.

Beth turned to Terry and smiled.

"Thanks again for the advice," she said, offering her hand. He took it to shake, his eyes crinkling in that way she found so alluring.

"Think about it," he replied. "And call me if you want."

Beth patted her pocket where she'd put his card. He sounded so genuine she was tempted to tell him she was interested in his offer. But she held her tongue. The more she'd thought about it the more she realized that this was supposed to be a solo journey.

"I have to go catch the taxi," she said apologetically, giving his hand another squeeze before letting go and turning away.

Outside in the fresh, chilly air she trotted along the dock waving to catch the water taxi driver's eye. He already had a half dozen passengers, and when she got on board he pushed away from the dock.

SIXTEEN: UNCERTAINTY

"Hell!" Beth rubbed at the sore spot on the back of her head and collapsed onto the floor of the cockpit. She felt like a ball of grease and sweat. With a concussion from hitting her head on the lid of the lazarette.

The problem was the engine: It had been hard to start the last couple days – sometimes it turned right over, sometimes it was completely dead. Currently it was in the latter mode, and in an hour she would be at the mouth of the Elizabeth River in Norfolk, Virginia at the mouth of the Chesapeake Bay. If she couldn't get the engine started she would have to find a place to drop the anchor under sail, and the weather wasn't making that a very attractive option.

The temperature had been unseasonably warm, but a wicked breeze had picked up in the last hour, whipping up the surface of the water so that it slapped asynchronously against *Trouble*'s sides. Off to the west the sky was darkening with clouds, and off to the east it was darkening with nightfall.

Beth was certain that the batteries were not dead – the starter would at least churn a little if that was it. And the intermittent nature of the problem – until now – made it much harder to diagnose. She had traced the leads from the batteries in their compartment down in the cabin to the starter on the engine under the cockpit. Then she'd traced the connection from the starter to the engine control panel here in the cockpit. But that was the hardest part – the panel was mounted on the combing – the backrest for the cockpit bench to the right of the helm. Beth hadn't been able to figure out how to remove the panel to check the connections, so she had to contort herself in the lazarette to look up behind it from underneath.

It was no use: even if she could see it clearly, she didn't know what she was looking for.

Frustrated and desperate, she pulled herself up onto the seat, then stood and looked around the boat. This was a major shipping area, not to mention the enormous Naval base just ahead. But *Trouble* was sailing along in open water with no close traffic. As she watched the jib shuddered and re-filled as the unsteady breeze shifted.

"One more time, my dear," she said, and reached out and turned the ignition key.

The engine roared to life, revving too fast because she'd left the throttle engaged. She quickly pushed it down and the engine slowed to a humming idle. Beth shut her eyes and blew out through her nose, then shut the lazarette.

She rolled up the jib and dropped the main, tying it to the boom in quick, expert folds, the result of much experience. Then she went below and checked all the systems, confirming that the batteries were fully charged, and turning on the hot water heater and the refrigeration. Norfolk was an important stop for her, where she would provision for the next leg going down along the Intracoastal Waterway through the Carolinas and into Georgia. Or she might go out into the Atlantic instead – throw up the sails and make a long run for it. It depended on the weather, and whether this starter problem got fixed.

She radioed the marina that she'd telephoned two days ago and confirmed her arrival. The voice on the other end sounded competent, if artificially friendly. She had reserved a mooring, but when she mentioned that she would need to have someone look at a starter problem he informed her that she'd need to be in a slip for that. Biting her tongue about the cost, she listened to his instructions and explained that she was single-handed. He promised to have someone on the dock to take her lines.

The someone was a young woman bundled up in a fleece top over khaki shorts and sneakers. She grabbed *Trouble*'s spring line from where it lay coiled on the side deck and walked her forward into place. Beth left the engine running as she hopped onto the dock to secure the stern, then climb back aboard to go forward and toss her the bow line.

"Can I plug in to shore power?" she asked the young woman.

"Sure. You want to pass me your cable?"

Beth returned to the cockpit and hauled the heavy yellow cord out of the lazarette, paying it out as she walked forward until she passed the end over to the woman. Then she went back to the cockpit to shut of the engine and plug the cord into the boat. There was a second cord tucked away in the lazarette that powered the boat's air conditioner. But that was an unnecessary luxury at this time of year.

"You're all set," the girl called out a few minutes later. Beth went below and flipped the switches to transfer *Trouble's* systems from the direct current batteries over to good old land-based alternate current. She climbed back out into the cockpit to finish making arrangements with the dock girl. She had to go check in at the office, she learned, and she could contact a mechanic through them. They would also give her a packet of information about the facilities and local events. By the time Beth had accomplished this – after changing into her cleanest trousers and sweatshirt – she felt like she had just checked into a nice hotel. As it was already after five the mechanic from the local marine repair shop wasn't available until tomorrow, but she telephoned and arranged for him to visit *Trouble* in the morning.

A long, hot shower and a cold beer in the cockpit later she felt human again. She flipped through the brochures from the marina office, trying to decide what to do next. Her budget was going to have to go on life support if the engine problem was serious – the slip charge alone would consume her planned expenses for this stop. She needed some groceries, although she could scrounge something from the galley for tonight's dinner. But the thought of boiling dried pasta and slicing open a carton of long-life marinara sauce put a big damper on her appetite. She wanted something different. Something with fresh vegetables and maybe some seafood. There seemed to be plenty of options in the neighborhood.

She ended up eating steamed shrimp and drinking PBRs sitting at the bar in a sprawling, friendly waterfront pub where the locals had gathered to watch football on the big-screen TV. After three days sailing down the bay, anchoring at night without going ashore, she found the crowd both comforting and overwhelming. The stress of the engine problem had taken more of a toll on her than she'd realized. Before she knew it she'd consumed three beers and was a little unsteady when she got up to go to the restroom. She splashed water on her face and chastised herself for her excess – she didn't mind a little alcohol buzz, but she hated getting drunk and she really hated hangovers. Back at her place at the bar she found a mug of black coffee. Catching the bartender's eye he nodded toward it pointedly. *They'll probably get fined if their patrons have an accident on the way home.*

The coffee warmed her and sobered her enough to make a sure-footed exit after paying her tab. She caught herself being particularly conscious of her surroundings as she walked back to the marina a few blocks away. The neighborhood was no worse than parts of New York City that she'd regularly traversed on foot, but here in Virginia the groups of people sitting on front stoops and loitering on the corners seemed more threatening. She knew that various pairs of eyes followed her progress as she kept to the outer edge of the sidewalk, but nothing more threatening occurred before she pressed the combination on the marina night gate and got safely inside.

"Your starter's shot. I think I've got one in stock, but I'll have to go back and check. It'll take a couple hours to install."

"You're sure?" Beth asked, peering down at the suspect starter. "It seemed to start right up – when it worked. Couldn't it be a bad connection or something?"

The mechanic was a big man dressed in stained coveralls. One of his ears had a notch missing along the top, and his bulk was obviously mostly brawn, not fat. He had the menacing look of an unsuccessful boxer – a man with something to prove and no qualms about teaching any challenger a lesson. He squinted at her, his mouth slightly agape.

"So you know about engines, do you Miss?" he asked in his rumbling drawl.

"I know that it seems like the starter works fine when it kicks in."

He shook his head as he wiped his hands on a rag that he pulled from a pocket.

"Well then, you can count on it – when it decides to work."

Beth watched him drop his pliers, screwdriver, and flashlight into his tool box, which lay open on the cabin floor. He shut the case and looked up at her.

"You want it to work, I'll replace it. Otherwise we're both wasting our time."

"How much?" Beth asked, panic rising at the notion of reliving yesterday afternoon.

"Two hundred for the starter. 'Nother one twenty for labor."

Beth gulped hard. Plus the sixty dollar slip fee.

"Fine. When can you do the work?"

The mechanic's demeanor changed immediately. He grinned salaciously and picked up his tool box.

"I can be back this afternoon. How's around three suit you Miss?"

"Fine. I'll be here."

"See you then," he heaved his bulk up the ladder and Beth followed, feeling cheated.

She sat in the cockpit thinking about calling another mechanic for another opinion. But she felt desperate, the pressure of her journey forcing her to get this taken care of. The next leg of her journey would take her deeper into the south, and if this place was an example, she wanted to avoid having to deal with the locals if she could.

If it still won't start after he installs the new starter, I can just make him check again. She assured herself, knowing as she thought it that she would have a hard time confronting him. And for the first time she had an inkling of what the water taxi driver and Terry had meant. *Right here in the US. What will it be like when I get to the islands?*

Being a self-assured woman in New York was no small feat. But this experience had taught her that out of the urban context some men's assumptions were different. The mechanic assumed he could intimidate her, and he had with words alone. In other contexts – more rural settings, or the islands, such a man might think nothing of using more forceful means. Beth hated to think in terms of stereotypes, but she had to be ready to recognize potential dangers. She would rather be embarrassed by misjudging a good man than be injured or lose *Trouble* because she trusted an evil one.

Beth's uneasiness continued through the afternoon while the mechanic installed the new starter. *Trouble's* engine purred to life over and over again after the work was done, the mechanic sitting behind the wheel starting it and shutting it down repeatedly while grinning smugly at her.

"Thanks," she said simply, handing him the wad of cash that she'd gotten from the cash machine in the marina. He scrawled out a receipt and tore off her copy.

"Pleasure doing business with you Miss," he said, almost chuckling.

After he was gone she turned the key again. The engine roared to life.

"Fine. That's what you wanted," she said aloud, then leaned back on the bench and took a deep breath before forcing herself to plan her next moves.

Another shower headed her list. Then checking out of the marina – she'd stay tonight since, like a hotel, once it was past noon she was in for a second day. But she'd get out tomorrow morning. That meant that groceries were her next priority. A couple loads of laundry. And another look at the book exchange up in the office. She had learned the value of these shelves of books tucked in the corner of many marinas. It was an honor system where sailors dropped off books they'd finished and took an equal number. Some volumes she'd seen looked like they'd circulated around the world, and one or two even had names and dates inside the cover of some of the readers who'd carried them.

With a plan in her head Beth felt better already. She got up to gather her laundry, canvas grocery bags, shower kit, and used books.

SEVENTEEN: LESSONS

"On no. Do *not* tell me this," Beth rubbed her face with one hand and tried the key again. *Nothing.*

The starter had worked consistently for the last two days so Beth had decided that the mechanic had been on the up and up after all. And she'd regained her complacency about her boat's systems and slacked off on precautionary measures. That was why she was trying to start the engine just a half mile from the entrance to Roanoke Channel.

I should have just kept it on. I shouldn't have sailed at all. She chastised herself. The Intracoastal Waterway was already getting to her. The Goldbergs back on City Island had warned her about it – about the miles of unbelievably narrow channel that was only barely deep enough for *Trouble* to pass through. If she strayed outside of the dotted line of channel markers by so much as a foot she'd drive her boat's five-foot deep keel into solid mud. Looking at the charts she'd thought it looked simple enough. Go from buoy to buoy and watch the depth.

But she hadn't considered that it meant paying constant attention. The auto pilot could not watch for buoys. And she hadn't considered the effect of current and wind on her vessel. She'd nearly run aground in the first stretch of narrow channel when the current carried *Trouble* just a few yards to the east. She'd been watching the pair of buoys ahead, but failed until the last moment to look back and discover that she was no longer lined up with the last pair. Her depth gauge was beeping madly in alarm when she realized the danger she was in and yanked the helm hard to the left to get back in the middle of the dredged channel.

After that she wished for eyes in the back of her head as her neck grew sore from straining around.

She had naively planned to make forty miles a day through the waterway. After her first three hour passage during which she'd had to throttle back to five knots due to traffic and to wait for draw and swing bridges to open, she re-calculated her pace to half her original estimate.

When she'd entered Albemarle Sound with its miles of twelve-foot deep water she'd pulled out the jib and killed the engine. Sailing for two hours in a moderate breeze did a lot to ease her nerves before the next narrow channel. She'd known that she should raise the main to go faster, or leave on the engine. But she'd allowed herself to laze along instead, studying the charts and picking several possible anchorages to stop at in a few hours, once she was through the Roanoke Channel.

Now she knew she would have better spent her time studying the tidal charts, because then she might have tried to start the engine sooner to beat the change and get into the channel before she had to fight it all the way. But she hadn't, so now she was sailing against the tide toward a thirty-foot wide channel with three-foot depths all around it, and her engine would not start.

"At least if I don't do anything the tide will push me away from the channel," she said out loud. Then she looked behind her and realized that she couldn't drift far in that direction either before running aground. She tried the key again.

Nothing.

I'm in shallow water. The wind is dropping. It's getting late. I can't navigate that channel without power. I have to do something.

Days in the shallow Chesapeake Bay had gotten her used to sailing in water barely deeper than *Trouble*'s keel, in depths that, in Long Island Sound, would only be suitable for anchoring. She forced herself now to revert to that mentality. By her Long Island Sound standards she could anchor just about anywhere in Albemarle Sound. She stood up and looked around at the low islands that protected the Sound. She spotted a pair of white masts off to the west near an island. If she hauled in the jib she could sail over there. She studied the chart, identifying the anchorage as off the town of Nag's Head. There was a big marina, but it looked like it was too shallow for *Trouble*. And she didn't need a marina, just a safe place to stop and breathe and think through her engine problem. *Again.*

She changed course first, setting the auto helm but leaving the sail loose to cut her speed and give her time to go forward and prepare the anchor. She had practiced anchoring under sail once with Doug, and although he'd stood back and made suggestions while she did all the work, she'd been bolstered by his capable presence. To recapture that feeling now she recalled his voice and the way he made suggestions rather than telling her what to do.

It worked. Thirty minutes later she turned up into the wind and ducked in under the flapping jib to lower the anchor into eight feet of water. When all twenty feet of chain and another twenty feet of rope were out she went back to the cockpit and rolled up the jib. If she'd had the mainsail up she would have pushed it back against the wind to move the boat backwards and dig in the anchor. But with the current running at least two knots she could wait for it to pull *Trouble* along and drag the rope and chain out across the bottom. Which it did, gradually. She watched landmarks shift as *Trouble* slowly aligned herself with the current until the changes in her position became imperceptible. Then she went forward and hauled in on the anchor rode, feeling tension on it and trying to judge whether it would hold. With so much chain in such shallow water it ought to withstand a lot stronger breeze than was predicted for the rest of the day and the night.

Standing on the bow she took a long look around. The other two anchored boats appeared to be unoccupied, their sails removed. This close to shore she could see the channel markers leading into the marina. As she watched a small fishing boat came out of the entrance and followed the markers, increasing its speed as it reached the outer marker and then took off on a plane, engine buzzing. The shoreline was lined with wooden cottages – houses built on stilts to protect them against occasional high water. She knew that the Outer Banks were, collectively, a huge summertime vacation destination. But there had to be at least a small year-round population – the fishing boat supported that theory. But it didn't mean that the marina was open to transients.

I don't need a marina, she reminded herself, striding back along the side deck to the cockpit.

Her faith in mankind had pretty much evaporated when the engine failed. She didn't need a marina because she didn't trust any mechanic who might agree to look at her engine. She had paid three hundred and twenty dollars to be taken advantage of in Norfolk.

She climbed into the salon and picked up her cell phone. *At least I've got service here.* She looked at the mechanic's business card tacked to her bulletin board. And then she reached out and tore it down, crumpling it into a stiff wad. Her eyes moved to another card on the board, creamy ivory with a name, phone numbers, and an email address.

"Hello," she recognized Terry's voice immediately.

"Hi Terry, it's Beth Anderson. From Annapolis?"

"Beth! Is everything all right?"

"Well, mostly," she hedged. She didn't want him to think she was just calling for help. Except that she was.

"What's wrong?"

"It's not an emergency," she looked out the salon window at the derelict looking boats anchored nearby. What if they had the same problem as me? Anchored here and went ashore and never came back? Don't be silly!

"I've been having trouble starting the engine. I had a mechanic look at it and he replaced the starter. But it's still happening. I think – I wondered if your offer is still open? I think I do need company."

"You're sure the problem was the starter?"

She noticed that he hadn't answered her question.

"No. I wasn't sure, but it was all he would do."

"It could just be a bad switch in the panel."

Beth cringed – that was exactly what she'd been trying to see when she was twisting herself into the lazarette. Not that she knew what she was looking for.

"I know. But he said it wasn't."

"Well, he may have taken you. You need to have someone test the switch."

She sighed, understanding his unspoken message. She'd blown it back in Annapolis.

"Beth, I'm sorry. Some business issues have come up that I have to tend to right now. I'm flying to Germany tomorrow."

"I understand," she replied quickly. She did, but she was deeply disappointed.

"I'm still sorry. Let me have your number – I'll call you when I get back. In the mean time – where are you?"

"Nag's Head North Carolina."

"Hey, good for you! How are you liking the Intracoastal?"

"I hate it."

"Yeah, I'm not surprised. I've done a few stretches of connecting the dots myself. But you're safer in there at this time of year. Nag's Head ought to be big enough to have someone around who can look at your starter switch. But be clear with them, Beth – don't buy another whole starter."

She could hear the encouraging smile in his voice and it cheered her a little bit.

"Thanks Terry. I'll be firm with them."

"You go, girl. Safe sailing!"

And then he was gone.

He didn't say how long he would be gone. Maybe I could just wait for him to get back and join me. She switched on the gas and lit the stove to boil water for tea. I could go into the marina, rest for a few days – a week. Find some temp work.

The following morning the sun glittered on the water and the pine trees on shore were a beautiful deep green. The tide had turned and swung *Trouble* around, but the anchor had held and the water was deep enough in her new position. Beth dragged the dingy from its storage position on the deck in front of the boom and slid it overboard. It took her a half hour to carefully secure the dingy across *Trouble*'s stern, put a safety line on the outboard motor and lift it down into the dinghy. Positioning it and tightening the screws was nerve wracking with no one to steady it while she worked. But finally it was done. She climbed back up the swim ladder to get her backpack, locked the boat, and set out on her expedition.

She took a turn around the empty anchored boats, knocking on the hull of one and then the other and calling out "Hello? Anyone aboard?" But she could see from close up that they were both locked with padlocks and stringy green algae was growing on their anchor rodes below the waterline. So she pointed her little boat toward the marina channel. She could cut across the shallows in her dinghy, but the little outboard did extend a foot or so into the water, so rather than risk finding out just how shallow it was by breaking the shear pin she played it safe.

The marina was half full of motorboats and a few small sailboats. She puttered around the ends of the docks until she spotted a low one with two or three dinghies tied to it and one pulled up and overturned on it. She secured hers with the others and walked up a ramp to a faded wooden building with a sailcloth blue awning. White lettering on the awning proclaimed it as "Nag's Head Marina." A red and white sign on the door below the awning said "Open."

"Morning," the wiry redheaded woman seated at a desk behind a counter said as she stood up. "Can I help you?"

"I got here late yesterday, but I anchored out because I wasn't sure about depths inside," Beth began. The woman beckoned her over to a big framed chart on the wall.

"What do you draw?" she asked.

"Five feet."

The woman tsked a few times.

"It's tight at low tide," she said honestly. "But an hour either side you'd be fine. Once you're in, the outer slips are all good." She traced the channel as she spoke and Beth noted the depths marked. At mean low tide the shallowest spot was exactly five feet – which mean it was probably a little less since the chart had been made a few years ago.

"What are your rates?"

"This time of year, dollar a foot – you draw five feet? Must be 35? 36?"

"Thirty-eight foot Island Packet."

"Nice. I figured you must have something solid to be cruising at this time of year. So you want to come in? The tide's low at noon, so you have time now."

"I have a problem, actually. The real reason I anchored out was that my engine wouldn't start. Is there a mechanic around?"

"Ole Jess Midgette over at A-One Auto."

"He knows boats?"

"Hon, this time of year most of the watermen find shore side work to keep food on the table. You want his number? You'll have to take him out in your dink – I assume that's how you got here."

"Yes. I can do that."

The woman pulled a telephone book out from under the counter and slapped it down. She flipped through it and stopped at a page where the ad for A-One Auto was worn and smudged. She stepped back to grab a scrap of paper and a pen from her desk and copied the phone number.

"You need to use the phone?" she asked, and Beth decided she liked her.

"Thanks, no – I have a cell phone. Can you also direct me to a grocery store?"

"That's a little harder Hon. You'll need a ride for that."

Beth sighed and nodded and the woman watched her for a moment.

"You know, I can't leave the marina. But Jess may be willing to help you out. If he's coming over here to look at your boat, he might be able to run you to the store."

"He'd do something like that?"

"This time of year the island's pretty quiet. Folks like you coming through by boat, you're quality – you know? More like us than the summer people. But I can't make any promises for him. All I'm sayin' is that it wouldn't be out of line for you to ask."

"Thanks for the advice. My name is Beth Anderson, by the way."

"Welcome to Nag's Head, Beth. I'm Ella Midgette."

"Related to Jess?"

"Oh, us Midgette's are all related, either by blood or marriage," she chuckled. "But I couldn't tell you just how Jess and I are connected, off hand."

"So it's a common name?"

"Common as blue crabs in the sound," she laughed – a coarse sound that suggested too many cigarettes. "'course, those are getting harder and harder to find."

Beth smiled appreciatively and picked up the scrap of paper with the phone number on it.

"I guess I'll call Mr. Midgette first, and then see about the grocery store," she said. "You don't happen to have a book exchange, do you?"

"Over in the laundry," Ella Midgette said. "You might as well take this," she pulled a sheet of paper listing marina information from under the counter. "And let me know if you're going to come in to a slip. I got plenty available," she laughed again.

"Thanks. I will."

EIGHTEEN: KENNY

How long will Terry be in Germany? She wondered idly as she watched Jess Midgette examine *Trouble's* engine control panel. She'd been embarrassed when she watched him pop it out of its hole – no screws required, just pressure in the right places. *Can I afford to wait? Would he come, or was the whole thing just an excuse to get me off the phone?*

"That's it," Jess said, lifting the panel up to carefully turn the key to test it before re-installing it.

The engine rumbled to life.

"That's great – but will it work every time?" Beth asked skeptically. Jess straightened and looked at her curiously.

"There was a faulty connection in the switch," he said, his pale green eyes sliding over toward the panel and then back to her. He had a weak chin covered with a stubble of beard, and now he rubbed at it with one hand. His nails were filthy. "I could have soldered the connection, but there was some corrosion on the contacts, so I went ahead and replaced the switch. It must have been giving you problems for a while."

"Yes," Beth sighed.

"Well, I guarantee that my connections will hold."

"I'm sure they will," she said. "I'm sorry, I didn't mean to suggest your work wasn't good. It's just that the mechanic in Norfolk insisted that it was the starter, so he had to replace it."

Jess wrinkled his nose, his face pinching oddly. Beth realized that it was an expression of sympathy.

"Did you keep the old one?" he asked.

"Yes, actually. I figured I might need it for parts or something," she shrugged. The Norfolk mechanic had been reluctant to leave it with her, but she'd insisted. It had felt like a small victory at the time, but then she'd felt silly and shoved it in its cardboard box into the aft berth.

"Can I have a look at it?" Jess asked. Beth went and got the box, setting it in the cockpit in the wintry sun. Jess picked it up and turned it over in his hands.

"Miss, I can't be sure without installing it, but I think this starter is just fine."

"Please don't tell me that," she groaned.

"Okay, I'll just tell you to keep it around in case the one you've got now gives out. And one other thing."

"What?"

"You don't want cardboard boxes like that on board."

Beth looked at the old liquor box the Norfolk mechanic had put the starter in. "Why?"

"Them cockroaches lay their eggs in the glue. Once you get roaches on board you'll never get rid of 'em."

"Ugh!" Beth grimaced and eyed the box suspiciously.

"You have more like that on board?"

"No, thank goodness."

"We can take it ashore with us," Jess assured her, then he turned back to the panel and shut off the engine before beginning to reinstall it.

"Thanks again, for everything Jess," Beth said, shouldering her backpack and picking up her grocery bag from the floor of the car. He had driven her to the market, claiming that he could take care of a few errands of his own and meet her in thirty minutes. That had given her plenty of time to pick up some fresh produce, milk, coffee, and frozen bread from among the market's meager off season selection.

By the time he'd fixed the starter switch it had been two o'clock in the afternoon and she'd decided to take *Trouble* into the marina – at least for the night. So now she tossed Jess a last wave as he pulled out of the parking lot in his pickup truck, then turned and trotted down the dock through the propped open security gate.

It feels good to be home.

Beth stepped up onto *Trouble*'s side deck and froze. There were three empty, crushed Bud Light cans piled in the corner of the cockpit.

A wave of unease washed over her as she stepped down onto the bench and then the cockpit sole, her eyes never leaving the alien trash.

And then her head popped up and she scanned the area. *Trouble* was in a slip at the very end of the dock that stretched out from in front of the marina office. Her nearest neighbors were the group of powerboats near the shore end of the dock, more than one hundred feet away. There were no boats moving around the marina – in fact, it seemed particularly desolate, which made the intrusion even more disturbing somehow.

Her hands were shaking as she unlocked the companionway and slid the hatch back. She realized as she looked below that she was actually afraid. The evidence of the intact lock should have assured her that nobody was aboard, but she wasn't thinking rationally. Still, *Trouble's* interior – what she could see of it through the open hatch – was undisturbed.

Concentrating on slowing her racing heart, she removed the washboards and climbed down, grabbing her grocery bag and pack as she backed down the ladder. She flipped on the master switches and then all of the cabin lights to banish the threatening darkness. After making a quick inspection and finding nothing amiss, she stepped up on the ladder, slid the washboards back into place and pulled the hatch shut.

She stood at the base of the ladder and looked around again, sucking in a deep breath. Everything is okay. It was just some kids checking out the new comer. As she stored her groceries and set out the can of soup she was going to heat for dinner she decided to go up to the office to speak to Ella. A few minutes later she knocked on the locked office door. But the sign in the window said "closed" and the lights were out. It was four p.m. She walked around the building, which housed the laundry and showers in back, and paused on the wooden walkway that led to the parking lot and street beyond.

The gate was still propped open. Ella had not given her a key for the lock.

You're not going back out. And if someone else gets locked out, too bad. There's a security gate here for a reason.

She strode quickly over to the gate, knocked the wooden wedge out from under it with the toe of her sneaker and let it swing shut. It locked with a clank that made her feel unaccountably better.

But not better enough. She warmed her soup and dipped the last of her stale bread into it, huddled in the closed-up cabin. She had flipped on the television and played with the rabbit ear antenna until it pulled in a snowy image on one channel. The programming rolled by – stories of urban murder and arrest, crime lab workers, and people looking for love and money. Several times Beth realized that she was staring blankly at the screen, her thoughts whirling as she paid no attention to the images presented there.

She reviewed the path of her life for the last year, recalling the stagnation of her relationship with Peter and the changes she'd begun to make that had led to their breakup. He was right – it had been her doing more than his. She missed him sometimes – she missed having someone to cuddle with, a kindred spirit to share silly observations and secret jokes with – but she was having less and less difficulty balancing these needs with the negatives. He was picky about his belongings and surroundings so that she'd always felt like a guest in his apartment. When they traveled together, he had to make the arrangements. When she did it he was obviously uncomfortable with feeling like he was "along for the ride." He had avoided any mention of formal commitment.

He had, she realized, made her skittish about men. She blamed herself for that – for walking on eggshells around him for so long that she could no longer trust her instincts. If she'd behaved more like herself with him and gotten angry at him when she wanted to their relationship might have ended a lot sooner.

She lay awake in her berth, *Trouble* so steady in the slip that she forgot she was on a boat, trying to draw a connection between her personal life and her first layoff. Had her work suffered after the breakup? *I don't think so. I think I worked harder, to ignore the pain.*

The first layoff had been a huge shock, and the disappointment and sadness at rejection had piled on top of her lingering feelings over Peter. She supposed that the combination had been enough to drive her to the drastic action that had brought her here to a marina in Nag's Head six months later. When she'd needed to move, she'd taken it as a chance to flee. And she'd been fleeing ever since. But now her flight had taken her too far. She was entirely alone facing the realization that she wasn't ready to be.

Which brought her back to Terry. A man she'd known for one day. Ignoring the flush of excitement the memory of his velvety voice and the crinkles around his eyes inspired, she forced herself to think rationally. She barely knew him – knew nothing about his background, his business with Jeff. She didn't, she realized with alarm, even know where he lived. *Near Annapolis? No – they were all in a hotel. Where did Jeff say he had come from?* Grace *had been on a guest mooring, so they must have sailed her there from somewhere else. Beth, you're an idiot. You're waiting here for a stranger. You're marking time again, just like with Peter. Except this is even worse – at least Peter was there for you in the small ways, even if he wasn't going to go any further.*

By the time the hatch over her bunk went grey she had developed a new plan. And as always, merely knowing what she intended to do made her feel infinitely better.

"Beth?" the voice was accompanied by a knock on *Trouble*'s hull. Beth put down her coffee and stepped up on the ladder to slide open the hatch. She'd peeked out earlier, but it was chilly and damp, so she'd resealed her cocoon until after breakfast.

"Good morning Ella," she replied, glancing up at the grey sky. It wasn't raining, but it looked like it might start.

"Good morning Beth. The gate was locked last night – do you know anything about that?"

Beth swallowed hard. It had felt right at the time, but facing with a clearly annoyed marina manager made her question her decision.

"Yes. I – Someone was on my boat yesterday afternoon. What's the point of a security gate if it's wide open for people to come in?"

"Well Joe Hamelin over on *Mako King* got locked out. He had to shout and whistle until his wife Sara came and let him in. You wouldn't have heard the commotion way out here, of course." Ella's tone clearly implied that Beth had intentionally shut Joe out knowing that she wouldn't be disturbed. Beth felt herself bristle and fought to remain cordial.

"I'm sorry about that, Ella. But I was very disturbed to find those empty beer cans in my cockpit," she pointed at the pile, which she had not touched. Ella glanced at them and shrugged dismissively.

"Probably just some local kids. It doesn't mean anything," she said. "Please don't close the gate again – Thomas, the owner, has the only key, and he's only here a couple days a week. He does not appreciate getting called at all hours to come open the gate."

"Okay," Beth replied, stifling the urge to ask all the questions that came to mind – why didn't they make more copies of the key? Why didn't they just permanently unlock the lock somehow? Was he called last night? – it didn't sound like it. And how did Ella herself get in this morning? *Of course, Joe and his wife re-opened the gate. So it was open all night anyway.*

Ella nodded acknowledgement of her agreement and walked back up the dock. Beth slid the hatch shut and plopped back down on the settee.

"We're getting out of here," she told *Trouble*. "But not without some company, if we can possibly manage it. I need some advice."

She picked up the phone and scrolled through the directory until she found Ori's number, then pressed "talk."

"Start talking!" the voice on the other end of the line sounded awesomely distant, emanating from a bright, safe place so far away Beth could never join her there.

"Hi Ori. It's me, Beth."

"*Beth!* I can't believe it! I was just telling someone about you today."

"Good, I hope," Beth said automatically. As so often happened when she had imagined a conversation too many times before actually having it, the other person didn't follow her imagined script. And that was enough of a distraction to lift her mood a little.

"Of course. What's up? Still honoring those commitments?"

"No. I'm in North Carolina."

"Really? Don't tease me --."

"Really. So much has happened, Ori – but the short version is I was able to pay off my loan, so I decided to get while the getting was good."

"Barely," Ori acknowledged. "It's already winter."

"But I'm already half way to Florida."

"Beth, I am so proud of you I'm about to burst. Did you get my letter? Was that why you did it?"

"It played a part," Beth admitted, smiling. "So where are you?" She had wanted to talk about the beer cans, about the intruders. But already their significance had faded in the face of Ori's adventures.

"St. Thomas baby!" Ori cried. "And I've been partying every night with this bunch of Rastas. Man are they sweet kissers!"

"*Ori!*" Beth really was astonished. She was no prude, but the risks of casual intimacy with strangers were real.

"Oh stop it, it's de Islands, mon. When in Rome ..."

"You eat pasta," Beth retorted. "Are you staying out of trouble, Ori?"

"I mean it Beth, these guys will do anything for me because I party with them. That's how you get by down here."

"I'm glad you're having fun, then," Beth replied, disguising her concern for her friend since there was nothing she could do about it. Ori would not sit still for a lecture. No more than Beth would slug down Bud Lights with whoever had left the cans in her cockpit. "What's your plan? Will you be there long?"

"I'm waiting on some sail repair," she replied. "My jib tore wide open on the way here from PR."

"That sucks – was it bad weather?"

"Just a bit of a blow. The sail's pretty old, but I'm determined to squeeze a little more out of it. Anyway, that'll take a couple more days then I'm going over to St. John. A couple of the guys want to take me on a hike to see some Indian hieroglyphs or something. But I think I'll be moving on to Tortola pretty quick after that."

"That sounds great. I can't wait."

"Why don't you give me a call when you get to Miami. We'll see where we are and if we can rendezvous – okay?"

"Okay, that sounds like a plan --."

"Great. Gotta go kid – I'll be thinking of you!"

She let an hour pass during which she cleaned the salon and her berth and ran her little dust buster in the aft berth around the gear stored there. Then she refilled the water tanks and checked the levels in the fuel and holding tanks. Fuel was at half – enough left for several days of motoring. The holding tank was more than half full, but she could probably go for nearly a week before it would have to be pumped out.

Ori's solution was not hers. She could not arrive in a marina with a problem and go partying rather than dealing with it. But just hearing Ori's voice had made some of her "Devil may care" attitude rub off on Beth. Adding the empty beer cans to her bag of trash, she carried it and her shower bag up the dock, hoping the marina manager was sufficiently cooled down from their morning discussion.

"I'm planning to head on south through the ICW," she explained to Ella. "But after the day before yesterday I realize that it would be a lot easier with two sets of eyes to watch for buoys. I wonder if you know of anyone who'd be interested in going along with me for a few days?"

She watched the other woman consider it. She had intentionally omitted any reference to payment, although she suspected that in a community of watermen this sort of trip would be regarded as work, not fun. Still, she clung to the vague hope that there would be someone looking to go joy riding.

"You might try Kenny," Ella said. "Don't know his last name. He's still over on *Gaucho* until the end of the month."

"Who is he?" Beth asked, looking for some background to help her form some questions for the man.

"Crew," Ella shrugged, as if such creatures were interchangeable cogs in the boating community. "*Gaucho*'s owner sold her and the new owner gave Kenny until the end of November to do some brightening up. He's not too happy about it."

"So you think he'd jump ship early?" Beth wasn't sure she liked that attitude, but it was hardly fair to make such a judgment based on Ella's version of the story.

"Worth asking, that's all I'm saying," Ella replied.

"Thanks."

"You checking out?"

Beth felt a little of the morning's acrimony resurface. She paused with her hand on the doorknob.

"I'll let you know before noon," she replied.

"Fair enough."

Having set a deadline, Beth deferred her shower and instead wandered the docks looking for *Gaucho*. She found her – a big old Chris Craft cruiser with attractive wood details and lots of fittings to hold fishing gear. The sliding cabin door leading into the cabin was ajar.

"Hello? Anyone home?" she called, rapping on the gunwale.

A shadow moved inside, and then the door slid open the rest of the way. A skinny man with uncombed hair wearing painter's pants and a white tee-shirt squinted at her.

"Yeah?" he drawled. Beth was struck by how similar he seemed to Jess Midgette. Could Kenny also be a Midgette and Ella not know it?

"Kenny?" she asked.

"Yeah."

"I'm Beth Anderson. I came in yesterday on the sailboat out at the end," she pointed toward *Trouble*. He turned his head and looked out through the interior windows toward the boat. She wasn't convinced he could actually see her boat that way.

"Saw you," he acknowledged in a knowing tone that gave her the creeps, but she chalked it up to her overall sense of uneasiness.

"I'm heading out today or tomorrow, going south down the ICW. Ella thought you might be interested in riding along for a few days, helping spot the markers and keep her on course."

Kenny stepped out on to the aft deck, then wrapped his arms around himself and rubbed his bare forearms with his hands. Beth was glad to see some muscle definition – he wasn't as skinny as she'd thought at first – he looked like he could grind a winch or handle the wheel in heavy weather.

"Ain't much of a sailor," he said.

"Ain't much sailing in the ICW," Beth countered. "I'm looking for someone who can read a chart, drive in a straight line, and keep to the channel. I'd guess that you know the channels in this area pretty well."

"Sure, and the shoals," he replied, his mouth splitting in a lopsided grin. Beth had to chuckle with him.

"I've been trying to avoid those," she said.

"How far you goin'?" he asked.

"Miami, in and out of the ICW – depends on the weather. But I'd appreciate company for any stretch of it."

"I'd need to get back – you payin' bus fare?"

Beth struggled to keep a straight face. He's asking for bus fare? It didn't occur to him to demand airfare?

"I can do that," she replied, nodding slowly as if considering it. Actually, she had no idea how much that might be. But it had to be cheaper than a flight. "And cover all expenses, of course – food, fuel, water, dockage when we don't anchor out."

Kenny squinted at her again and she knew he had understood the unspoken part of the deal – she was not offering to pay him.

"I got a couple more things to do on *Gaucho*," he said glancing back over his shoulder into the dim cabin. "Gonna take the rest of the day. You said you want to leave today?"

"Tomorrow's okay," she replied, realizing that she'd need to re-arrange some things on *Trouble* to make room for him.

"It's a deal," he said, stepping closer to extend his hand. She reached across the gunwale and shook it. His grip was surprisingly strong.

"Great. What's your last name, by the way? Ella didn't say."

"Oakes. Kenny Oakes."

"Okay Kenny Oakes. You want to come by tomorrow morning? I'd like to shove off by nine a.m."

"Sounds good," he said and Beth started to turn away. "Ah, Miss?"

"Yes – please call me Beth."

"Beth, I'm real partial to Fritos – you mind getting some in the provisions?"

Beth smiled. "Sure Kenny. Any other favorites? What do you drink?"

"I'm a Coke man myself," he said. "And Bud Light, if you mean beer."

Beth felt another little chill run down her spine, but she shook it off. *Millions of people drink Bud Light.*

"Sure – I'll get some of each. Gotta keep the crew happy."

"Thanks," Kenny smiled again. "This is gonna be fun."

"Right," Beth nodded and turned away, forcefully ignoring all the meanings she was inferring from his tone.

NINETEEN: TERRY

Beth telephoned a taxi for her second grocery run and purchased Fritos, a case of Coke and one of Bud Light, along with cereal, rice, and more produce and frozen bread and meat. More than ever she needed to anchor out and not pay mooring or slip fees, now that she was feeding two and would have to come up with Kenny's bus fare – whatever that would be.

By the time she got back to *Trouble* she felt tapped out – once again she'd blown several days of budget at one shot. She stowed the new supplies, then set about clearing out the aft cabin for Kenny's use.

The many storage spaces in the main cabin had always seemed like a lot of room when it was just her, especially after she stored so much stuff in Mrs. Johnson's garage. But suddenly all the under-seat compartments were full and she was tucking sealed containers into the cubbyholes under the floor, too.

And although she felt better about her situation now, knowing she'd have someone to share the driving through the waterway and a male presence on board, she was also fighting a nagging concern about her new crew. She couldn't interpret Ella's suggestion of him as a recommendation, and even if it were, she hardly knew anything about Ella herself. Kenny's demeanor was foreign to her – rural and southern and a little suspicious of strangers – so that she didn't know how to read him. At the end of her reorganization spree she carried the eight-inch sheath knife that had come with the boat – a scuba diver's knife, someone had told her – and tucked it under her pillow. She had no illusions that she'd be able to use it on another human being, but at least where it was no other human being was likely to find it. She also moved the computer into her cabin. She fought the impulse to hide her other portable electronics – the GPS, VHF radio, and cell phone – but she needed them on hand.

She shut the door to her cabin for the first time in months. It had a courtesy lock on the inside that at most would deter someone if they accidentally tried the door. If her new crew decided he wanted in, he'd have little trouble breaking it.

"So they told you they were cutting your job, and a week later they were advertising to fill it?" Kenny took a gulp of beer. "That's harsh!"

"I never saw it coming," Beth agreed.

"So after that you just decided to go cruising?"

Beth took a sip of her own beer to think about her answer. *Kenny thinks I'm rich – that's not good.*

"Not exactly. I worked in an electronics store while I planned for the cruise. I had to save as much as I could, and figure out every way I could to cut monthly expenses."

"What expenses?" Kenny chuckled, looking around the cozy salon. "No rent, no car --."

"Health insurance, boat insurance, cell phone, food, dockage, fuel . . ." Beth let her list trail off. Kenny looked suitably amazed.

"Insurance!" he said. "That's a luxury."

Beth shrugged. Her plan had backfired. "It's a stretch," she said. "But I need to know that if I get sick or hurt out on the water I can get help. And *Trouble* is all I own of any value. I have to know that she's still worth some money if I have an accident and need it."

"Summer time when the big cruisers come through the waterway, some of 'em carry enough cash to buy this boat twice over. Just for tips," Kenny observed, playing with the dregs of spaghetti on his plate with his fork. Beth let her brows rise in surprise.

"I gotta say, I admire someone like you – doing it on a shoestring – more than those guys. It means something to you."

A wave of guilt for her assumptions washed over Beth, but she suppressed it. *He might just be a good liar.*

So the knife stayed under her pillow, and Kenny stayed in his cabin in the stern. And they worked their way south through narrow channels and streams, bays, and sounds. Chased by the winter weather, they dealt with bone-chilling squalls full of drenching rain, and more times than Beth wanted they dropped the hook mid-afternoon rather than entering another long channel with a wicked cross breeze.

Beth's comfort level with Kenny increased as he proved himself competent at the helm even in tight situations. But she did have a real problem by the end of the second night: they were out of beer, and she had only had two. She was glad that she'd hidden the bottles of rum and gin.

"Ah, that always happens," Kenny groaned the following afternoon when she told him she didn't think there was any Bud Light left. He climbed back out of the cabin with two Cokes and handed her one.

"You run out of beer half way through the trip?" she asked, popping the top, just trying for conversation. She didn't imagine that *Gaucho* had ever run out of beverages.

"I get cut-off half way through," he laughed good-naturedly.

"Kenny, we're really out – I only bought a case."

"Hey, we're cool. I drink the stuff like water. I know it – everyone tells me."

"So do we have a problem?"

"You mean, am I going to go through some kinda withdrawal?"

"Well, yeah."

"Nah. Never happened before. But I'll warn you: we'll probably run out of Coke next."

Beth had to laugh and shake her head at his easy-going manner. If all he was going to cost her was extra beer and soda she counted herself lucky.

At the end of the fifth day they tied up at Georgetown Landing, South Carolina – a big marina with fuel, power, water, and groceries nearby. True to his word, Kenny had switched from beer to Coke with no observable change in temperament or physical condition. And when the Coke ran out he switched to water. But by the end of five days the holding tank was full to bursting and they were running low on almost everything. And Beth badly needed to walk on dry land.

She split up the tasks with Kenny, trusting him to launder her clothes only because she'd limited herself to jeans, t-shirts, and sweatshirts. The notion of him handling her underwear made her pause, but she got over it. In five days he'd been, for lack of a more accurate term, a perfect gentleman. She called a taxi to take her to a supermarket where the bright lights and wide aisles were disorienting. She doubled her previous beer and Coke purchase, refusing to buy more even though she suspected they'd need it.

That evening Kenny suggested that they walk up the road to a local bar. His treat.

She was so surprised she had to accept, although she made sure to order the inexpensive, basic hamburger and the cheapest tap beer. The bar had a video trivia game so they teamed up to compete against the other patrons. Beth was good on the literature and history questions while Kenny could answer most in the sports category, except for the golf questions. Their weakest category was current events, which didn't surprise Beth. Part of the pleasure of this trip was detaching from the turmoil of the larger world. She knew she couldn't escape forever, but a short break from the hostilities in the Middle East and starvation and slaughter in Africa was good for her soul.

Walking back to the marina in high spirits from the warm meal and the fun game Kenny threw his arm around Beth's shoulders. The weight of it felt surprisingly comfortable and she realized that she hadn't been touched like that by another person in almost a year. She resisted the urge to wrap her own arm around his waist, although it would have been easy and natural. Very easy – but then she'd have an even harder time stopping things, if Kenny pressed. And if he didn't, she'd feel all the more rejected.

He didn't press, but parted with her at the marina heads. Like all cruisers, she had learned to take advantage of land-based plumbing whenever possible. She used the facilities, then washed her hands and face using the provided soap, delicious warm water, and rough paper towels. That just left brushing her teeth, and she could do that aboard. By the time she was done Kenny had already returned to *Trouble* and retired to his cabin.

Beth brushed her teeth and changed into the sweat pants and shirt she slept in – warm, comfortable, and presentable if she needed to get up for an emergency in the middle of the night. She wished Kenny a good night through his cabin door and he replied with the same.

"Is that your cell phone ringing?" Kenny asked. He was steering *Trouble* along a very narrow stretch of the waterway south of Charleston. Beth was sitting up on the deck watching for obstacles and traffic. She cocked her ear down the companionway and heard the jingling that

Kenny was referring to.

She swung her legs around and down through the companionway to the top of the ladder.

"Hello – this is Beth."

"Hi Beth – still afloat?"

Terry. Her heart raced and her hands broke out into a sweat. She glanced out through the companionway at Kenny, then dropped down onto the settee at the navigation desk.

"Sure am," she replied. "I'm so happy to hear from you Terry."

"I'm glad to be able to call – finally," he replied. She pictured him behind a desk with his feet up, a sweeping view of city rooftops through wide windows behind him. She imagined a model sailboat on a credenza then stopped herself before filling in the details of his attire.

"Are you back in the US?" she asked.

"Yes – yesterday."

"How did your trip go?"

"Very well. Jeff and I will be signing a lucrative training contract very soon. How's *your* trip going?"

"Slower than I expected," she replied. "I had no idea that it would be this boring."

"Yeah, nobody warns you because they don't want to discourage you from making the trip," he chuckled. "Including me. I hereby apologize."

"Accepted," she said. "I did get some company for this leg, though."

"Oh?"

"A local in Nag's Head agreed to ride along. He's at the helm now."

"He is? He's a sailor?"

"He's crew from a Chris Craft. He can drive the boat and read a chart. We haven't done much sailing."

"Good. Just what you needed."

"Well, mostly," she said. "He's getting off in Miami. I'm still looking for some help getting to the islands."

"Is that an invitation?"

"More like a plea," she replied, hoping she wasn't coming on too strong. Terry chuckled.

"Well, it's nice to still be wanted after I was so useless last week."

"I understood. You had to take care of business."

"And I still do – for at least until after Thanksgiving. You'll get to Miami before that. I wouldn't want to hold you up."

"But you'd be available after that?"

"I would."

"What about Christmas?"

"I love Christmas in the tropics."

"I meant, don't you have family that expects you to spend it with them?"

"Don't you?"

"I've already warned them that I can't afford to leave *Trouble* and fly to California. They've accepted it." Even as she said it Beth felt a pang of guilt. *Who knows how many more holidays Dad will be up for?*

"Well, mine accepted that I couldn't be relied upon a long time ago. I used to cancel family plans at the drop of a hat when business came up."

"Are you saying I can't count on you?"

"No. I've changed since Jeff and I got the business on solid footing. I have more flexibility with my priorities now. But I haven't let on to my folks. I like my freedom."

"But what if they need you?"

"I'd be there for them. They're flying to Nice this Christmas and my sister and her husband and son are going with them."

"Sounds lovely," Beth tried to imagine Christmas on the French Riviera. Then reminded herself that she'd be spending the holiday somewhere in the Caribbean if all went as planned. That sounded pretty glamorous too. *And the way we're talking, I might be spending it with Terry.*

"Terry, this probably sounds absurd, but where do you live?"

There was a moment of silence on the line and then he laughed. "I guess that's a fair question. I can't believe I never said. Georgetown, in DC. A long walk from our office."

"Are you in the office now?"

"Yes."

"And are your feet up on your desk?"

"As a matter of fact – how did you know?"

"Just a guess," Beth was grinning.

"Hang on a second," he said and line went quiet. A moment later he came back on. "Germany is calling. I have to take it. Can I call you later?"

"Of course."

"Hang in there Beth – there is an end to the Waterway."

"Your sister?" Kenny asked as she climbed back out into the cockpit carrying two Cokes. She had discovered that if she fed him Cokes he drank fewer beers.

"No. A friend," she replied, still feeling buoyant from her talk with Terry. *Georgetown. I think that's supposed to be pretty upscale.*

"She give you good news or something?" Kenny asked. "You look happy."

"It looks like I've got someone lined up for the leg after Miami," she replied, then watched his face fall.

TWENTY: MIAMI

It rained for the next four days and Kenny's mood seemed to match the weather. Each time Beth's phone rang he withdrew a little more, although on a couple occasions the calls were actually for him. Beth had told him to give her number to someone at home and he had – Kenny's uncle Jess checked up on him every few days. Beth had not been in the least bit surprised when she'd learned a couple days out that Kenny Oakes was actually a Midgette – on his mother's side.

Beth spoke to Trish every few days and her parents once a week, always listening for signs of confusion in her father. These conversations were the hardest, and after them she felt as grey and drained as Kenny and the weather looked. The best conversations were the ones with Terry, who had taken to calling every afternoon. At the sound of his voice her face would flush and if she was at the helm, Kenny would get up and move away – often all the way up to the bow.

Beth tried to convince herself that it was just the weather getting to Kenny, but even when it cleared, the sun warming *Trouble*'s decks and drying out the towels Beth hung along the lifeline, his mood remained dark. *I haven't done anything to lead him on, and I can't believe he's actually hurt because I'm looking forward to having Terry aboard.*

But the evidence was there when her phone rang late one afternoon. They had just dropped the hook in the best anchorage available before entering the last stretch of narrow canal before Miami. Beth heard the jingle of the phone and opened her cabin door just in time to see Kenny pick the phone up off the navigation desk and press a button on the side that silenced it. He dropped it back on the desk and heaved himself up the ladder.

Frowning, Beth went to the phone and saw the "missed call" message with Terry's number below it on the display. She looked up the ladder to see Kenny standing at the back of the cockpit looking out across the water.

She went to the refrigerator and hunted in the bottom for one of the last beers, then grabbed her water bottle and climbed outside.

"Hey Ken, want a beer?" she asked. He turned his head, giving her a sidelong glance over his shoulder.

"Sure," he replied, then turned around and took the can from her.

"You must be starting to feel homesick," she said, opening her water. "Just one more day, plus the bus ride."

"Yeah sure," he replied.

Beth pursed her lips. *Why am I doing this?*

"Have you ever cruised for this long before? I mean, did the owner take *Gaucho* out on long trips?"

"A couple times a summer," he replied before taking a big gulp of beer.

Because he's a nice man and I think I've hurt him.

"So you've got more experience at this than me. I'm glad you came along."

His head came up and he looked at her curiously.

"Really?"

"Oh yeah. I would have gone crazy doing this alone – on the helm the whole time? And I think that we may have set some kind of record – we didn't run aground once!"

"'cept back near Ocracoke," he reminded her. They had found a patch where the channel had shifted, but they'd been able to back off the shoal and into deep – six foot deep – water before *Trouble* got really stuck.

"Oh right. Shoot, there goes the record," she smiled at the memory. She'd been completely freaked out when *Trouble* ground to a halt, but Kenny had reached for the throttle and gear shift and moved the engine from forward to neutral and then reverse before she could think. Then he'd taken the helm and worked her backwards, explaining that the first thing you always do is try to back out the way you got in. After sailing in Long Island sound where there were plenty of damaging rocks to run aground on, the attitude of a sailor used to soft sand and mud had taken her by surprise. But when *Trouble* suddenly shot backward, her keel freed, Beth was converted. And she owed it to Kenny.

"You taught me a lot, Kenny, I'm really grateful."

"Yeah? Doesn't seem like it."

"But I am – I'm sorry if I don't show it --."

"No, I mean, it doesn't seem like you had much to learn from me."

"Don't be modest, Kenny. You set up the watches. You showed me how to make spaghetti in just one pan, you proved to me that hardboiled eggs keep longer and they're perfectly fine for breakfast. And you taught me what to do when I run aground on the mud – even if I only did it the one time. And there were tons of other things too. This has been a great cruise Kenny. I'm glad you've been here."

Kenny sucked at his beer and didn't meet her eyes.

"You don't think so?"

"Nah, I do. I've had a great time too. Never been further south than Charlotte before."

"Well then," Beth said, unable to think of what else to say. She sighed and tried again. "So what's bothering you?"

"I figured that you must'a asked that other person to come aboard in Miami 'cause yer sick 'a me."

Beth noticed that his statement was gender non-specific. But he must have figured out that Terry was a man.

"Sick of you? Not at all. But Miami was our deal and I wouldn't expect you to keep going with me. It's nearly Thanksgiving now, and I'll be sailing through Christmas. I wouldn't ask you to stay."

"You could'a."

Beth sighed again. *He isn't going to let it go.*

"Kenny, I had arranged for Terry to join me before I asked you. He was delayed, and I needed someone for this leg. Now he can meet me in Miami. So I have to honor my commitment to him."

"So that's all it's about?" he asked, finally meeting her gaze.

"Of course it is, Kenny. I've enjoyed your company. I hope we can still be friends – some day I'll need to make this trip north," she chuckled.

For the first time in over a week he smiled. "Maybe I could help you take her back to New York," he suggested.

"Maybe you could," she nodded. *I hope he doesn't read anything into that.*

Beth waved good-bye to Kenny as the taxi she was paying for to take him to the bus station pulled away. The Miami Marina had a wireless network and she'd gone ahead and paid the fee for a month of service since it was equivalent to a few individual days. She'd brought the laptop to the patio area where the network worked and researched bus fares with Kenny looking over her shoulder. Then she'd gone to the cash machine and withdrawn the $135 fare plus an extra $50, plus cab fare and handed it over. They'd exchanged a long hug as the cab pulled up in front of the marina office, and Kenny had reminded her to send him postcards as he tossed his duffle bag into the car and got in with it.

And now he was gone and Beth was already lonely.

I'm tired, and relieved, and excited to be here, and broke. I need a plan.

Although the temperature had been increasing steadily as they moved south, suddenly it seemed excessively hot. Beth went back to *Trouble* and laid out the second power cord, the one she hadn't used since August in New York. At first she'd thought it utterly decadent to air condition a boat. But living aboard in the sweltering humidity that was The Bronx in August she had learned to appreciate it. And since power was included in the slip fee her only guilt was for the environmental impact. But she justified it by reminding herself that she didn't drive a car.

Here in Miami the slip fee also included power, and the heat and humidity felt worse than summer on Long Island Sound. She had noticed that every other boat of any size was spitting the telltale stream of recycled salt water that indicated either air conditioning or a generator, or both.

With the hatches and ports all shut *Trouble* was soon delightfully comfortable below. Beth sipped from the bottle of diet Pepsi she'd bought at a vending machine on the dock and typed up her to-do list.

Call Ori.

Find a job.

Call Terry.

Celebrate arrival! (Again)

Call Mom and Dad

Laundry.

Clean *Trouble*.

Groceries.

Book exchange.

The caffeine jiggered her spirits long enough to get her through the last item first – she dropped all the books she'd finished into a canvas bag and carried them up to the book exchange in a corner of the marina bar.

She took an equal number from the shelf – several mysteries and the second fat volume of a fantasy saga, an old cruising guide to the Leeward Islands of the Caribbean, and a self-help book that had been a best seller last year. Then she asked in the office to look at the telephone book and noted several employment agencies. The attendant in the office saw what she was doing.

"Wally world downtown has been hiring holiday help – the sign was still up yesterday," he said, using the common nickname for a huge discount franchise.

"Oh yeah?" Beth flipped through the phone book to find the listing for the giant chain. "I've heard they don't pay very well." In fact, she'd heard and read far worse, but she was beginning to understand how high ideals could easily crumble in the face of desperation.

"I guess it depends on your point of view," he replied. "It might be easier to get something there than the places around here."

Beth noted the store's phone number and thanked him, then went back to *Trouble* to make some calls. Reviewing her list, she tried Ori's number and got her voicemail. A little disappointed, she left a message announcing her arrival in Miami. She had called Trish last night when they got in and learned that she was driving out to their parents' house a day early for Thanksgiving to take Dad to his appointment with the doctor. They wouldn't know anything until after the holiday, but Beth still owed her parents a call to tell them she was safe.

Her mother answered and related much of the same news that Trish had. She sounded glad about Dad seeing the doctor, but Beth detected a hint of fear in her voice nonetheless.

"Are you okay, Mom? You sound worried."

"I can't help but be, Bethy. First it's your Dad, next it'll be me."

"Oh Mom, don't talk that way."

"It's life, Bethy. We get old, things start to fail. I'm so glad you're out there doing things. I tell the girls in mahjong what you're up to and they're so impressed – the say you have to come do a slide show for them when you get back."

Beth smiled at the notion, then thought about the hundreds of photos on her laptop and realized it wasn't such a bad idea to organize them into a show.

She talked to her father when he came in from the yard and she could picture him, tall and lanky, rubbing at the short hairs on the back of his neck while he talked. He habitually paced the kitchen, the long cord on the wall phone whipping around and tangling on the chair legs. Alf, the big ginger cat, would be swatting at it from the floor.

She ended the call feeling more lonely and homesick than ever.

"Can you start tomorrow, evening shift?" the matronly store personnel representative asked. Beth nodded. "You'll need to come for orientation at noon, then you can start your shift at three."

"Okay. I can do that. When does the shift end?"

"Twelve."

Nine hours. At six dollars an hour, give or take.

"Do, um, busses run at that hour?" she asked hesitantly.

The personnel representative frowned.

"Yes. You don't have transportation?"

"The bus, or a taxi," Beth shrugged.

"Listen, I don't have any other shifts right now. But if this becomes a problem I want you to come to me and I'll see if anything has changed."

"All right," Beth was even more hesitant. *What should I be afraid of? Can Miami at midnight possibly be more threatening than Manhattan? The Bronx?*

It was, if only because it was so different. The walk to the bus stop across the giant parking lot past the RVs camped out with their generators humming was almost as long as the walk to the marina at the other end of the bus trip. But those weren't the scary parts. The bus in mid-afternoon was just as alarming as it was at midnight — maybe more so, and Beth chafed at having to ride it. Despite her years in New York she was a Californian at heart, and although she supported the concept of public transportation, the reality of it had always been hard for her to embrace. And Miami was definitely not a city that had embraced it either.

It was the other passengers that put her off the most. Not the raucous Cubans, for whom the air conditioned, clean bus was a luxury, but the others – starved-looking white girls from the mid-west with stony façades covering animal panic that escaped through their eyes. Older women with frazzled hair and needle tracks stitched along their inner arms and ankles Men whose clothing had absorbed so much booze and sweat it emitted a sour, non-specific odor. Some of them studied racing forms; others just stared out the window at some other world.

Riding with them all made her feel lonelier and poorer than she had ever felt before. And the wage she was receiving didn't make her feel much better. But the marina attendant had been right – before resorting to the big discount store she'd canvassed the shops and bars near the marina and realized that she lacked the look and the wardrobe required for those establishments. It was the first time in her life that she'd felt like an outsider. Even the snobby clerks in the most upscale Madison Avenue shops hadn't intimidated her like the reedy sales people in the South Beach boutiques. Every store clerk, let alone manager, had instantly identified her as boat trash, their noses lifting so that they could peer down them at her. Even though the wages might have been better there, she'd given up looking in favor of trying for a job she knew she could get.

During her interview when they asked her to work Thanksgiving Day – for time and a half – she'd known that if she wanted a job she should agree without hesitation. On Thursday of her first week at Wal-Mart she telephoned her parents and wished everyone a happy Thanksgiving, then she warmed up the one quarter roasted chicken, two sides, and corn bread that she'd picked up the night before. She ate it for lunch with the repeat of the Macy's parade scrolling by on the TV, then grabbed her backpack with her smock tucked into it and ran for the bus, which was late.

Nine hours later at the end of her shift she was setting out across the parking lot when Myra, one of the mangers, called out to her.

"The busses are on the Sunday schedule today, you know," Myra said. Beth frowned, unsure of what that meant: she hadn't tried to ride a bus on Sunday. Then she remembered that she thought the bus had been late that afternoon. "You'd have to look at the schedule at the stop, but I think they run hourly after nine – you could have a long wait."

"Well, I guess I could call a taxi," Beth said, stifling a yawn.

"Where do you live?" Myra asked.

"Miami Marina."

"On a boat?" she sounded a little surprised.

"Yes. I'm just passing through – I'm just working here to bank some money until my crew gets here."

"And then you'll sail away, huh?" she shook her head slowly. "Lucky you. Well, come on."

"Pardon?"

"I'm heading over the causeway. I'll give you a ride."

"You don't mind?"

"Come on."

"Do you live on the island?" Beth asked when they were buckled into Myra's Ford.

"Me?" she snorted. "Hell no. I'm meeting my boyfriend for a drink at one of the bars."

"Oh – that sounds fun."

"Have you been hanging out at the bars?" she sounded surprised.

"No," Beth admitted. "I wandered around a bit the other night when I was restless. It's quite a scene."

"Ummm. I like it. But you don't seem the type."

Beth decided not to take this as an insult, although she thought it might be intended to be one. She was too tired to care, or wonder why this store manager would feel the need to abuse a lowly clerk.

"I'm more a daytime person," she said. "I got to the beach yesterday morning for a little while. And I tried a Cuban coffee. Wow!"

"Strong, huh?" Myra laughed with her. "I guess the only other place you'll find those is in Cuba, and that's off limits. So enjoy while you can."

"I like strong coffee, but that's a bit much."

They came off the bridge and turned right, Myra navigating expertly to the Marina gates.

"You know where it is," Beth observed as the car came to a stop.

"Yeah, I dated a guy with a boat for three months. Name's Pauly – if you see him in there, give him a shove off a dock for me."

"Okay," Beth laughed, although Myra didn't seem to be joking. Then she got out of the car, offering her thanks and waving as the car pulled away.

Her cell phone rang as she was walking down the quiet dock. Immediately fearing the worst – something wrong with her parents – she stopped to dig it out of her bag.

"Happy Thanksgiving – belatedly," Terry's voice purred in her ear.

"Same to you – belatedly," she replied joyfully.

"I hope it's not too late. I know you were working tonight. That must have been interesting."

"Oh yes. You'd be amazed at how many people buy their turkey at noon on Thanksgiving, and then start their Christmas shopping right after they eat it."

"Trying to beat the rush?" he laughed. "How about you – did you have Thanksgiving dinner?"

"I had a hot dog."

"Oh Bethy, that's awful!"

"Hey, it had relish and onions. I liked it."

"Okay, okay. But I wish I could have FedExed you a care package."

"Did you actually spend Thanksgiving with your family?" Beth asked. She had learned that his parents and sister all lived in southern Virginia."

"Yes I did. I'm on my way home now."

"I'm glad. I'm living vicariously these days."

"Well, if I come down there will you start living for real again?"

"The moment you get here," she agreed – finding it hard to believe she sounded like a girlfriend talking to a man she'd spent all of eight or ten hours with, and none of it alone. But if you counted telephone time it was more like four straight days, and she had opened up to him about many things that she rarely shared with others.

In any case, he didn't seem to question her response. She knew she should look at this from other angles – he might just be too self-involved to notice that she was falling for him long distance. But since he was going to come, and she wanted him there, she deferred her rational assessment until he was present.

"I know I said right after Thanksgiving, but this German deal is dragging. I need another week. But I could fly down this weekend," he said.

"You mean fly down and go back to work on Monday?"

"Yes. I don't want you to think I'm trying to back out. I'm really looking forward to sailing with you again. I just can't leave things hanging here. We have to get the contract signed."

Beth was too startled to formulate a response. What is he thinking? Is he proposing, like, a weekend-long date?

"But Sunday is the busiest travel day of the year. You'd never get a flight."

"I'd go standby. I do it all the time. I just feel awful for abandoning you."

"Terry, it's all right. I mean, I should work another week anyway. I need the money."

She heard him sigh, wondered if he was considering offering her money as well. Wondered what she'd say if he did.

"It is a bit nuts, isn't it?" he asked. Suddenly, surprisingly relieved, she laughed.

"A bit."

"Well, I'm not sure what it is about you Beth, but you seem to have that affect on me. Not too many girls will sign onto a racing yacht full of jocks at a moment's notice. Even fewer head out on an open-ended cruise all by themselves. I'm fascinated. I don't want to lose the chance to get to know you better."

"We've done pretty well on the phone," she replied, stepping up onto *Trouble*'s side deck and sitting down on the cabin top to catch her breath. It was the first time he'd even remotely alluded to an emotional interest in her.

"It's not good enough for me. I'm a face-to-face kinda guy. I'm just afraid you'll find someone else to take my berth. Promise me you won't?"

"I promise Terry. What do you think got me through all those miles of waterway? There's a spot for you on *Trouble*. You just come when you can stay for a while."

"Okay. As long as you're sure. Because thinking about spending Christmas with you is what's getting me through this deal. Jeff says I've gone mad, the way I'm pushing the Germans."

"Terry don't risk your deal – what else does Jeff say?"

He laughed. "Oh no, I don't have to tell you the guy talk. I'll just say that he's not unhappy – the Germans *need* pushing. Oops – I almost missed my exit. I'd better go."

"Good night Terry. I'll talk to you soon – and just remember that your spot's waiting here."

"Good night Beth."

TWENTY-ONE: DATE NIGHT

She worked eight of the next nine days before Terry's arrival, adding up her wages at the end of each shift and comparing them to her expenses. The day after Thanksgiving she moved *Trouble* to a much cheaper mooring, although it meant that she had to leave her dinghy at the dinghy dock all afternoon and evening while she was at work. And she couldn't use the air conditioner. She started sleeping out in the cockpit where the feeble night breezes cooled her skin, Every night a squall passed through sending her below for an hour or so. She tried calling Ori again and left another message. At the end of the next week she called Trish and asked about her father.

"We met with the doctor this morning to hear his analysis," her sister sounded subdued. *It must not be good.* Trish sighed, then went on. "Let's see, what did he say? Dad is in the earliest phase of the disease. The doctor wants to run some more tests to see whether he's a good candidate for some of the experimental drugs. They're working well on some people."

"I know, I've read about them. Oh Trish please just give me a second. I can't believe he really has it," Beth swallowed down an unexpected sob. "How long until he starts to forget us?"

She heard Trish sob as well. "I'm sorry – are you at work? We can do this later."

"I am. But you need to know."

"Not right this second, Trish. Why don't you call me tonight – after ten your time."

"That'll be one a.m. for you."

"It'll give me time to get home from work."

"Oh God I forgot. Okay honey. We'll talk then."

Beth went to work and struggled through her shift, endlessly gathering discarded clothes from the floors of the ladies department and re-hanging them where they belonged. It was ridiculously exhausting work, and she vowed never to leave a fallen garment on the floor or in the fitting room again. *If I ever have money and time to shop again.*

Beth's cute Annapolis haircut had grown out and the ends were split and frizzy in the Florida humidity. She brushed it, sprayed it, and brushed it again. Then wet it down and let it dry again. All in the hour between Terry's call from the airport and his arrival by taxi at the marina.

She felt herself hopping from one foot to the other as she stood in the shade of the breezeway watching a green and white taxi pull into the parking lot and roll to a stop near the office. She had put on her crisp, white, collared tank top over her tan shorts that had the fewest stains. And she had stopped on the way to work yesterday to have her finger and toenails painted a flattering dark red. It cost ten dollars, but she could never have done it as neatly as the diminutive Asian woman who performed the service. She'd been using sunscreen liberally, so that her skin was an even brown but not burnt. She felt that she looked as good as she possibly could, and if it wasn't good enough for Terry then, well, that would be that.

He unfolded himself from the taxi and met the driver at the back where they removed two bags and an odd-shaped bundle that at first she couldn't identify from the trunk. Then he turned toward her and she realized that it was an enormous bouquet of flowers.

"Welcome!" she called out, trotting out into the sun to him.

"Beth!" he opened his arms, one hand holding the flowers, and she stepped into his friendly embrace. It felt so good to be held, and to hold on, she had a hard time letting go. But she did, taking a half step back to look into those lovely, crinkle-edged eyes.

He presented the flowers to her with a proud smile.

"For you."

"Thank you. They're beautiful." Once upon a time she had bought flowers for her apartment nearly every week. But these days they were an extravagance. She pressed her face into them and inhaled their perfume.

She had thought about moving back to a slip for his arrival, but in the end decided that he should see how things really were for her. It wouldn't be good to start things on artificial pretenses. So she guided him to the dinghy dock and helped him arrange his bags so that the boat was balanced when they both got in. The dinghy was made for four adults, but it seemed most comfortable with two.

Shouting over the outboard motor she asked him about his flight. He described it equally loudly – small talk at high volume to fill the few minutes between dock and boat.

They worked together to load his bags up onto the deck and then themselves. Beth guided him below and indicated the aft cabin as his, then put the flowers in a pitcher of water while he dragged his duffle bags down into the cabin. By the time he had settled them on his berth she had dug out the chilled bottle of Spanish sparkling wine she'd gotten for the occasion. He stood in the doorway of his cabin and watched her twist off the cage and carefully pull out the cork with a pop.

"Shall we sit outside?" she asked. "I'm sure you like being able to. Was it cold in DC?"

"Frigid," he agreed, carrying the two plastic stemmed glasses up the ladder. She followed, and they settled in on opposite sides of the cockpit, the bottle tucked into an oversized cup holder on the binnacle.

"To fair weather," he said, touching his cup to hers.

"To good friends," she countered, wishing she could be cleverer when she was nervous.

"Something's wrong," he said, eying her. She frowned. She had been brooding about her father since her late night talk with Trish on Friday. Although both Trish and her parents had told her they understood that she couldn't be home for Christmas, she still felt awful about it. That Terry could see her upset through the joy she was feeling at his arrival meant that either she was more upset than she thought, or he knew her far better than he ought to, given their limited experience together.

"Family stuff," she said, trying to be dismissive. He watched her for a moment.

"Tell me. Is it your father?"

She had told him of her fears over the last few weeks. He had a right to ask.

"Yes. He has it. He has Alzheimer's. They're doing more tests to figure out how to treat it."

"How long have you known?"

"Officially? Since Friday. I've been pretty sure that's what they'd find for weeks. But hearing that it's true is really hard."

Terry got up and moved to the bench beside her, then put his arm around her shoulders and drew her to him. She felt herself shudder with emotional relief. Nobody had held her like this – offered a comforting shoulder to lean on in a time of need – in months. She was Beth – the independent one, the strong one. She didn't panic. She didn't need advice or sympathy. She made her own decisions and lived with the consequences. She was a role model, although she wasn't sure for whom.

"I understand if you need to go to California," Terry said quietly. Belatedly she noticed how good he smelt, and how solid his arm and chest felt. She forced herself to sit up, to leave his sheltering embrace just a little and reach up to wipe her damp eyes.

"No, I've talked to them. There's nothing I can do to help. It's such a slow disease, Dad will not notice any change for months – or rather, we won't notice a change in him. And if they can use some of the new treatments, they may be able to stop the progress for a long time."

"Still, he's your father. If you need to see him you should go."

Beth shook her head. "I'm not that kind of daughter," she said, realizing that it was true. She'd sprung from the nest mid-way through college and never gone back. As the younger sister there had been fewer expectations. Trish had been the one to think about their parents' retirement and old age. Trish had found a reliable husband and settled nearby. Beth had been allowed to fly away to the east coast, remaining single and unfettered by responsibility to her elders.

"Meaning you're not a 'daddy's girl'?"

"Something like that. My sister is there. I talk to all of them. If I went there, it would be great for a while, but then I'd begin to resent it. I couldn't give up my life just to be with them and they know it. I am with them, in my heart."

"Okay. You know what's best."

Beth pulled away from him a little more and looked into his eyes.

"Who are you to talk, Mr. 'I don't want my folks to know that I can get away from work when I really need to'?" she asked with a smile. He chuckled.

"Touché," he smiled back.

"Besides, if I was going to leave I would have called you last night before you headed down here. It would be really rude of me to lure you here and then take off. And stupid!"

"Well, I'll give you that. But I just want you to know that I understand that things change sometimes. If that happens, you just tell me. You can leave me guarding the boat while you go take care of business. That's only fair considering how long you've had to wait for me."

"That's okay. In fact, if I'm going to get back on budget I need to keep working this next week. Besides --."

"Beth, I've been meaning to tell you, if I had booked this trip as a vacation, I would expect to pay a couple thousand dollars. Let me help out --."

"Besides, there's a low pressure zone whipping up some nasty weather out in the Atlantic. We need to wait for the high pressure that's over the Midwest to move it – at least three days according to the reports."

"Well, in that case, I'm sure I can find something to do. But my offer stands. That job sounds like a horror show."

"I've been moved to the day shift starting tomorrow. I'm sure that will be better," she replied. His offer was hard to resist, but if they were to build the sort of relationship she wanted she knew it couldn't be based on money.

"Okay. So what about the rest of today?"

"I'm off."

"I meant, what do you want to do?"

"Well -- seriously?"

"Yes. Is there something you've been wanting to do but haven't had time for?"

"Parrot Jungle."

"Parrot what?" he laughed.

"You heard me. I've seen all these brochures and ads for it. I want to see it."

"Tell you what. Why don't I rent a car until we leave? Then I can drive you to work, too."

Since she wouldn't accept his money directly, that sounded like an excellent compromise. Although he seemed skeptical of her proposed adventure, he collected his wallet and a small digital camera and telephoned his favorite car rental agency. She called for a taxi to take them to the nearest rental office, and they were off.

In many ways the afternoon felt like a first date. Terry had rented a white convertible and he drove it like it was a racing sailboat. Beth leaned her head back and enjoyed the sun on her face and the pleasant feeling of trusting someone else to take her where she wanted to go. It had been a long time since she'd relinquished control, and it felt good.

At Parrot Jungle they oohed and awed at the colorful birds and exotic animals, and posed for pictures with rows of heavy macaws on their arms. When they finished they found a brochure on the car window for another attraction, so they drove over to the Coral Castle and played hide-and-seek amid the fanciful stone structures. On the way home Terry spotted a restaurant that looked like a hole-in-the wall local place to Beth. But she followed him inside where they had a bucket of fresh steamed clams followed by shrimp and some crab claws. They stripped cobs of corn with their teeth, butter dripping down their chins, and washed it all down with icy cold white wine of indeterminate vintage or origin.

Near midnight they climbed down the ladder into *Trouble*'s salon. When she reached out to flip on a light switch Terry caught her hand.

"Wait Beth," he whispered near her ear, turning her around with a hand on her other shoulder. "Thank you for a wonderful day," he said. Then he released her hand and stroked her cheek with one finger. His lips brushed hers ever so lightly, sending a jolt of desire keening through her body. She inhaled sharply as he stepped back into his cabin. "Good night," he said, a knowing smile crinkling the edges of his eyes as he looked at her standing in the pool of moonlight falling through the open companionway. Then he shut the door to his cabin.

Beth plopped onto her bunk still tingling from his touch. If he'd been trying to seduce her, he'd succeeded. And not following through had made it all the more powerful. He had her now and judging by the look in his eyes before he shut the door, he knew it. *But does he know that I have him exactly where I want him, too?*

TWENTY-TWO: RULES

The daytime shift on a Monday was as bad as the late shift in its own way: It was boring. There was a lot less to do because there were far fewer shoppers. The ones who were there were mostly overworked moms with undisciplined small children. Now Beth understood why the clothing departments always looked a shambles when she came on at 3:00. It wasn't the adult patrons who were slobs – well, they were too – but their children, who they let run wild while they tried on cartloads of cheap clothes in the dressing rooms.

When she emerged from the store at six she was a little surprised to see the shining white convertible sitting in the fire lane with the engine idling and the air conditioning blasting.

"Trying to air condition all of Miami?" she asked jokingly as she climbed in. The cool air blowing on her face felt great.

"It's a rental," Terry shrugged. "If they didn't want people to do it, they'd disable it while the top is down. But speaking of air conditioning, as crew I have a request."

"What's that?" she sighed, turning her face to cool the side.

"I'd like to move *Trouble* in to a slip so we can turn on the AC. I'll pay for the difference between that and the mooring."

Beth turned her face back to look over at him. *Be stubborn about the money, or be realistic?* He reached down and maxed out the cool air with a devilish grin.

"Deal," she said simply. *What the hell. I'm too old to rough it if I don't have to.*

She stopped in the office to find out if there was a slip available while he moved some shopping bags from the car to the dinghy. He kept them shut tight and his mouth closed about them while they moved *Trouble* and hooked up the shore power. Then he urged her to go enjoy a nice long shower. She had the distinct impression that he was trying to get rid of her, but she went with it.

She returned forty minutes later with clean hair and in a clean linen shirt and shorts to find the cockpit table set, including wine glasses and candles. As she stepped on board and her weight rocked the boat a little he stepped up into the companionway with two foil serving dishes.

"Good evening miss. If you'll have a seat, dinner is served," he said.

"So that's what was in the bags," she observed, setting her shower bag in the corner and stepping down into the cockpit to sit down at the table.

"I didn't cook it all up while you were in the shower, if that's what you're thinking," he admitted, bringing up two more dishes. "I ordered it."

"It's wonderful Terry. Thank you," she assured him as he served her fish stuffed with crab, steamed green beans, and some sort of mashed squash, and filled both their wine glasses from a bottle nestled in a bucket of ice.

They ate and discussed their day – he had spent some time on the phone with the office, and done some odd jobs on the boat – lubricated a squeaky winch, put fresh tape over the lifeline cotter rings, rebound the ends of the jib sheets. She told him about the bratty children in the store and shared her untested philosophy of child rearing, adding that she never had the nerve to discuss it with her friends who actually had kids for fear they'd tell her she had no right to an opinion. He agreed, and shared a couple stories of Jeff's two kids, who according to Jeff and his wife were little angels. Beth refrained from asking Terry why he hadn't yet married and had kids, and he paid her the same courtesy.

She insisted on washing up – what consisted of throwing out all the disposable containers and washing the plates and flatware. Terry refilled their wine glasses and they sat side by side with their backs to the marina lights. They talked long into the evening just as they had on the telephone so many times, but with the added pleasure of visual and physical contact. Beth patted his thigh to emphasize a point. He rested his arm on the combing behind her, letting it touch her upper back lightly. She still couldn't get her fill of his flashing eyes and handsome, weathered face, and she watched him intently as he spoke of his childhood in suburban Virginia.

When the candles had burned down to nubs and the wine was long gone Beth realized that she was terribly sleepy. Terry's voice had become a warm, comforting sound near her ear, but carried no words to her brain. She turned her face to his, not realizing how close together their heads were, and her mouth brushed his cheek. The stubble of his beard on her lips tingled deliciously. *You've got it bad when beard burn feels good,* she thought idly as he turned his face to hers and caught her lips with his. It was no light brush this time, but a solid, grasping kiss. She sank into it, wondering why they'd waited so long. One hand snaked up to his collar, the other rested on his chest feeling the rapid beating of his heart. His arm shifted from the combing to wrap around her shoulders, holding her against him possessively.

When it ended he smiled into her eyes, then placed another tiny kiss on the tip of her nose.

"I was hoping you'd do that," he whispered. "I couldn't stop talking. I don't even know what about."

"Me neither," she winced, guilty for her inattention. "Terry, I'm so sleepy if I don't go below I'll fall asleep on you."

"And that's bad why?" he squeezed her a little tighter. She understood his message. *Too fast,* a little voice in her head admonished. She always listened to it.

"It's not bad at all," she said, pulling away gently but firmly. He released her. "Just not – yet."

He watched her stand up, his expression enigmatic. She took his hand, stroked his fingers.

"I'd like to be sure of the ground rules," she said.

"Your boat, your rules, skipper," he said softly. She didn't doubt his sincerity. But it wasn't him she was talking about. This had all happened too quickly and she was afraid of ending up right back where she'd been with Peter. What did he want? A tropical Christmas fling? She could do that – God knew she wanted him. But she needed to know going in if there was a finite duration. She needed to protect herself now from the emotional rejection.

"Thanks Terry," she said. "For everything."

She escaped to her cabin to get ready for bed, grateful for the air conditioning that masked the sound of him coming below a while later.

"Kenny thought that was funny too," Beth chuckled and Terry set the cartoon torn from a daily calendar down quickly. He'd found it tucked into one of the books on the shelf over the port settee.

"So this Kenny guy left quite an impression here," he said, "Including a pair of shorts in the aft cabin." He forced a laugh as he stepped into the cabin and back out again dangling a pair of dingy boxer shorts pinched between the tips of two fingers.

"What?" Beth's eyes widened as she giggled, pressing a hand to her mouth. "I can't believe I didn't find those – I'm so sorry!"

"No worries – they were under the cushions. But I do have to wonder about the guy who'd pick these. You seem to mention him a lot." He looked at the underwear quizzically. They were printed with a maroon and brown paisley pattern.

"They are rather atrocious," Beth agreed, still giggling. And then the rest of what he'd said sank in.

"When you're with someone twenty-four seven for a couple weeks, you tend to think about them a lot," she tried to explain. "It takes a while to unweave them from your thoughts."

"So how much longer do you think that will take?" Terry asked, still smiling.

Beth shrugged. "I'm working on it. Look, that's really all it is – Kenny was pleasant company, but we had very little in common. It was an education for me to hear about his life, and I guess it was the same for him. But I was glad to see him go. I have a couple pictures, if you'd like to put a face to his ghost." Without waiting for a response she seated herself at the navigation desk. She had brought the computer back out after Kenny left, openly admitting that she trusted Terry more – for no rational reason other than first impressions. She started up the photo software. Terry stepped up behind her while they waited for it to load, the warmth of his body radiating out to caress her back. She fought the urge to lean back just a little: to make contact.

The most recent photos that she'd downloaded from the camera appeared on the computer screen. She clicked on one of Kenny taken about a week into their journey.

"This is a good one," she said. "We had run out of beer a couple days before, so he was more alert. And we'd both gotten to know one another, so we were relaxed."

She leaned to the side away from Terry and turned her head to look up at him, to see his reaction. He bent a little and studied Kenny's toothy grin and squinty eyes.

"Looks like he laughed a lot," he observed. "You had fun."

"He did laugh a lot. And I wanted to make the best of the situation, so I laughed too."

"You have a beautiful smile, Beth. I hope you'll keep sharing it now I'm here," he said, looking down at her. Beth did just that, and he smiled too.

"Kenny was a pair of eyes and hands to help get *Trouble* through the ICW," she said.

"And I'm eyes and hands to get her to the Islands?" he asked, still smiling even though his words were loaded with pitfalls. Beth's heart was pounding, her eyes locked with his.

"What do you want to be?" she asked, her voice unintentionally breathy. He dropped to the edge of the settee beside her, his back to the desk that she was facing. His gaze never left hers, his smile never faded, although there was tension around his eyes.

"Let's take a little more time to figure that out – okay?"

"Okay," she nodded, still sharing his gaze. His eyes were hypnotic. For a moment she thought he would kiss her again and every fiber of her being anticipated it.

"Okay," he said, much louder than her. He squeezed her shoulder with one hand, then stood up. She covered her embarrassment by busying herself with shutting down the photo software. *Imagining things. That's what you're doing. He just wants to – he just wants – What does he want?*

"Hi honey, how was work?" Terry called from *Trouble's* bow as Beth came along side on the dock.

"Murder – I hope you've got my martini ready," she quipped back. "The Kaplan account is a mess and Mr. Dithers yelled all afternoon."

She continued speaking as he followed her back to the cockpit and down the companionway.

"I am so glad to be done there. It was a friggin' mad house for the last week – all the frantic buying, like the only way to say 'I love you' is by giving some cheap junk that the person doesn't need or want." She watched him turn toward her at the base of the ladder and found an odd expression on his face.

"Is everything okay?" she asked.

His face cleared and he smiled. "Sure, fine. I'm sorry you disliked the job so much."

His head tilted toward the navigation desk, drawing her gaze there as well. A thick stack of spiral bound charts topped with a big red bow were sitting on it.

"What --?"

"Merry Christmas," he said.

"But –."

"You've got those old charts your friend in New York gave you. I know. But I prefer that the vessel I'm on have complete charts for any possible landfall. Makes me feel safe."

Beth stepped over to the desk and examined the pile of chart books. Collectively they covered southern Florida and all of the Caribbean in enormous detail. She had dreamt of having such a complete library and discarded the notion immediately when she'd calculated the cost.

"They're worth a fortune," she said.

"You and *Trouble* are worth a lot more. I see it as a sound investment."

Beth faced him, struggling to decide what was appropriate. She gave in to impulse and put her arms around his neck to pull him into a hug, at the last moment turning her face away from his. *My boat, my rules. So I have to stick by them too.*

He wrapped his arms around her and held her tight for a moment that went on and on. She wanted to turn her head and kiss him, but since they'd both agreed to give it time, she was afraid he might reject her. And then he was rubbing her back fraternally and pulling away from her. She dropped her head to avoid confusing eye contact, directing her eyes back to the charts instead.

"Thank you so much," she said, realizing she hadn't said it.

"My pleasure," he replied, a purr in his voice that was full of suggestion. But she couldn't look at him. If she was imagining it, seeing that to be the case would hurt too much.

TWENTY-THREE: ESCAPE

"Maybe I should try to get my job back," Beth lamented, laying down the Monday morning newspaper folded open to the weather. The low pressure system hadn't budged and conditions out in the Atlantic were still dreadful for sailing. They were not much better aboard *Trouble* in her slip in Miami, either.

"Whatever you want to do," Terry replied, his eyes not leaving the sports section as he took a sip of coffee. Beth stared at him, wondering how she'd gotten into this strange situation: living with a man who she hardly knew, but with whom she was desperately in love, and to whom she could hardly talk because of the tension between them. She knew it was mostly her doing: she could not convince herself that he was there as crew and did not want or need to be in charge.

Over the weekend while they'd waited out the weather she had caught herself feeling threatened by his presence, imagining an invisible challenge to her authority. She had started to counter his every suggestion and to interrupt him when he undertook some helpful task like re-organizing the refrigerator or hosing the decks. She had her reasons each time, of course: she was about to go shopping, so she'd do the fridge when she was adding the new provisions; she was going to put a coat of varnish on the brightwork, so she didn't want it wet. They were spurious reasons – the fridge could always use some organization, and no varnishing was actually done. She was privately appalled at the control freak that she had become, but just the same she could not stop herself.

She knew there was more to it than simply having another person in her space – after all, she'd been comfortable with Kenny for the entire trip down the ICW. He'd taken on chores without asking, offered advice, even taken control of the helm when his greater experience was needed. None of that had bothered her. She had appreciated his contribution and respected his experience as a waterman. So why didn't she feel the same way about Terry? He certainly was an experienced sailor, and he was in a position to make a significant contribution to their trip if she would let him.

Because I want him to be my boyfriend, and I can't be in charge if he is.

By Sunday afternoon Terry was reacting to her edginess by closing up. He left the decision about Sunday dinner to her, so even though he probably would have treated them both to seafood somewhere, she made economical spaghetti on board. He asked if he should wash up, and asked if the trash was ready to go up to the dumpster. By the time he returned to the boat Beth had felt drained both from the self-imposed burden of command and the growing tension between them. And he'd put on the final straw by assuring her in the sincerest tones that she was in charge, this was her boat, and she could count on him to be good crew.

She believed he was sincere, she just did not believe that any man could really want to be subservient to a woman – either on a sailboat or in a relationship. And the truth was she did not want him to be. His continued insistence that she was in charge grated on her because what she wanted was a partner and she didn't know how to achieve that balance. *Trouble* was her boat, so she had to be the captain. How did she invite Terry into her life while maintaining her authority?

By Monday morning when she snapped at him for putting the coffee pot on the wrong burner his attitude had deteriorated to a passive-aggressive neutrality regarding everything.

"You don't really want me to go back to work, do you?" she asked, getting his attention. He lowered the sports section where she saw he had been reading about jai-alai. "Wouldn't you rather we both go to the beach?"

"I'm not much for lying in the sand. But you should go." He replied. She felt herself grow pale beneath her suntan. Disappointment blended with suspicion then turned to self-doubt.

"Okay," she said carefully. "What are you going to do?"

"Make some calls."

Her stomach lurched. To airlines, for reservations home? To Jeff, to tell him he was over it and how foolish he'd been. They'd have a good laugh over a beer. She could not think of anything to say, so she got up and collected their breakfast dishes, carrying them over to the sink.

"I'm going up to Starbucks," he announced a couple minutes later. "Shall I have a look at the long-term forecast and the radar."

"That would be great. Maybe I should come along." *Because lord knows I can't trust you to interpret the weather correctly,* she scolded herself sarcastically.

"If you want to do it ..."

"No, you can do it. But I should check email and send some pictures to my sister."

She was certain that he resented her presence as they got out of the car and walked into the Starbucks in a hot Miami strip mall. They each carried their own laptops to a café table, and Beth wondered if she should sit at her own.

"What would you like?" Terry asked as he took out his wallet.

"Iced latte please, tall," she said, opening her own weathered nylon wallet. "Here," she extended a five dollar bill.

He waved it away as he turned toward the counter where a short line of people were waiting to place their orders. Beth put her money away, ashamed to be grateful that he was treating her to the expensive coffee. She started up her computer, quickly logging on to the Internet using the short-term account she'd bought when she got to Miami. She was studying a radar map of the region while checking email when he returned with their coffees.

She momentarily forgot her uneasiness as she turned her computer so that he could see the screen, "Look – the cold front is moving southeast." She switched to a forecast map that showed the jet stream – the west to east current of air that influenced all US weather – swinging south across the great plains states. It pushed a mass of cool air ahead of it, which in turn would push the warm, calm, heavy air currently enveloping Florida out to sea.

"We can expect rain tonight or tomorrow morning, and then a couple days of good breezes!"

She knew her grin was contagious. He handed her the latte and raised his own – the same, she noticed – touching the rims of the plastic cups together. "To getting underway."

"To *finally* getting underway."

They spent a companionable hour together, each wrapped in their own digital world reading emails and on-line news. Several times Terry left the table to stand outside and make or take a phone call. That was one of the things she loved about him – he respected her and the other coffee house patrons and would not subject them to his phone conversation. She banished any notion that he was actually out there arranging a flight home. This was reinforced by a peek at his computer screen, which displayed an email from someone discussing the schedule for training on a new sales management system. It occurred to her that she knew very little about his work despite all their long phone conversations. She had a vague idea that he and Jeff sold training services, sending their teams of corporate trainers all over the country – and the world if Germany was any indication – teaching people how to use corporate software.

Based on her publishing background she couldn't imagine it being a profitable business – publishing houses never spent money on formal training. But then she remembered from her brief stint at the financial company that they had an ongoing schedule of courses for all sorts of things. She had always been a "let me at it and I'll figure it out" sort of computer user, but she had encountered people who flatly refused to use a computer program for work if they were not formally trained in it by their employer. It had never struck her as a very team-spirited attitude, but she supposed that companies that did offer training in everything encouraged it.

He came back to the table and downed the last of his latte, then methodically quit from each of the programs running on his laptop and shut it down. Beth looked at the blog about a television star she'd been reading and realized she'd been marking time waiting for him to be through for the last fifteen minutes. She didn't mind – the only part of it that bothered her was that the on-line time cost money. She logged off the Internet.

"Don't shut down because of me," he said.

"No, it's okay. I dealt with all the email."

"How's your dad?"

She watched the iBook cycle through its shutdown procedure. She had read her sister's message quickly, storing it on the hard drive for later review. She did not want to think about it right now, but she forced herself to answer honestly.

"He says he's fine and he doesn't need any medication," she said softly, realizing as the words came out just how upset they made her. Terry covered her hand on the table with his, squeezing gently.

"Could you convince him?"

"You mean if I went out there?"

"Yes."

"I doubt it. Mom will have to do it. She's the only one he'll listen to. He certainly won't take the advice of his little girls."

"I'm sorry Beth. I can't imagine how hard this is."

"I feel so –." A sob welled up unexpected and she pressed her free hand over her mouth, squeezing her eyes shut. His arm encircled her shoulders, pulled her close. She realized that he'd moved his chair right next to hers from a third of the way around the table where he'd been sitting.

"Shhhh. Come on, let's go for a walk."

He maneuvered her to her feet, collecting their computers and leaving their empty coffee cups for the staff to clear. She ducked her head to hide her blotchy red face and let him lead her out by the hand. He stowed both computers in the trunk of the car, then, standing with it still open, enveloped her in his arms. She relaxed against him, laying her head on his shoulder, and fought back the tears.

He stroked her back slowly, his face pressed into her hair as he murmured soothing sounds to her. She won her battle, choking back the flood of emotion and swallowing it down. Finally she turned her head and leaned back a little to look into his face. He continued to hold her, peering into her eyes with concern.

"Okay?" he asked.

She nodded, resisting the urge to lean back into him for another long hug. Instead she raised one hand to her face and wiped at the sweat forming on her brow. It was hot for December.

"Come on," he guided her around to the passenger side of the car and opened the door for her. She got in, wincing at the hot seat beneath her bare thighs below the hem of her shorts. He went back around the car, shutting the trunk as he went, and got in behind the wheel. He started the engine and turned on the air conditioner full blast. Beth smiled and raised her head as the cool blast hit her in the face.

"That's like a bucket of cold water," she said.

"I'm sorry I upset you."

She turned her head to look at him. He was staring out the

windshield. For the first time she wondered whether he had some history – some difficult memories that were affecting his behavior. Perhaps he'd been involved with someone like her before – *a crazy control freak.*

"You didn't. It's life that's upsetting – mostly because I feel so out of control."

My God, did I just say that?

"With the weather holding us here, and Dad sick – but there's nothing I can do. I just --."

She stopped short, struggling to sort out the emotions from the truths, and to deal with her revelation. *I can't control the weather, and I can't control Dad. So I'm determined to control what I can: Terry. But I can't control him either. I'm driving him away.*

"I hate being stuck here. You know, I think I really hate Miami."

Terry chuckled and turned his head to look at her.

"I know what you mean. Once we get away, I'm looking forward to the hours of sailing. Just skimming along – you and me and the boat. I can't wait for that. Even if we end up motoring, it's still the thing that makes all this waiting worth it."

"You and me," Beth repeated quietly. Terry took her hand from her lap, uncurling her fingers to study her palm.

"That's what I said. That's what I want. All those hours, talking, laughing, holding you. . ." he trailed off and she realized he was watching her face.

All she could think was, *you can't still want me after the way I've been acting!*

"That wouldn't be against the rules, would it?" he asked tentatively. "Hold you now and then?"

"No," she breathed, afraid to ruin the moment by saying too much. "That wouldn't be against the rules."

Idiot with your idiotic rules.

"We're casting off first thing in the morning," Terry said. He was sitting at an outdoor bar that was part of the marina complex with a stiff gin and tonic in front of him. He had left Beth in a frenzy of pre-departure organization. He would have helped, but her territorial expression had been enough of a warning sign to send him up the dock.

"The forecast looks spectacular. You were wise to wait," Jeff replied, obviously looking at a weather report on-line.

"Yeah? Well what does it forecast for me and her?"

"What do you mean? Trouble in paradise? Oh – well I guess that's a given isn't it," Jeff laughed at his own witty reference to the boat's name. Terry groaned.

"I think she's still really torn about having me here. She wanted to do this herself, you know?"

"You mean you haven't romanced the girl into your cabin?"

"Strictly speaking I'd rather be romanced into hers – it's bigger. But no, I'm not here for that."

"Sure you aren't."

"I tell you Jeff, there's something about her. She's competent, brave, clever --."

"I got it Terry. You're smitten, and that's okay. I think we all got that after one day in Annapolis when you wouldn't stop talking about her."

"I don't know what you're talking about."

"You were drunk."

"We all were. But that doesn't matter. I was still in love."

"And now, after several days with her?"

"What do you think?"

"That you always fall hard when you fall. Just be sure she isn't another Linda. We don't have the luxury of nursing you back from another fall like that. Business is too good."

"Don't remind me," Terry rubbed his face with his free hand and took another sip of his drink.

"It may surprise you to know that I didn't call you for advice about my love life. I just wanted to give you our rough schedule so that you can call out the Coast Guard if we don't turn up."

Terry proceeded to relate the plan that Beth had outlined when they'd gotten back from Starbucks. They would island hop, touching down only briefly in the Dominican Republic and Puerto Rico – or skipping one of them if they had no need for supplies or repairs – before making landfall on St. Thomas. The US Virgin Islands were Beth's first goal and Terry could understand the lure. For someone who'd never been to the Caribbean, the security of US territorial waters would be very appealing. He just hoped she would not be discouraged by the tourist factor in Charlotte Amalie. First chance he got he would try to get them over to St. John. But he did not mention any of that to Jeff. It made the trip sound way too open ended for his patient business partner to tolerate.

"So how is this expedition funded?" Jeff asked, a question that Terry thought was a bit out of line.

"Beth keeps a careful budget."

"You're not contributing?"

"Not materially. Now stop prying."

"I'm just looking out for you. You know when things started going down the drain with Linda."

"Beth is nothing like Linda, Jeff. I really did learn my lesson, so you can stop lecturing."

"Okay. 'nough said. Have a great sail. I'll be thinking of you out there while the rest of us are covering for you."

"Yeah, thanks. You know I made up for it closing the deal with the Germans. So I won't feel any guilt at all. I'll be in touch in a week or so."

"Bon voyage."

Terry suppressed the thoughts of his ex-girlfriend Linda as he walked back down the dock to *Trouble*'s slip. As he approached Beth emerged from the companionway with several plastic grocery bags. No, she was nothing like the high-strung, high-heeled model that he'd dated for three years. For one thing, he did not believe Beth had ever used any recreational drugs, and he knew for a fact that she kept down any food she ate.

"Trash?" he asked from the dock. Beth nodded.

"I tried to get it all. It's amazing how quickly stuff accumulates."

"Let me take it up."

"You just got back."

"I'm on the dock already."

Realizing it was a ridiculous point to argue about, she passed him the bags.

"I'll be right back. Then let's go out for dinner. My treat."

Beth's smile, which had been scarce lately, was the best reward.

"I'd like that."

"That's me, professional rail meat," Terry took another gulp of beer and watched Beth's reaction to his claim. It had struck him somewhere during his second beer that what he'd thought was simple impatience to be off on her part was actually more complicated. He had suddenly connected her comment back at Starbucks about being out of control with her behavior over the last three days. He thought he understood: he was the more experienced sailor, and she thought he wanted to take charge. He was sure if he could convince her that being the skipper wasn't important to him that it would go a long way toward repairing their nascent relationship.

"I love to drift around the boat adjusting things, making it go faster, handle better. There was this one race last season . . ." he launched into the story, making his timely easing of the main halyard seem like the thing that had won them the regatta. He watched her face, so interested, absorbing every detail as he explained the principles of his adjustment. "Jeff manages that gang of thugs he calls crew. I'd much rather focus on the sailing and leave the decisions to him."

"Or me," Beth said, almost under her breath.

"Or you," Terry replied with a smile.

"You weren't supposed to hear that." She was blushing. It was adorable.

"Beth, you asked for company and help and I'm very glad to provide it. But *Trouble* is your boat and you're her skipper. I have no problem with that. And it has nothing to do with our personal relationship."

Beth's eyes widened and he had the rare experience of thinking that he'd read a woman's mind.

"I'm really confused Terry," Beth let the words tumble out, committed once she'd said that much. "I didn't have this problem with Kenny: he was hired crew. End of discussion. But you . . ." she trailed off, terrified of committing to anything more than friendship.

"What about me?" he prompted with a sly grin.

Beth sighed, staring down at her empty plate. She'd consumed a huge amount of shrimp and now she was feeling overstuffed.

"I'd like us to have something more like a partnership," she finally said. It was a woefully inadequate description of what she hoped for, but as shorthand it would suffice.

"And you don't mean a partnership in the boat, right?"

"No. She's mine – she's all I've got. I mean – you brought it up," *thank heavens I didn't have to*, " – our personal relationship."

"Good." Terry flashed her a delighted grin. He had followed Linda around like a pet because she was gorgeous and demanding. That Beth wanted a balanced relationship was a tremendous relief. It was a great place to build from.

"That's it?" Beth said, feeling a little deflated. She'd been holding it all in, driving herself and him crazy for three days with her inner turmoil, and in the end, when she declared her terms for their relationship all he could say was *good?*

"Well, to be honest, if you said you wanted a man you could lock below and take advantage of I would probably still be interested," he teased. "But I think we'll do much better as equals, except where the boat is concerned. There someone has to be in charge, and it's you."

"And you can do that?"

"Honey, I can do anything you want me to," he drawled, finishing off his beer.

TWENTY-FOUR: WATER

"Beth, where's the handle for the manual bilge pump?" Terry called from the companionway.

Beth's heart skipped a beat. "Up here," she replied, patting the port lazarette with one hand. He climbed up and opened the compartment, retrieving the long, cylindrical handle. "Why?" she asked cautiously.

He fitted the handle into a socket near her left leg and began pumping it up and down.

"Terry?"

He pumped a few more times and looked up at her. "The bilge pump has been running constantly while I've been below. I just checked and the bilge is almost full."

"We're taking on water faster than it can pump," Beth felt panic rise in her throat and swallowed it down. *You're the strong one. You don't panic.*

"Or the electric pump isn't working," he said, pumping by hand a few more times. "I don't feel anything happening with the manual pump either. I think it won't prime."

"It can't get a vacuum. That would mean a leak in a hose that both pumps use."

"You must have a portable hand pump."

She nodded. "In the deep lazarette. Did you look for a leak?"

"No."

"We should not have that much water in the bilge just because the pump is broken. You go look for a leak. I'll dig out the pump."

He moved to follow her orders without question. She checked her sails and course, then flipped on the auto pilot. She had to dive almost all the way into the deep lazarette to reach the grey plastic tube with the plunger and attached hose. Then she got the bucket out of the aft lazarette where it lived with the deck brush and cleaning supplies. By the time she carried them to the companionway Terry had removed most of the floorboards to reveal various compartments in the bilge and the companionway ladder to look at the engine.

She could see that water was reaching the rim of the main bilge compartment near the foot of the ladder, covering the hoses and valves mounted there and sloshing out onto the floor when *Trouble* heeled over.

"Jesus," she breathed, swallowing down panic. Terry looked up at her, then reached for the bucket and pump. "Did you find anything?" she asked.

He was already plunging the pump into the rising water, using long strokes to suck it up into the tube, then push it out through the hose into the bucket.

"There's a flow of water under the engine," he replied. The bucket filled, but the bilge didn't seem any lower. He stood up and dumped the bucket into the sink, which drained directly overboard.

"An aft seacock could have failed," she said, then turned back toward the deep lazarette. It was difficult to get to the fittings that provided drainage for the cockpit – two hoses attached to seacocks – valves that could be shut off, but never were, affixed to the hull of the boat. If a seacock or the attached hose broke, seawater could flow in. The natural path it would take to the lowest part of the boat was beneath the engine.

She could see the seacocks on the drains only by climbing all the way into the lazarette and practically laying on the bottom along the hull of the boat. She was neither short nor skinny, but somehow adrenalin helped her to contort herself into the space, holding her nose against the combined odor of diesel and mildew. She squinted in the dim light, cursing herself for not bringing a flashlight. Then she reached out to the nearest of the two seacocks and felt around it. Dry. She couldn't reach the far one, but she extended her hand to the midpoint of the hull further down and didn't feel any water – surely if the seacock were leaking she would feel moisture.

It was easier to get out than in, she discovered, wiggling her legs back out of the narrow space she'd wedged them into and standing, then pulling herself up onto the edge before swinging them out. She straightened her rumpled clothes and went back to the companionway.

The water in the bilge was perceptibly lower. She breathed a relieved sigh and forced herself to think. Out of habit she stood up straight and looked around. The breeze was a steady twenty knots – enough to move *Trouble* along under working jib and reefed main. The seas were a couple feet and growing. They were twenty-five hours and a hundred and sixty miles out from Miami. She didn't see any other vessels, especially not the Cuban rafts that she and Terry had joked about while toasting their departure.

And while she breathed and cleared her head, her brain kicked into gear. She bent back into the companionway.

"Terry, is the shower sump pump on?" she asked.

He was in a rhythm, stroking the twenty strokes it took to fill the bucket, then turning to dump it and begin again. He finished stroke twenty and looked up at her, puzzled.

"I don't know," he shrugged, lifting the bucket.

"Can you check? Turn it on if it isn't."

He dropped the bucket to the floor and stepped over the various open compartments to get to the panel of switches over the starboard settee. She could imagine him rolling his eyes, although she could only see the back of his head.

"Lower left," she prompted. He reached out and flipped the switch. Somewhere in the bowels of the boat a pump came on. He turned to look at her curiously.

"Its intake is in the bilge too. It's not as powerful as the main bilge pump, but it will help," she explained. He smiled, then grinned and shook his head.

"Anything else?" he asked, arms dangling at his sides as he looked up at her waiting for further orders.

"No. Keep pumping. I'll come take a look at the bilge pump – unless you did."

"Not yet. I've just been bailing."

She lowered her legs through the companionway and dropped to a patch of intact floor near his cabin doorway. Then she went into his cabin and removed an access panel to the side of the engine. The big bilge pump mounted next to the engine was covered in black dust. Frowning, she blew on it, then coughed at the dense cloud she'd raised. She reached in and felt the pump, wiping it off with her bare hands. It was warm from having been running for a long time. The wires connecting it to the battery seemed solid. Then her hands fell on a ragged edge and she traced it around a fitting. And then she realized why her mental picture of the pump didn't match what she was looking at.

Terry had emptied about half the water from the main bilge.

"There's a rubber gasket – more like a bellows – that expands and contracts as the pump moves," she said, holding up her black hands. "Or there was anyway."

"Disintegrated?" he asked, pumping away.

"Completely. The pump can't create a vacuum without it. And the manual pump won't work without a vacuum either."

"So one mystery solved. How about the aft seacocks?"

"The hull under the cockpit is dry. It's not them, or anything else that far back."

Terry set the pump aside and picked up the bucket. He looked weary as he held it over the sink until it emptied, then set it back on the floor and picked up the pump. "That's a hundred gallons, give or take," he informed her.

"Hand me that flashlight," she replied, unable to comprehend how a hundred – two hundred, since the bilge was still half full -- gallons of water could be have flowed into the bilge without their noticing.

Terry handed her the light he'd used to inspect the seacocks and through-hull fittings. She returned to his cabin, angling the light aft and under the engine. She could see the flow of water he'd mentioned – not a gushing river, but more than a trickle. Enough to fill the bilge in a few hours. She put her head near the floor and played the light around until she found what she was looking for.

"It's the stuffing box," she called out.

"That's supposed to leak a little," Terry replied, pumping away.

"Not this much," she countered. Scrambling back to her feet. "Let me spell you."

They switched places, and by the time she'd filled a bucket and heaved it up to the sink he had conducted his own inspection.

"Do you have any oakum?" he asked. She frowned at him and he grinned.

"That's what they use to stuff the stuffing box – grease soaked fibers. It lubricates the prop shaft and forms a seal – until the fibers wear out or the grease dries out. They used to pick apart old rope to make it on sailing ships.

"No, I don't have any oakum. Nor do I have old rope and grease," she replied as *Trouble* pounded over an extra high swell and the water in the bucket splashed her. Fortunately, *Trouble*'s bilges were fairly clean so the water wasn't terribly vile. "Check our course, will you?" she added, knowing she sounded testy. But she had a right to be. Her boat – her home -- was sinking.

Without a word Terry climbed out to the cockpit. Beth emptied two more buckets into the sink before he came back. She had started to wonder if he'd gone out to get away from her.

He was wearing the ship's binoculars around his neck when he came back down. He went directly to the navigation desk and looked at the chart spread there. She dumped another bucket and paused to look at him. He looked up from the chart, a devious, charming expression on his face.

"What?" she asked, wiping her forehead with the back of her hand before she realized that it was still covered in black dust – at least what hadn't washed off in the bilge water. He grinned at her.

"You've got --."

"I know," she sighed and picked up a damp dishtowel to wipe her face. He nodded, serious again, although she suspected he was still amused.

"The wind is slightly north of east. If we try to sail back to Miami it'll take twice as long as it's taken to get here," he said as if beginning to build a case for something.

"Agreed," she nodded. She had already considered that.

"We're on *Trouble*'s best point of sail. We're making seven and a half knots – eight or more with the current," he went on.

She nodded, an inkling of what he was about to propose popping into her head.

"Motoring will just make it worse. I guess we're lucky we had the engine in reverse to keep the prop from turning or it might be worse already."

She cocked one eyebrow. He was stalling. He understood the expression and looked back down at the chart, ready to get to the point.

"The nearest landfall on our current heading is the middle of the northern coast of Cuba. If we fall off a little we'll be dead on Havana."

She stared at him, sorting through a rush of possible responses. *It's illegal for us to go to Cuba* lost out very quickly to *I don't speak Spanish*, which was replaced by, *How do we know that they'll have what we need?*

"I'm listening," she finally said.

"Most Americans forget that we're the only ones who aren't supposed to go there. There are luxury hotels and marinas that cater to Europeans and Mexicans and Canadians."

"We don't have visas. And we can't use our Visa cards."

"The Cubans don't care if we're American, only the Americans care whether we contribute to the Cuban economy. And I have cash – in various currencies."

"You just want to go there to say we did."

"Yes."

"Really?" she was taken aback by his honesty. He laughed.

"No. I really think it's a good option – the only reason it wouldn't be the first, best choice is because of politics. I do business with countries all over the world, including some regimes that are a lot worse that Castro's."

"Politics aside, what are the risks?"

"We have to be sure nobody stamps our passports – but they're aware of that. We'll have to buy a Cuban flag – I assume *Trouble* doesn't have one in her courtesy flag locker." Beth shook her head and he went on. "There's a risk of being searched – both by their authorities, and by the Coast Guard if they see us coming out of Cuban waters. We have to be sure that we don't carry away anything that's identifiable as of Cuban origin."

"So we have to ditch the flag and file the serial numbers off any parts we buy?" Beth smiled. She was getting into the spirit of it. And discussing options – a plan – was calming her fear of losing most of her worldly possessions.

"No using Cuban coconut fiber in the stuffing box," he nodded seriously, then grinned. "Look, if we can find the rubber gasket for the pump at all, it'll probably be from a French manufacturer, or Asian. We just have to be sure not to buy any cigars. Or rum."

"Or we'll have to smoke and drink them before we leave."

"Or that," he nodded.

Beth bent to pump another bucket of water. "Will you plot the course and put the waypoints in the GSP?" she asked.

"I'm on it," he replied eagerly.

"Beth, get the life raft. The life raft. *Beth!*"

Beth charged through the salon past Terry where he crouched by the open bilge bailing water with a coffee mug into the bucket. She grabbed the handles on either side of the companionway and started up the ladder, but her legs wouldn't lift. She listened to him shouting at her, begging her to help, and struggled to drag her right foot up onto the first step.

"I'm trying," she cried. "I'll get it."

Icy water sloshed over her bare foot.

"Keep bailing!" she screamed down at Terry, who was crouching on the floor at her feet. He looked up at her, mug in one hand, a wad of fabric that she knew was a Cuban flag in the other. "Please Terry, please keep bailing."

"Beth!" another voice – no, Terry's voice, but real, not dreamt – broke through her panic. Strong hands grasped her shoulders and shook her, but her feet still wouldn't move.

"I can't climb up," she said. "Terry, please keep bailing."

"Beth! You're dreaming honey. Wake up."

"I can't – ," Beth's eyes popped open and took in the dimly lit cabin and Terry leaning over her. "Oh. Terry. Oh God." She gasped, the vestiges of her panic leaving her breathless. "Oh God, we were sinking."

He hitched one hip onto the edge of the bunk and wrapped his arms around her, pulling her into a tight hug.

"Shhhh. We're not sinking. Everything is under control. Remember? We emptied the bilge. We've pumped out twenty-gallons an hour since then."

She did remember. She'd set up watches using Kenny's method, with an hour of overlap followed by four hours solo for each of them. During the overlaps the person who'd just come on would bail and cook while the other watched the helm, then the helmsman would go off watch leaving the fresh one to take over. With the auto pilot working perfectly, the helmsman's real job was to monitor the breeze and the weather reports and trim the sails. They had been going for fifteen hours in this way. The reliable trade wind kept blowing and *Trouble* eating up the miles on her heading to Havana.

"I'm sorry," she muttered, embarrassed. She pushed away from Terry and he eased his hold on her. "You were bailing with a coffee mug, and I couldn't lift my feet to climb the ladder."

"A coffee mug? Well you should have known it was a dream. I'd never dirty a coffee mug with bilge water," he teased. She managed a smile at the truth in his words. He rubbed her upper arms with both hands, watching her carefully. "Are you okay now?"

She nodded.

"Because I need to get back on deck. I've got two more hours."

"I'll bail a bucket full," she said, swinging her feet to the floor as he stood up.

"Okay, but no time credit at the end of your watch," he teased as she followed him out into the main salon.

Trouble was moving through the water with ease. She could feel it now. Terry squeezed her shoulder with one hand as he passed her and climbed the ladder back out into the cockpit. She crouched beside the open bilge and fitted the hand pump down into it. All she got was a half a bucket before the pump sucked air. She dumped it out and stepped up the ladder – just to prove to herself that she could – and looked around. It was the darkest hour of the night – the moon had set and dawn was still a while off. But the sky was awash with starlight. The Milky Way was a clearly defined swath across the sky. And just like last night it took Beth's breath away. She'd seen starry nights during the Intracoastal Waterway journey, but none had been as clear and bright as this. The open sea and their distance from any land lights contributed to a magical view that helped her to understand why poets and artists were moved to write about and paint the night sky.

"It's beautiful, isn't it," Terry said from behind the wheel. His face was dimly lit by the instruments on the binnacle.

"I can't get enough of it," she replied. "Be right back."

She got a light blanket and pillow from her berth and carried them out into the cockpit. She could have changed into warmer clothes, but this felt more like she was still getting her rest.

She stretched out on the starboard bench wrapped in the blanket with the pillow under her head. She could see the stars and Terry. Nothing could be better.

"I thought I should do this alone," she said. "I told you about Ori, didn't I?"

He nodded and said, "Yes," very quietly, as if respectful of the night.

"I really admire her. But I think I'm beginning to understand that I'm not her."

His mouth curved in an inward smile, as if her words were a private joke. She studied the stars for a while and realized that there were so many she could not distinguish the familiar constellations amid the crowd.

"I always thought I was a loner. It took facing the prospect of being really alone to show me that I'm not."

"I think you like your privacy," Terry said. "And you're better at taking care of yourself than you realize."

She lifted her head to look him in the eye. He met her gaze, curious. "Does that intimidate you?"

He grinned. "No."

She dropped her head back on her pillow. "Good."

"Because I know it doesn't mean you don't want to be taken care of. Just that you can manage if nobody does."

"And you?"

"Can I take care of myself?"

"I know you can. But do you want to be cared for?"

"Bethy, we all want to be cared for, one way or another."

"That's Havana, it has to be. And I see the two domes. They're here on the chart," Beth pointed to the spot on the chart. "Have I thanked you again for this chart book?" she added. Back in Miami when she'd seen that the pile of charts he'd given her included Cuba she'd thought he was more frivolous than thorough. She hated to be proven wrong, but she could admit that it was a good thing in this case.

"Like I said, any possible landfall," he replied from behind the binoculars. "I see the two domes, and I can make out the harbor entrance. According to the cruising guide, Marina Hemingway is another ten miles west. Do you see it on the chart?"

"Yes. There's a detail inset. I guess I should try calling again."

Beth had found an entry on clearing procedures in a cruising guide she'd acquired from a book exchange up the coast. It was a few years out of date, but procedures like this didn't change very much. So she had put up *Trouble*'s yellow quarantine flag and started radioing Marina Hemingway as soon as the GPS told them they were in Cuban waters. So far they'd not received an answer.

Nor did she get one this time.

"The chart shows a customs dock," she said. I guess if we don't hear from them we should head for that. Otherwise I wouldn't know where to go – it's a huge marina."

Terry nodded, stepping down from the bench and lowering the binoculars. "It will be interesting to see how many of the boats in there are American. I'll go bail."

Beth checked their heading, the sails, and traffic, then tried calling again. This time the radio crackled with a response. In Spanish.

"Ah, *hable Ingles por favor?*" she tried, using her best street Spanish.

"Si capitan. I speak English. Please switch to channel seventy-eight."

Beth changed the VHF radio channel from the hailing channel they'd been on to the general use channel. The man's voice was already there: "Vessel calling Marina Hemingway, please respond."

Beth provided their position and explained that they would be seeking repairs. He told her to call again when they were approaching the marina and gave her landmarks to look for. She returned the radio to channel sixteen and set it on the cockpit table so she could get ready for their final approach.

TWENTY-FIVE: HAVANA

A little over an hour later they lined up *Trouble* with the entrance buoys and started the engine before dropping the sails. Terry was stretched out on the cabin floor with the flashlight pointed in under the engine illuminating the stuffing box where the propeller shaft pierced the hull.

Beth put the engine in gear and the shaft began to turn.

A moment later Terry stood up and leaned out the companionway. "It's leaking more," he shouted over the engine's roar. "But we don't have far to go. We can keep up with it."

From behind the wheel Beth nodded, then returned her attention to the markers.

A uniformed man was standing on the cement quay to take their lines. He and Terry secured them and Beth shut off the engine. He explained in halting English that the officials would be with them soon to inspect their boat and that they should not leave the boat. Beth glanced down the companionway, imagining the bilge overflowing while the officials were on board. *Maybe it would speed up the process.*

The heat was stifling, but Beth had read and been told that Caribbean customs officials were particularly formal, so instead of stripping to a swimsuit, she changed into her tidiest outfit and got her ship's papers together. Within ten minutes she was soaking with sweat again, but it least it wasn't bilge water. Terry pumped out a bucket of water while they waited.

Thirty minutes after they had arrived the first official came on board – the doctor was there to examine them and, if they passed, lift the quarantine. He had a look into their eyes and looked around the boat then accepted an ice cold can of Coke from the bottom of the refrigerator. He filled out and signed a form, then tore off a carbon copy for them.

"You may now remove your quarantine flag and fly the Cuban courtesy flag," he said. Beth glanced at Terry, but his expression was enigmatic. She thanked the doctor and stepped up onto the side deck with him, moving toward the flag halyard as he got off the boat. She took down the yellow flag and returned to the cabin where Terry was watching the bilge water level visibly increase.

"Do you think it's okay that we don't have their flag?" she asked.

"We should get one. I'm sure they can tell us where. The leak is worse."

Beth watched it for a moment and saw that he was right.

"We can't do anything but wait," she said. "And pump."

He sighed as he bent to do so.

The Customs officer was next, and while he was reviewing his list of questions with Beth a small coast guard launch came along side and discharged two people – one was an officer who inspected *Trouble*. The other was a diver who somersaulted into the water and disappeared under *Trouble*'s hull. When this visitation was over and Terry told Beth, who'd been below, about the diver she could only laugh at the irony.

"Do you think he could have repaired the stuffing box?" she asked.

Terry grinned and shook his head.

Immigration was next, a dour officer whose English was weak, held his rubber stamp over Beth's passport and looked at her questioningly.

"No, please," she shook her head. He took a slip of paper from his bag and stamped it, then tucked it in between the pages of her passport. "Thank you," she smiled. He performed the same favor with Terry's passport after studying the numerous stamps on its pages.

"Do you think there are more?" Beth wondered when he was gone, supplied with the last of the apples.

Terry was pumping again.

Another call from the dock answered her question. This time it was a marina worker come to direct them to their assigned slip. Beth explained that their boat was leaking and they were in need of urgent repairs. The worker scratched his head at her urgent demand, then came below to examine the problem for himself. Beth bristled at this, but Terry's calm gaze soothed her. *Play along. Be courteous. Be patient.*

The worker peered at the water streaming into the bilge and *tsked* a few times. Then he stood up and took a paper from a portfolio he carried. He spread it out on the navigation desk and beckoned to Terry to look at it. Terry made room for Beth at the table.

"Here. You will take your boat to the lift," he said. "The repairs can be done, but not today. Today is a holiday."

"But they can lift her out of the water today?" Beth asked. The worker looked at her sharply, then at Terry.

"You will ask," he said. Beth caught his meaning – that Terry should do the talking – and inhaled a slow breath. *It doesn't matter. I have nothing to prove.*

The worker gave them their slip assignment as well – a spot along one of the four canals, telling them that they could move there after the repairs were made, and to come to the marina office to check in then. Beth wondered if they'd get to the spot and find another boat in it, if they didn't check in now. But she held her tongue. Doubtless it would be worked out. She needed to concentrate on repairing the leak.

She hated putting the engine in gear again, but there was no choice. Terry stayed below pumping against the rising water. She held the marina map up matching landmarks on it with reality as she drove *Trouble* slowly through the busy waterways. And after several turns and a momentary panic that she had made a wrong turn she spotted a big, blue boat lift straddling an empty slip. There was a rotund man with a cigar in his mouth standing on the shore at the back of the slip. He waved her in as she slowed the engine to a crawl.

Terry poked his head out of the companionway.

"I hope we're almost there," he said.

Beth's eyes darted to him and then back at the man on shore. "Come get ready with the bow line," she said.

"It might fill up," Terry warned her.

"Can't help it – I think we'll have her out of the water in a few minutes."

Terry bounded up from below and went forward, taking in the sight of the lift as he moved.

He tossed the line to the man, who secured it to a cleat. Beth put the engine in neutral and plunged below to pump just before the water reached the rim of the bilge compartment.

Outside she heard voices – Terry's and then a deep Spanish one. She heard Terry moving around on the deck and the sound of a motor nearby. She kept pumping and dumping the water in the sink. The flow from the stuffing box was ten times what it had been, but it must have been even worse when the shaft was turning to bring in this much water so fast. She thanked heaven for Terry – not only just having him on board, but that he hadn't panicked when the water surged in.

Trouble lurched and Beth left off pumping to poke her head out the companionway. The big man was operating the lift. Two thick, wide webbing straps were positioned under the boat's full keel. Beth knew that she'd been hauled for the surveyor to inspect her when she bought her, but she hadn't been at the marina to see it. The sensation of floating as she was lifted was strange – after all, the boat floated all the time. But there was a strange, sideways swaying now as *Trouble* settled into the slings. Beth eyed them suspiciously, but they held as her boat was lifted from the water.

Saved, she thought. *We're saved.*

"No *seniora*, we don't have that," the rotund man looked at the drawing Beth had made of the bilge pump gasket. "Try Garcia, over in Mariel."

"Is that a marine parts store?" she asked. The man looked at Terry, who was standing beside Beth in the hot little office.

"Is it?" he asked.

"Nah," the man laughed. "Garcia, he makes things. Maybe he could make that."

"Out of rubber?' Beth frowned.

"Never know," the man nodded thoughtfully. Beth thought they were being lied to.

"What about our other repair?" Terry asked.

"*Mañana*," the man said.

"And for the night – we can't go back in the water – we'll be up all night pumping."

"You pay the charge, you stay in the slings tonight. We get to work tomorrow."

"What's the charge?"

"Three hundred."

"Dollars?" Beth gasped. Terry put a hand on her shoulder and stared at the man.

"Fifty Euros," he said.

The big man turned and spat into a bucket behind his desk, then looked up at Terry.

"Euros?" he said, sounding skeptical. Then he shrugged as if the type of currency didn't really matter to him. "Two hundred Euros."

"One hundred."

The man nodded, planting his hands on his desk to stand.

"You pay now."

Terry withdrew his wallet from his pocket and took out the agreed upon amount. Beth did the math in her head and kept silent – it was less than half of the original price.

The outdoor heat seemed pleasant compared to the office when she and Terry stepped out and crossed the dirt yard to where *Trouble* hung in the slings over the gravely ground. Beth climbed up the ladder the big man had provided and kicked off her dirty shoes on the side deck before climbing down into the cockpit.

At the bottom of the companionway ladder she stepped over the brimming bilge compartment, then turned to look down at it. A pump was chugging away – the shower sump struggling to overcome the tremendous volume of water. She stepped over to the panel and switched it off.

At the base of the ladder Terry gave her a quizzical look.

"We're not taking on any more water. Might as well give it a rest."

"I'll pump out a few more buckets," he said.

"Terry --."

"Don't even mention the money," he interrupted, although his tone was kind.

"No. I wasn't. I – um – can I have a hug?"

"Oh," he dropped the pump back into the bucket and stepped over the bilge opening. "Of course you can."

He enfolded her in his arms, pressing his face to the side of her head. She wrapped her arms around his waist and held on.

"I'm sorry," he murmured near her ear.

"For what?" she asked, turning her head a little so that their cheeks touched and her lips were near his ear.

"For not realizing you needed it. I'm not good at that – at reading people – women."

"You seem to do pretty well most of the time."

"I seem to be at sea with you."

"How about we forget about any rules," she said, the words out of her mouth before she could stop them. And his lips were on hers before her next heartbeat. His kisses consumed her overheated flesh, his mouth wandering over her face and caressing her throat as she let her head drop back. She heard herself moan and stroked one hand up his back, the other down. He shifted against her, the evidence of his desire a solid presence between them.

In an illegal country, her boat fatally leaking, the heat enough to drive her mad, the only rational thing she could imagine doing was making love with this man. She felt elated, completely in control, as she dragged him with both hands toward her cabin.

And then they were on her berth, arms and legs tangled, one of his hands cupping her breast through her shirt, the other tangled in her frizzed hair. She slid her hands beneath his shirt and felt the smooth flesh of his abdomen, moist with sweat. He drew in a sharp breath as her hand ranged up his chest, fingers passing over his nipple.

She smiled wickedly and did it again and he responded with an equally enflaming pinch on her own taut nipple.

"Terry," she said, her hand moving downward, inching over his belt. She had his attention. He stopped kissing her and waited. "Do you have any condoms?"

He snorted a laugh and fell back on the berth, turning his head to look at her. She raised her eyebrows in alarm, her hand still resting flat on his stomach, inches from his groin.

"I don't have anything," she said, almost apologetically. He rolled back onto his side and put his arm around her waist, stroking her. She slipped her hand under the waistband of his shorts where they bagged in back. *I'm touching Terry's ass.*

"The thing is," he said, bringing his hand up to draw a finger along her jaw. "If I say yes, you'll think I was planning on this when I joined you in Miami. But if I say no," he touched her nose, then leaned close to press a chaste kiss on her lips. She returned it, trying to extend it, but he pulled away, smiling. "If I say no, then this will end right here, won't it?"

"I wouldn't give up that easily," she said, cupping his solidness with her hand on the outside of his shorts. "There are alternatives."

"Ah, I see," he said, his smiling turning into a grin. "Well, I'd like more options."

He pulled away from her and got to his feet. "Take your shirt off while I'm gone, Captain."

Beth obliged, suddenly wanting very much to be naked. She reached around and unhooked her bra, letting it fall just as he came back and dropped a ribbon of connected condom packets onto the berth. She looked at them and giggled.

"That's optimistic," she said. He pulled off his own shirt and smirked at her.

"I was in a hurry," he replied. "This woman I'm crazy about was waiting at the other end of the ship."

Beth swallowed hard, her giggles banished as he stretched out beside her, their bare flesh touching for the first time with an electric jolt. He ran his fingers through her hair, pulling them out when they threatened to become tangled. She watched the corners of his eyes crinkle as he smiled at her.

"So tell me more about this madness," she whispered, as he lowered his face to her breast. His lips triggered a sharp wave of heat that made her wrap her legs around him and gasp.

"You have it too?" he asked, his eyes returning to hers. She swallowed, her mouth dry.

"Oh yes. I'm insane," she whispered.

"Thought so," he nodded sagely, then returned his attention to her breasts.

A while later they lay spooned together, sated and content, feeling the slight swaying of the boat as the breeze picked up.

"You didn't really think so," she said.

"Hummm?" he placed a row of kisses on her shoulder.

"You didn't really think that I'm crazy about you. I've been so – such a pain."

"Have you? I thought you were just being female," he chuckled, his chest rumbling against her. "You've been crazy about me forever."

"I haven't known you forever."

He sighed, his breath tickling her neck.

"You came here to seduce me," she said with no hint of malice.

"I came here to find out if you really were as good as you seemed."

"As good?"

"Well, back in Annapolis you were too good to be true. I couldn't stop thinking about you. Jeff practically put me on the plane, I'd become so annoying."

"Jeff?"

"Keep up love. Don't you have any idea how disappointed I was when you refused my offer that first night?"

"No. I had no idea." She was still trying to get past the little four-letter word he'd just used. *He called me "love" and he's not a 1940s British movie star.*

"Well I was. And I was even more disappointed when you did call and I couldn't help you. The truth is I had arranged the Germany trip to get my mind off of you. I mean, it was good business, but I pushed for it. And then you go and call the night before I'm leaving. Actually, I was a little angry with you – although that wasn't fair."

"Certainly not."

"Oh well. Maybe it was for the best – all those boring days on the ICW. We might have been at one another's throats. And as it is you got to spend that time with what's his name."

"Kenny."

"Right. Kenny of the ugly shorts."

Beth burst out laughing, raising up to roll over and face him. He smiled at her, repositioning his arms around her once she was resettled.

"Terry, I have been imagining this since we met – so if you want to call that forever, then I guess that's how long I've wanted you."

"But hold on. Are we talking physical attraction here, or emotional?"

"Both?"

"Just so we're clear."

"So it is both?"

"Oh God yes. I'm in love with the whole package."

Her heart skipped a beat.

"And I'm the luckiest woman in the world."

"Anything else?" he asked pointedly.

"I'm the luckiest woman in the world because I've had the good fortune to fall in love with a man who loves me back."

"Okay then," he squeezed her tighter. "That's over with. Can we make love again?"

Beth reached above their heads to a small shelf and dragged down the string of condom packets.

"I think so," she laughed.

TWENTY-SIX: MARIEL

The intense heat in the forward berth finally drove them out half naked into the main salon. Beth dug into the refrigerator for bottles of water, and when she turned back she found Terry pulling on his shorts.

"Oh," she said, the cold bottle half way to her lips. He stepped close and pressed his body up against hers suggestively.

"I'm going to see if we can plug her in – our friend out there must have power here. And we still need a Cuban flag," he explained, taking the bottle from her. He took a long gulp and handed it back.

"I suppose we do have to get the flag right away," she sighed.

"Look at it this way," he slid a finger beneath her jaw to lift it a little, "once it's raised, and we have the air conditioning on, we can hole up in here until the morning."

He dropped a kiss on her mouth, then pulled away, carrying his shirt with him up the companionway ladder. Beth gulped down some water, then turned back toward her cabin to find her clothes. Only then did she realized that he had taken charge. And as she sorted out her sweat-sodden blouse and bra she realized that she didn't mind at all. She was exhausted, and relieved that he was willing to do it. And aside from all of that, she could not quite stop thinking about the fact that he was out there going commando.

Terry returned a while later, his weight on the ladder making the boat sway in the slings. Beth climbed into the cockpit to meet him, then joined him in hauling the yellow power cords out of the lazarette. He said that the mechanic told him the closest place to get a flag was the marina office, but it was now closed. They would have to stay on the boat until the morning. But he had been able to get approval to plug

Trouble in, if the cords were long enough. Terry thought they were.

He climbed down and Beth fed him the cords as he dragged them across the ground to a portable power stand – a galvanized pole cemented into an old tire with several electric connection boxes bolted to the top and a cord as thick as Trouble's fed out the bottom, across the ground, and inside a decrepit shed. Terry found the appropriate plugs on the top of the pole, so Beth went below and switched on the AC power. Seeing the proper indicator lights come on she reached for the air conditioner switch, then stopped. A wave of frustration threatened to dissolve her good mood as she climbed back up into the cockpit and looked down to the ground for Terry. She had expected to see him waiting by the power stand for word that all was well, but he was gone. Then he appeared from behind the shed carrying a coil of what looked like garden hose.

She was about to tell him that their water supply was sufficient until they got to a slip, but instead of stepping up the ladder to give her the hose, he disappeared under the hull.

"Terry?"

"You didn't turn it on, did you?" he called back. Beth frowned.

"We can't. It's water cooled. But I guess you realized that …" her words trailed off as he stepped back out from under the hull and looked up at her.

"Toss me one of the spare lines – that old furling line you've got coiled in the lazarette would be good."

She opened the lazarette to find the line and tossed it down to him.

"Go to the other side so I can toss you the end, okay?"

"Okay…" She was still puzzled, but she had an inkling of what he was trying to do. It seemed nuts. A few minutes passed, and then he appeared on the other side of the hull and tossed her a coiled line – but it was only a fraction of the total length. "Now the other side," he said, disappearing.

She crossed back over and accepted another coil.

"Now take that one forward," he instructed. She climbed out of the cockpit and walked along the side deck to the shrouds. "Good. That's the spot. Can you take it around the shroud and back to the sheet winch? Maybe it can run through the sheet car?" he asked. Beth considered what he was asking. "We need to put a lot of pressure on both lines. Equal pressure," he added.

Beth took the coiled line forward of the shroud and then fed the end into the sheet winch on top of the jib sheet. There was plenty of room for both lines. Then she brought the line aft, removed the sheet from the winch, and wrapped the new line around it. Before tightening it she took the line that Terry had tossed up on the other side forward and rigged it the same way on that side.

"Both are rigged. Can I grind in one, then the other?"

"No, don't wait a sec."

She watched him carry the end of the hose across the ground and drop it over the seawall.

"I would have felt very silly if it wasn't long enough," he smirked as he appeared at the top of the ladder. "Now let's both tighten the lines at the same time.

They each took a winch and started pulling the line tight.

"Do you really think this will work?" Beth asked, having figured out that the line was holding the hose in the through-hull fitting that the air conditioner normally sucked seawater through.

"No idea, but I had to try something. I really want us to be comfortable tonight."

Beth could not stop herself from shooting him a loving smile across the cockpit as she gave her line another tug.

"That's all I can get without grinding it. Should we at least try it first?"

"Yeah. I'll go down and see what happens. You turn it on."

Beth went below and waited to her a muffled "Okay, go" from outside. She switched on the air conditioning master switch and then went to the main salon thermostat and turned it on. The motor came on and warm air started to come from the vents. She climbed back into the cockpit, and, unable to stand by for word, down the ladder to see what was happening.

Terry was looking at the hose jammed into the fitting. It was visibly vibrating. The real indicator of success would be a stream of water coming out the output fitting. But it was dry.

"It may not be able to suck the water that far," Beth said, "You're sure you got the right through-hull?"

Terry smirked at her, then frowned and looked at the various holes on the hull above them. Then grinned. "Yes. I'm sure. But you may be right. It's a stretch for it to draw the water this far."

"What if we cut the hose just long enough to reach the ground, and put it in a bucket right under the output fitting? Then maybe it can pull it the shorter distance and recirculate –." She cut herself short as a trickle of water started dripping from the output.

"Yes!" Terry cheered, pounding the hull above his head with his fist. "I can't believe it!"

Beth threw her arms around him as they both hopped up and down a few times, laughing and giddy with pride and surprise.

Back on board the main salon was definitely cooling down. Filled with relief and a sense that the partnership she so desperately craved was within reach, Beth rewarded Terry for his ingenuity in ways that they both enjoyed immensely.

"What are you doing?" Beth peered over Terry's shoulder into the engine compartment. She had just returned from the marina office with a small Cuban flag that looked like it had been sewn from discarded clothing but had cost almost as much as a night's slip fee. Terry had both arms extended inside the engine compartment and she could hear tools clunking. He straightened, resting both hands on his knees as he looked around at her. Her heart skipped a beat at the sight of his brilliant eyes. They were both still in what Beth thought of as a falling-in-love daze, when the very sight of one another caused a flutter of elated desire.

A loud thunk outside interrupted their gazing. The Cuban work crew had been at it for an hour now, after the mechanic had scolded them for Terry's use of the hose and demanded that they not only remove it, but unplug the boat entirely. The rising temperature had driven Beth on the solo expedition to buy the flag, leaving Terry showering in the cramped, humid head.

"Don't be surprised if we have to replace the entire pump," he said, turning back to his work.

"But if we can get a whole pump, why can't we get just the gasket?" She felt stupid the moment she finished the question and was glad that he didn't stop working to answer. "Because we may have to get a different model," she concluded with a sigh.

He grunted as something finally came loose, then set down his wrench and straightened again, this time lifting the damaged bilge pump out of the compartment.

"It's not a big deal," he said, returning his gaze to her. It had its usual effect, which was far more reassuring than his words. "I don't think this one is original either. So long as we can connect the hoses and the power, and mount it somehow, the make and model aren't important."

Not important mechanically, but from a budgeting perspective the cost of new bilge pump was very significant. Beth held her tongue, sure that her financial obsessing irritated him. He would pay for the pump if she let him know that it was a financial burden for her, and she didn't want that. She had already given up her goal of sailing alone, she hated to also concede that she couldn't finance her own lifestyle.

"I can put this in my pack if you'll carry an extra bottle of water for me," he said, rising and setting the pump on the counter.

"Sure. Thanks."

Terry had used three beers to placate the mechanic and purchase more advice about how to get to the town where the man who knew pumps was located. When he'd related the mechanic's suggestion to Beth she'd had to fight an urge to refuse instantly. *Do you trust this man?* She'd asked herself. *Would he suggest doing something that was truly dangerous?*

The way he'd watched her she was certain he could read her mind.

"It will be an adventure," he'd said, flashing her his most conspiratorial smile. That had been all it took for her to agree to hitchhike to the town where Garcia, the man who knew pumps, would be found.

They left *Trouble* still hanging in the slings with two workers still repairing the stuffing box. Walking along the dirt drive between high stands of cane Beth glanced back over her shoulder at her boat, resisting the urge to indulge in wondering if she'd ever see it again. Terry caught her arm as she tripped over a rut. Her hiking shoes, dug out of a deep compartment for the occasion, felt heavy and unfamiliar. She was glad she'd taken the advice of marina friends who'd urged her to bring them. Apparently they'd known she would have to make this kind of trip somewhere along the line, although they hadn't warned her.

Ori did, she realized, remembering her friend's letter and the story of hiking through the woods to a road. Beth glanced sidelong at Terry and felt a contented smile creep across her face. He noticed her look and grinned back, sliding his arm across her shoulders for a quick squeeze before releasing her. It was too hot to walk that way for long.

"This must be the place," Terry said a while later as they approached a group of people standing under three ragged beach umbrellas by the side of the road. They had found the paved road – a dusty two-lane highway between stands of cane and empty open land dotted with trees, shrubs, goats, and an occasional small house. They'd followed the mechanic's directions along the road for a quarter mile to the crossroads.

"It's an official pick-up spot?" Beth asked, still not sure that she believed there was a government sanctioned hitchhiking program.

"That's what he said. I've seen stranger things. Like the free bikes in Amsterdam."

"I think I'd prefer the bikes."

"Come on, this will be fun. What's the point of cruising if not to meet the locals?"

He had a point, she just hadn't anticipated meeting them in the back seats of their cars.

They joined the group of Cubans waiting for rides in the hot shade. A boy with a Styrofoam cooler offered to sell them a chilled mango, but Beth demurred, taking a gulp of water from her bottle instead. A car appeared through the heat mirages down the road, gradually resolving into a long, dusty red American sedan that came to a stop beside the umbrellas. Two men, apparently the next in line, leaned in the window to speak to the driver, then straightened and called out "Alamar."

A woman with a woven shopping bag pushed her way through to the car and leaned in the window to confirm the destination, then climbed into the back seat.

"We want Mariel, right?" Beth muttered to Terry. He nodded, watching the car drive away.

An hour passed with cars stopping every few minutes. Some were shabby little Russian models, but most were stately, old American cars the likes of which had not been seen on US roads for decades. The third one was going to Mariel, but two men who had been there when Beth and Terry arrived climbed in.

Someone purchased a mango from the boy and Beth watched him slice off the meaty sides and deftly cut a pattern of intersecting diagonals in the flesh of each piece. Then he inverted them so that the meat stood out on a dome formed by the skin. Mouth watering, Beth stepped over to him and negotiated a purchase, showing the boy a single US dollar. He accepted it without comment and sliced her fruit for her.

Most of the original crowd had gone and new people had come when a turquoise convertible Cadillac with lots of chrome and absurdly tall fins purred to a halt. Terry stepped up to it.

"Mariel?" he asked. The driver, a middle-aged man with streaks of grey in his hair and a round face that suggested strong Indian roots, looked from Terry to Beth and nodded.

"Mariel?" Terry repeated, to confirm it.

"Si," he nodded again. Terry opened the passenger side door and waved Beth in, but she shook her head and moved to the back. Something told her that her pride was not relevant here – small boys were one thing, but she should let Terry deal with the Cuban men.

"*Hable Ingles?*" Terry asked the man as he settled his pack in his lap.

"Si, a little," the driver replied, to Beth's surprise. "*Inglise?*"

Terry hesitated. They had not discussed whether to admit that they were Americans. The people at the marina knew, of course, but Beth was not sure whether it was wise to advertise the fact beyond that. She wished she had researched Cuba. Even if American's weren't supposed to come here, it was a tourist destination for the rest of the world, and there was plenty of information available on the Internet. It just hadn't occurred to her that she might end up on the biggest island closest to Florida. In retrospect she was ashamed of her shortsightedness, particularly since Terry had thought to get the charts.

"Canadian," Terry said so smoothly their driver didn't even blink. Beth smiled inwardly, relieved. It was the perfect cover unless they met a Canadian who quizzed them about their home.

Terry and the driver made awkward small talk as the big car lumbered along. The sun was stunningly hot, but the breeze helped. Beth imagined that a modern car without air conditioning would be miserable, so she resolved to enjoy the ride. Very quickly Terry and the drivers' voices became a comforting buzz beneath the roar of the wind. Every now and then a bend in the road on a hill would reveal the ocean and each time Beth caught her breath at the sheer beauty of it.

We crossed that, she thought proudly. In a sinking boat. We made it.

She didn't realize she was nodding off until Terry was opening her door for her. The car had stopped at a gas station on a stretch of road that looked a lot like the place where they had gotten in.

"Are we here?" she asked drowsily. Terry smiled indulgently as he took her pack from her and helped her out of the car. "Sorry," she said. "I didn't get much sleep last night."

His smile turned slightly sheepish and he turned toward their driver.

"*Gracias* Senior Morales," he said.

"Yes, *gracias*," Beth put in as the man waved and pulled away. "Terry, where are we?"

"Mariel," he replied, shouldering his pack. Beth took hers. "The western outskirts, actually. Senior Morales drove a little out of his way for us."

"That was nice of him."

"He was enjoying our discussion of his car's engine."

"You know about old Cadillacs?"

"My father was a Cadillac dealer."

"I think we have a lot more getting acquainted to do."

"I'm certain that we do," he replied, his meaning entirely more intimate than hers.

"Which way do we go?"

"We're here. Senior Morales said that there's a man named Garcia at this gas station who is known to be a good mechanic on small machines like our pump."

Beth liked the way he said "our pump." She wanted this expedition to be theirs, combined, and not because he provided the protection she needed in the islands.

She dragged her hand across her forehead, wiping away sweat and a strand of hair and followed him into the gas station office.

Garcia was a compact man. He was not threatening, but he looked like he could win a fight with much larger men through strength and guile. When Terry set the pump on the stained wooden counter between the mechanical cash register and a glass jar filled with something unidentifiable that was apparently edible, Garcia rubbed at his jaw with one hand and poked at the shredded remains of the rubber bellows with a ballpoint pen.

He clicked his tongue against his teeth several times, reminding Beth of her mother and, consequently making her feel absurdly guilty for not taking better care of the pump. She looked away, inhaling a breath of overheated petroleum flavored air, and let her eyes settle for a moment on a paper wall calendar hanging over Garcia's right shoulder. A nude woman peered coquettishly back at her through a shaft of dusty light coming in a side window. Beth envied the image for her nudity and shifted her day pack away from the sweaty patch on her lower back. Her guilt evaporated quickly when Terry began trying to communicate with the Cuban.

Garcia clearly understood why they were there, but after a cursory look through a greasy cardboard box that he dragged from under the counter he shook his head and looked mournfully at their pump. Beth was struck by the depth of emotion in his soft brown eyes. The broken machine seemed to truly pain him.

Through slow, deliberate gestures and pointing to the grimy label that listed the pump's capacity and power requirements Terry eventually managed to convey the concept of replacing the entire thing since no part was available.

Garcia's eyes revealed increased enthusiasm at the prospect of such a transaction and he studied the label carefully before disappearing through a door behind the counter.

Terry shot a relieved smile at Beth, then took a moment to look around. The gas station was a multi-purpose enterprise, with a shelf of used books and a rack of battered VHS tapes – some of them obviously home-recorded – a few DVDs, and a few beta format tapes. There were several shelves of groceries with long shelf lives: dusty boxes of pasta, cans with mysterious labels that did not provide clues as to their contents, jars equally mysteriously labeled, and equally hard to identify since the contents seemed to be congealed, discolored, and likely poisonous. Beth shuddered at the thought of the mother who bought the baby formula, although that might be one item that sold enough to keep fresh. She was tempted by the bags of greasy plantain chips, which made her realize that she was hungry. They'd made coffee and eaten muffins that were threatening to go moldy that morning. But that had been almost four hours ago.

"Are you hungry?" she asked Terry, her voice hushed. There were thumps and rattles coming from the back room and she didn't want to disturb Garcia in his hunt.

"Yeah," Terry said, walking over to look at a shelf of cans. He picked one up to examine the label more carefully.

"Don't even think about it," she said, certain that he must not be. He grinned at her and put the can back.

"Maybe Garcia knows of a café. Something with a good wine list and fresh seafood." His sarcasm stung, but he softened it with a smile. If he thought she wasn't completely into the native experience he was willing to forgive her.

But she didn't want forgiveness. She *was* into the experience, only she was sure that the natives avoided those dusty cans too, or they would not be dusty.

A car honked outside, the driver leaning on the horn longer than was appropriate just to summon assistance. Through the hazy front window they saw a green car of an unfamiliar make parked next to the lone gas pump. Beth realized that it must be a Russian model.

Garcia shot through the rear door and skirted the counter without a word or look in their direction. A rusty bell on the outer door clanked as he went outside and Beth sucked in the puff of fresh air that drifted in, only then realizing how oppressively hot and humid it was inside. Her skin was dripping and she could feel her body plunging toward dehydration.

She realized that the white metal box on the floor next to the counter was refrigerated as its compressor rattled to life.

"Oh!" she said, lifting the heavy lid. "Look!"

It was a freezer half full of ice cream bars, popsicles, and, looking out of place, packages of frozen fish – big, whole fish complete with fins and dull, staring eyes.

Terry came to look in with her, and after a minute they both realized they were taking advantage of the cool draft from the freezer. Beth shut it guiltily.

"I'm getting an ice cream sandwich," she said. "When he comes back."

"I love creamsicles – did you see any in there?"

"You mean those orange popsicles with vanilla ice cream inside?"

"Yeah. I love them."

"Really." Beth had to contemplate this. She had always hated them because they lacked any sign of chocolate, and in fact combined citrus with cream, which struck her as gastronomically unwise. Maybe it was time to reconsider. And that was Beth's biggest relationship problem: she had to resist redefining herself based on her partner. She knew it and had vowed not to do it again, and yet here she was reconsidering a lifelong dislike just because Terry liked creamsicles.

Garcia returned with a fist full of bills and entered a transaction into the cash register. He tore off the paper receipt and took it and some change back outside. As he slipped out he nodded toward Terry as if to acknowledge that they were still waiting.

He returned a few minutes later, passing through to the back without a word. There were some more thumps and clunks and an ominous cascading clatter of metal objects falling from somewhere. This was accompanied by expletives in Spanish. And then Garcia emerged carrying a filthy object that Beth had to assume was a pump.

He dragged an equally filthy rag from his back pocket and scrubbed at the pump, revealing a label. Then he poked the rag into the ends of the intake and output pipes. He lifted it and matched these to the pipes on their pump, confirming that they were the same diameter, then he pointed to the label and looked at Terry expectantly.

Terry leaned down and studied it. The lettering was nearly worn off where it wasn't coated with grease. But he smiled and nodded.

"It's slightly higher capacity, and the power is the same so we should be able to splice the connection right into the existing supply," he picked up a short length of two-lead wire with split, frayed ends. Garcia nodded. "And the pipes are the same, so we won't need any adapters."

Beth couldn't quite believe his enthusiasm. She understood how fortunate they were, but she couldn't get excited about installing the grimy thing aboard *Trouble*.

"*Com bien?*" she asked timidly. Garcia stared at her for a moment as if surprised that she could speak.

He rubbed at his chin again, looking down at the pump as if it were terribly valuable to him, a family heirloom perhaps. Then he named his price. Beth did a mental calculation and came up with close to three hundred dollars. She clamped her mouth shut, waiting for Terry to negotiate. He lifted the pump to look at the bottom, which had four holes to mount it with screws. He compared it to the old pump, noting that the holes did not match at all – they would have to improvise a mounting for it. He shook his head wistfully.

"One hundred fifty – dollars," he said in Spanish.

Garcia looked pained. "No, no senior," he said, his tone full of regret. "Two hundred fifty."

"One hundred sixty."

"Two hundred forty."

"Two hundred," Terry said, moving his hand horizontally over the pump – his final offer. Garcia squinted at him for a moment, then apparently realized that if they kept going that's where they would agree anyway. He nodded.

Terry saw Beth reaching into her trouser pocket and put his hand on her wrist, then took out his own wallet and counted out two hundred dollars in crisp twenties, a few tens, and two fives. Garcia watched in fascination as the green bills piled up. Beth wondered if he'd ever had that much American cash before. Apparently he saw no difficulty in spending it, though, for he scooped it up as soon as Terry put his wallet away. Then he found a large brown paper sack under the counter and shoved the pump into it, more to protect them from the dirt than for easy carrying. Terry crammed it into his pack, easing the zipper over the lumpy parcel.

"Can you take the old one?" he asked Beth. It just fit into her day pack. The transaction complete Beth pulled out her wallet and went to the freezer. She took out an ice cream sandwich and, after a brief hunt, found a creamsicle for Terry. Garcia accepted two more dollars for them and gave her a friendly smile in return.

They stood outside in the shade of the gas station awning for a few minutes, packs at their feet, eating their ice cream before it melted. Beth had a special way of eating ice cream sandwiches: she would lick the ice cream out from between the chocolate wafers all around the edges, then compress the edges of the wafers all around, turning the sandwich into a sort of an ice cream ravioli. Terry watched this procedure curiously while alternately licking and biting his orange and white treat. Beth caught him and shrugged to dispel sudden embarrassment.

"You always do that, don't you?" he asked.

"I guess so. It's like the reverse of eating an Oreo, I guess."

"How's that?"

"Well with Oreos you take two apart, eat one cookie from each, and put the two halves with all the filling together into a new, fat cookie."

"No, you do that. I just take one apart and scrape off the filling with my teeth."

"And with those double-stuff Oreos you get a really tall cookie," she added, ignoring his counter proposal.

He chuckled. "And that's even better?"

"Of course it is."

Terry peered up and down the road, smile lingering on his lips after he finished his creamsicle. He watched a woman step into the street through a gate in a low stone wall that surrounded a small house. She wore a floral print dress and carried a large, empty bag woven of red, white, and green fiber.

"That woman is going to the market," he said, glancing at Beth just in time to see her taking a sideways bite of her ice cream.

"Why don't we ask Garcia where to pick up a ride?" she asked, thinking only of *Trouble* and her hope that the boat would be back in the water where it could be plugged in and the air conditioner on.

"Because I don't know the Spanish word for 'hitchhike.' Come on, we came this far, don't you want to see what Mariel looks like?"

Beth had to admit that she was curious. This might be her only visit to Cuba. That thought spurred her to want to see all she could, and she was grateful to Terry for pushing her.

"Let's go," she said simply, depositing the wrapper from her ice cream in a brimming five-gallon bucket next to the gas pump.

TWENTY-SEVEN: ACCEPTANCE

Beth only realized as the buildings on either side of the road gave way to open spaces that they had found and nearly passed through the town of Mariel. The weathered cinderblock and wooden buildings were interspersed with trees and cars parked in unpaved lots.

Four boys whooped and shouted at one another as they dribbled a basketball and shot baskets on a one-sided, asphalt court next to a two-washer laundry. Two men sat across from one another over a small table stacked with dominos. Beyond them was a wooden structure that reminded Beth of a ball park concession stand, complete with a bright, seemingly random, paint job. It looked as if the boys had taken a break from their game to hurl coffee cans full of bright paint at the structure. Beth smiled, imagining their laughter at the colorful mess.

A third man stood inside behind the counter, a row of bottles with the labels peeled off on a shelf behind him. Further along between two buildings they found the market: half a dozen stands arrayed around a vacant lot. Most were farmers selling produce from the backs of their trucks, but there was one fisherman displaying his catch and one notions vendor standing over an array of tools, supplies, and toys spread on a colorful sheet on the ground.

"Looks like a New York street fair, without the mix CDs and tube socks," Beth whispered to Terry, forgetting that it was unlikely anyone here spoke English. He shot her a scolding look anyway and applied himself to examining a display of mangos. Beth's mouth watered. She was about to succumb to the bunches of baby bananas, hoping that the farmer would accept dollars – it had worked so far – when Terry put his hand on her shoulder and pointed across the market.

"What?" she asked, not seeing anything noteworthy in the vendors and other shoppers.

"A café. Let's go look at the menu."

Beth didn't believe him until he guided her between two fruit laden trucks to a pair of tables with umbrellas in front of a cinderblock building. Although the word "café" was painted on a board mounted over the door, it was the delicious smells wafting out from inside that convinced her.

There was a menu – handwritten on a chalk board leaning against the wall near the door. They stood in the shade of one of the umbrellas to read it. Or try.

"I have no idea what any of this is," Beth whispered.

"Neither do I. Let's be brave."

Before she could agree or decline a woman in knit trousers and a gingham blouse that gapped ominously across her full bosom, came through the door and gestured them toward the nearest table.

Terry mixed his dazzling smile with a flash of his wallet, pointedly showing her the American dollars. She frowned and he shrugged innocently. She studied him for a moment as if wondering if Cuban pesos would appear on his face, then nodded and took out her note pad and a stub of a pencil.

Terry ordered several dishes, indicating that they would share, and two bottles of beer that the waitress went and got from a cooler next to the door.

"Do you have any idea what you ordered?" Beth asked, drawing a line through the water condensed on her bottle.

"Not a clue," he replied. "I took one from column A and two from column B."

"That's Chinese, not Cuban."

"Don't you have those Cuban Chinese places in New York?"

Beth was caught off guard – he was right, although she'd never eaten at one.

"So we could be eating dog, or mule."

"I don't think they cook the mules here."

Beth noted his omission of dogs.

"Anyway, I think that's goat," he pointed at one of the items on the menu, "And that's conch," he pointed at another, pronouncing conch with a hard final "c."

"Conch," Beth said, sounding the "ch."

"They say conch."

"So it's conch shell, like you hit someone on the head with it?"

He took a gulp of his beer and grinned, and she couldn't help thinking of a big, satisfied dog.

The meal was moderately successful in that the beer was cold and one of the dishes Terry had ordered turned out to be a favorite: spicy conch fritters with even spicier sauce on the side. The next was a fish, whole and staring, with a lemony sauce that Beth tried to like but simply couldn't, although the fish – a snapper – was delicious. The third was a stew, heavy on the carrots and black beans, with lumps of meat that they decided had been the most ornery old goat in town.

While they were eating a teenage boy carrying a worn camouflage day pack on his shoulder and several fish on a line in his right hand came threading through the market and entered the café. He gave them a curious look and a shy "hola" as he passed by. A few minutes later he came back out wearing a white towel tied around his waist for an apron.

"Ingles?" he asked as he collected empty plates.

"Canadian," Terry replied, eyes darting to Beth, who nodded confirmation.

"I learn English," the boy said tentatively.

"In school?" Beth asked.

"Si – Yes. In school. Mi madre makes me."

Terry and Beth shared a chuckle with him at the whimsy of mothers.

"Can you tell us where to get a ride?" Beth asked, focusing on simple sentence construction and vocabulary.

"A car ride?" he asked.

"Si – yes. To the marina near Havana."

"You sail?"

"Si. We came here for a part for our boat."

"Apart?"

"Repairs," Terry tried. "From Garcia," he gestured in the general direction of the gas station. The boy's face lit up.

"Oh, si. Garcia make good repairs."

"We need a ride back to the marina."

The boy directed them to an intersection of the road they were on and the larger highway that they'd taken to get to Mariel, insisting in his limited English that there was a pick-up point there. Beth guessed that it was about a mile away.

Terry bought bottles of water from the café when he paid for their lumch – a staggering four dollars – and they set out along the road.

Beth felt like an old hand now as they found the pick-up point and waited in the shade of a single umbrella along with two men. The third car along was heading for Havana. It dropped them at the same point from which they'd departed that morning, and soon they were trudging along the dirt road into the marina, their packs with the two pumps hanging heavily on their shoulders.

"Look!" fatigue from the journey was instantly eradicated by adrenaline at the sight of *Trouble* floating in the water next to the work dock. The repair man appeared on an intercepting course as they hurried toward her, and for a moment Beth feared that he was going to prevent them from boarding.

But he was most interested in describing to Terry in great detail the work that his men had done. The proprietary way that held the shrouds as they climbed aboard did not ease Beth's concern. It implied that he had some claim on the boat until he was paid.

"Gracias, Senior," she said once she'd put her pack down in the cockpit and straightened her sore shoulders. Terry took her pack and his own down the companionway. The mechanic watched him go, looked at Beth speculatively, and then looked back at the companionway, clearly planning to wait for Terry to return. Beth stood in the cockpit, momentarily embarrassed, and then annoyed with herself for reacting that way. She resisted the urge to confront the mechanic, and instead stepped aft to check the stern line. But that put her in another awkward position: the spring line was cleated right next to the mechanic, but she didn't want to get near him to check it. She straightened and ran her hand through her sweaty hair, then gathered it into a pony tail with both hands.

"Ugh," she muttered, for show, and headed for the companionway to look for a hair clip.

She nearly tripped over Terry's legs – he was stretched out on the floor with his head inside his cabin and the access hatch to the engine open.

"Are you installing it right now?" she asked, too surprised to phrase her question better.

Terry twisted his head out of the compartment to look at her.

"Just checking the mount to see if we need something from our friend out there. And checking for leaks."

"Oh."

Beth made her way forward to her cabin and found an elastic for her hair, then returned to the main cabin and lifted the floor board over the bilge, nudging Terry's leg out of the way in the process.

"How does it look?" His voice was muffled.

She peered down into the compartment that had been full of water last night.

"Dry as a bone," she replied, hearing relief in her own voice. Terry twisted his head out of the engine compartment and sat up.

"He's waiting out there. How does the mount look?" she asked.

Terry got up and rubbed his hands together. "Do you want me to speak to him?"

"He doesn't seem to want to speak to me."

"That's not my fault."

"It isn't mine either!" The long hot day was getting to her. She instantly regretted snapping at him. "I'm sorry. That's not how I meant it. He just stood there ignoring me, waiting for you. So I came below."

"Bethy," Terry put both his hands on her shoulders, then slid them up to cup her head on either side of her neck. She resisted a cringe at his feeling how sweaty she was. "Don't let that bother you. It's as ingrained in a man like him as – as your independence is in you. I'll go tell him we're satisfied."

"He probably wants more money."

"I'll work it out. Don't you worry your pretty little head," his sheepish smile and the little shake he gave to her head before removing his hands forestalled any negative reaction to what was obviously a joke. He leaned in to kiss her on the forehead, then turned to climb up the companionway ladder. Beth stood watching his legs disappear, waging a mental battle to accept what she could not change. She had nothing to prove, and that would be all she was doing if she engaged in battle with the mechanic.

Instead she turned to the navigation desk to find the marina map that they'd been given when they checked in, the one that showed them the location of the slip they were renting. Terry came back down, but before she could ask him how it went he picked up his day pack that contained the new pump and went back up the ladder. She set the marina map on the desk and stepped over to the refrigerator. A cold drink was sure to soothe her frazzled mood. She stood sipping cold water from a bottle for all of thirty seconds, then gave in and climbed up the ladder to stand on the stop step.

Terry was on the dock crouched next to the mechanic. He was holding the pump upside down and the mechanic was tracing its bottom onto a piece of paper that looked like it had recently been a crumpled food wrapper. Finally they both rose, Terry lifting the pump, and nodded agreement about something. Then the mechanic strode away and Terry stepped back aboard.

Seeing her, he set the pump on the lazarette and reached for her bottle of water, which she surrendered.

"What's up?" she asked after he'd taken a long gulp.

"He's going to cut a piece of wood to size and drill pilot holes for the mounting screws. We'll have to attach the board somehow – maybe screw it to the old mount, or – we still have some of that two-part epoxy, don't we?"

Beth nodded. "I'm pretty sure there are a few more doses." She was referring to the one-ounce tubes of the stuff that he'd bought a quantity of rather than the larger quart or gallon cans. She'd understood his logic immediately – the larger containers were harder to store and their content was likely to age or dry out. Still she'd balked at the higher overall cost of the little "doses" until he'd pointed out that a cheaper quart can was useless – and a lot more expensive – if it dried out after you'd only used half a cup.

"So maybe we can epoxy it. Anyway, he said to come back tomorrow for it. We can go find our slip for tonight."

Beth's anxiety went into overdrive as they glided slowly up the fairway toward their slip. She had noticed the orientation of all the boats on their way in to the marina. But she only now faced the reality: she had to back *Trouble* into the slip – something she had never done before. Each narrow slip was bordered on one side by a pair of tall pilings and on the other by a short finger pier. If they went in bow first, the finger pier was not long enough to reach the widest part of the boat. Backing in would put *Trouble*'s fat waist right at the end of the finger, allowing them to step on and off without making a dangerous leap.

As she alternated her attention between the waterway and the marina map, she tried to remember the techniques for backing in that she'd only read about. They quickly formed a muddle of concepts and terms in her brain. Prop walk was important – but which way did *Trouble's* go? She tried to imagine the configuration of propeller and rudder, as if she knew enough to be able to tell from visualizing them, which she didn't. Then she tried to remember backing out of the slip back in New York. She'd always turned the wheel to the left and *Trouble* had obligingly angled her stern that way – but was it because she turned the wheel, or because the prop walked to port in reverse? She thought port was the most likely – something about most sailboats doing that – but the source of the information skittered away from her when she tried to pin it down.

"You okay?" Terry asked. She was grateful for the distraction from her addled internal monologue, and for a brief moment she considered asking him if he would dock the boat.

"Yeah. I little tense, that's all. You'll be able to get a line on a piling?"

His smile bolstered her confidence. Then he spoke: "First time backing in?"

She gulped and nodded.

"Piece of cake. Go past until the second piling is on your port quarter – go very slowly – then reverse and hard over. You can even move around to the other side of the wheel and drive backwards. I'll get a line on the port piling. Once we're part way in we can shove her to starboard to get a line on that side, if I can't lasso it. We're lucky it's pretty calm."

She knew he meant the wind, but she wanted to loudly contradict this statement – she was far from calm. There was still her first concern to deal with: was their assigned slip still empty?

Beth's mistrust of the marina's management turned out to be misplaced, for they found their assigned slip empty and a dock hand waiting to help them with their stern lines. Bolstered once again by this good sign, Beth followed Terry's earlier instruction, creeping forward and judging the moment to reverse to port very well. *Trouble's* bow obligingly swung to starboard as she tucked her stern into the slip. Beth quickly eased up on the reverse throttle and spun the wheel back to center so as not to overturn.

"Port line's on – slow , 'er down," Terry shouted as he lunged from the port side to the starboard amidships and grabbed the bow line that was coiled there. Beth slammed the transmission into forward and gunned it for a moment, arresting *Trouble's* backward glide. Terry tossed a loop of bowline over the starboard piling making it look easy. Beth put the engine back into idle reverse and turned to see the dock hand gesturing that she should continue backing in. He wore a welcoming smile that she returned. In a moment Terry was beside her grabbing a stern line that was waiting and tossing it to the dock hand. Then he squeezed behind her to the other side and repeated the toss with the second stern line. The dock hand cleated them and Terry disappeared again while Beth allowed herself a deep breath before shutting off the engine.

"Gracias Senor," she said to the dock hand, only then wondering how he'd known to meet them.

"No problem, captain," he replied in accented English. "Juan say you coming – next time you call, okay?"

"Oh! Okay. Sorry." They had told her to call when she was ready to come to the slip. Fortunately, the mechanic had guessed that they'd forget.

"We should have called?" Terry asked, reappearing beside her. "I thought of it about thirty-seconds before we got here."

"All's well," Beth shrugged, easily releasing the pent up tension now that they were secure. Terry was already fishing in a lazarette for the heavy yellow power cords. As he heaved them out she took them and passed the ends to the dock hand. While they connected them she went below and a moment later, at a shout from Terry, she turned on the shore power circuit. The indicator light turned a happy shade of green and, after she flipped a couple more switches, the air conditioning fan whirred to life.

"We're good," she called out, stepping in front of the nearest vent.

TWENTY-EIGHT: SMOKEY

"I'm exhausted," Beth admitted. "Maybe it's obvious."

They'd been secure in the slip for an hour, and all she'd managed to do was open a beer and drag herself and an open bag of stale tortilla chips into the cockpit. She sat with her back against the cabin and her legs stretched out on the rough, hard bench surface, too tired even to go get some cushions. Terry was similarly positioned on the other side of the cockpit.

"It's been a rough couple days. Don't apologize."

"I feel like I should make a to-do list. That's what I do when I don't want to actually do anything."

"I see. Good to know." Terry took a final gulp of his beer and swung his feet to the floor. She eyed him suspiciously, wondering whether she had to move too.

"Item one: find a restaurant on the water. Item two: shower. Item three: go out to dinner at restaurant from item one."

"And you're taking on item one?" she asked hopefully.

"That I am."

He stood up, bent down and placed a kiss on her forehead, and then stepped up and over her to the gunwale and then to the dock.

"I'm certain there are a couple restaurants in or near the marina. We won't have to travel far."

"Thank you," Beth called after him as he strode up the dock.

She drank the dregs of her beer and sighed, admitting that she had to repay his kindness with action of her own.

Ten minutes later she was in a clean, spacious shower in the bathhouse on the dock, standing in a tiled corner with her hands extended into the chilly stream coming from the shower head.

Reluctantly, she uncapped her shampoo and gingerly bent her head in under the water.

The cool flow actually felt good as it saturated her tangled hair and rinsed her sweaty scalp. She poured some shampoo into her hand and worked it through her hair, still shying away from plunging her entire body under the water. When she plunged her head back in it actually felt warmer. Sticking her arm in, and then a leg, she decided it really was warming up.

"I guess patience pays off when the water heater is two docks away. Or something like that," she muttered, enthusiastically lathering her hair again.

"Up for Cuban again?" Terry asked when she returned to *Trouble*. "There's a Spanish place, too, but the Cuban looks nicer."

"I'm game – I'll bet this restaurant has some English on the menu." Beth tossed her shower bag onto her bunk and stepped toward him where he stood by the galley sink.

"Not necessarily a good thing, but easier," he nodded, opening his arms so that she could step into them as if he'd read her mind.

"Ummm, you showered too. Busy man."

"How long did it take you to get hot water?"

"I don't know, maybe five minutes."

He chuckled, nodding, his face lowering to hers.

"Worth the wait," he murmured as their lips touched.

Their Cuban dinner was the antithesis of lunch. They were served in an air conditioned dining room with white cloths on the tables and linen napkins, heavy china plates and an unnecessarily large variety of flatware at each place setting.

Ordering from a menu that did indeed have English translations of the dishes allowed them to select favorites and try new things without having to guess. Unfortunately, the food itself was unexceptional. Terry asserted it was because it catered to the tourists, while their lunch had been strictly local. Beth didn't argue.

Despite the slightly tough chicken and slightly bland sauce on the shrimp their meal was desperately romantic. The fear and stress of the last couple days had clouded the memory of their brief, heated interlude in her cabin. This slow, candle-lit dinner cleared the haze and brought the newness of their relationship back into sharp focus.

Beth decided as they strolled away from the restaurant hand in hand that she was perfectly, ecstatically, joyfully happy for the first time in as long as she could remember.

Back on board they just sort of drifted into bed together, undressing one another in the dim light of the main salon and slipping effortlessly into the v-berth.

"Wow, what have you got there?"

Terry greeted Beth and her three canvas bags of provisions as she approached along the dock. He was sitting in the cockpit with the pump on the table in front of him.

The division of labor had been hers: she'd gone to explore a local market while he retrieved the new pump base from the mechanic. *It's just an errand*, she'd assured herself. *Hardly a learning experience.* And the market with its rows of tables heaped with produce, displays of livestock and butchered animals, and crafted products like honey and bread, had been fascinating. She'd gone overboard on fresh vegetables, herbs, and even had a quarter stalk of sugarcane sticking out of one or her bags. Terry eyed it skeptically as he took them from her.

She shrugged, blithely discarding any accusation of frivolity he might be trying to make. They were in Cuba! She may never visit here again. She wanted Cuban sugar cane.

When he came back up the companionway ladder she produced the item that she knew would appease him, if he needed appeasing: four plump, fragrant cigars.

"Rolled on the thighs of nubile Cuban virgins – isn't that what they say?" she said as she handed the paper wrapped package to him.

"Hah. Something like that. It's probably from a movie. Doesn't sound like Hemingway. Wow," he held the paper to his nose. "Did you smell these?"

"Yes. And I'll admit they smell nice. I may even try a few puffs."

"You may have to if we're going to get through them before we leave Cuban waters."

"You think we have to?"

"I think it would be prudent, and I'm not throwing them overboard!"

"Okay, hand me the wrench again," Beth said, reaching behind her back and wiggling her fingers. The heavy tool was placed in them and she twisted back to her task.

"As tight as you can get it," Terry instructed, crouching behind her and looking along her back at where she was working on the pump.

She fitted the socket over the bolt and tightened, putting all her strength into the final turn.

"Next one."

Terry dropped another bolt into her palm.

She pushed it into the hole, fit the wrench over it, and started tightening.

They had checked the alignment of the bolts out in the cockpit, and gone over the hose and wiring attachments carefully. When Beth had taken it from him and come down to do the hard work he hadn't said a word. It was hardly the first time she'd done mechanical repairs on her boat, after all.

"Okay, give it a try," she said a few minutes later, compulsively setting her hand on the motor cowling.

Behind her Terry stood up and leaned over the navigation table to flip the switch.

The motor purred beneath her hand. "Woo hoo!"

Then a sucking sound came from the bilge compartment: there was not enough water in the bilge for the pump to draw it out. Terry switched off the pump as Beth wriggled out of the narrow access hole dragging her tools with her.

She rolled onto her butt and sat for a moment, looking up at Terry.

"That's it then. We're seaworthy."

He nodded, bending to take the wrench from her and replace it in its box.

"Can you think of a reason why we should stay longer?"

"No. I wish I could. I wish I could take this opportunity to explore Cuba. It may never come again."

"But?"

"But Jeff expects me back."

"How soon?" she frowned. They hadn't really discussed his schedule – he had never set a deadline on their arrival on St. Thomas. His sheepish grin said a lot, some of it unclear to her.

"We weren't specific. He's a sailor too. But to really explore Cuba the way I'd like to would take more time than I can reasonably spend – I'd like to spend a month here. If we did that, I'd have to leave you here when we're done, and find a way to get back without getting arrested."

"Leave me here?" She had to force alarm into her voice, since she knew he would never do such a thing. And then as she watched him chuckle she thought about how just a few weeks ago she would have slapped herself for being so dependent. She could see from the way his expression changed from humor to concern that she had not hidden her thoughts.

"It's a tough country for a woman alone," he tried. She shook her head and he stopped talking. She climbed to her feet, then sat on the navigation station seat.

"I know. And if I'm honest with myself, I wouldn't want to be here alone. Dammit! What happened? I was going solo cruising! Now I don't want to anymore." She was shaking her head, staring across the salon at the galley cabinets. He stood still, just inside her peripheral vision. She was afraid to look at him, embarrassed by her outburst and her flip-flopping.

"Well Beth, I like to think it has something to do with me." His voice was a sensual purr that snapped her gaze to his twinkling eyes. Suddenly the sense of joy she'd felt last evening rushed back. She nodded, mouth curling into a silly grin.

"I suppose it does."

Checking out of the marina, and the country, proved less difficult than checking in, although more unexpected fees were collected. Stowing the tools, topping off the water tanks, and using the dinghy to ferry two five gallon jugs to the fuel dock for refill took an hour. While Beth took care of the paperwork and fees with the marina office Terry made a final check of the boat. Then they moved *Trouble* to the customs dock to inform the officials of their plan to depart.

Early in the afternoon they bid farewell to a bottle of beer and the final Immigration officer. Terry handled the dock lines while Beth drove them off the dock.

"We'll go straight north for ten, fifteen miles, get away from Cuba as fast as we can. We'll be able to keep up this reach in this wind. When we tack, we need to go as much to the east as we can, but with this easterly we'll have to go northeast," Beth said, tracing a northward line on the chart then angling to the northeast toward Andros Island in the

Bahamas. *Trouble* was reaching merrily through long four and five foot swells, the sails full and the degree of heel just comfortably off center.

"Time to start watches?" Terry asked from his seat on the high side of the cockpit.

"I guess so. Seven on five off with an hour of overlap? That seems to allow enough sleep."

"Who goes first?"

"It's four o'clock now. I'll come on at six. You join me at midnight. I'll make us dinner while you finish out this watch."

When they finished dinner Beth deemed their position far enough from Havana to change course. They hauled in the sails and adjusted course until *Trouble* was heeling nearly twenty degrees. Her bow thumped into the swells, sending splashes over either side of the bow that rushed aft to rinse the combing before draining overboard.

"Going to be a wild ride," Terry observed once everything was secure.

"I hope you can get some sleep."

"Don't worry about me. Shout if you need me."

He left her with a good night kiss and she settled into the aft corner of the cockpit with a lidded mug of instant coffee.

For the next four days they pushed *Trouble* into the trade wind and swells, tacking back and forth from east-northeast to southeast time after time. Because the breeze was coming from just south of east, the northerly tacks were twice as long as the south-headed ones, carrying them toward and along the shallow Bahama banks for hours until they had to tack or risk entering waters too shallow for *Trouble*'s keel. Each southern tack carried them back toward the north shore of Cuba, and each time they tacked just shy of the three mile line marked on the chart. There was no sign of U.S. patrols, nor any indication that their illegal visit had been observed.

The responsibility of watches and limited sleep was taking its toll on both of them by the third afternoon. When Beth caught herself almost snapping at Terry for no good reason she knew that they had to find a place to make a stop.

On the afternoon of the fourth day the eastern tip of Cuba was just visible through the lenses of the boat's binoculars. And to the northeast lay Great Iguana Island, the southern most island in the Bahamas.

"Man of War Bay," Beth said, holding up the chart. "Nothing there but some salt flats, but its shallow enough to drop the hook for a while."

"Tuck right in near shore," Terry said, studying the chart. "Should be calm. Uncrowded. Warm water…" he trailed off, smiling mischievously.

"Yeah, we need a break. I'll plot it. We can get there in the morning, spend a night and get going again the next day. It doesn't have to be a long delay."

"Are you saying that because of Jeff?"

"Yeah, I guess so."

"Forget about him. We'll stay as long as we need to."

"Well, I think we may want to stop on Dominica too, and that might be nicer. This is just a rest stop. Like a bathroom break on a road trip."

"Right," he snorted.

With its expanse of salt pans abutting a long stretch of the shore, Man of War Bay was far from the prettiest tropical bay in the islands, but to Beth and Terry it was paradise. They brought *Trouble* past Devil's point on the southern end and puttered along under power for an hour enjoying the sight of hills covered in shrubs and grass beyond the narrow beach. The sea was calm tucked in there behind the point, and they decided that stretch of bay was just fine for their purposes. Terry removed the lines that secured the anchor to the bowsprit and Beth steered them closer and closer to shore, one eye on the depth gauge.

Soon enough the anchor had dug into the sandy bottom. and the engine was off. Beth stood still behind the helm listening to the faint lap of ripples on the beach and birdsong in the bushes on shore as Terry walked aft along the side deck looking at her curiously.

"It's so peaceful. And level."

He nodded, and holding on to a shroud with one hand pulled each of his deck shoes off one at a time with the toe of the other foot. He left them there on deck and dove overboard in his shorts with a "whoop" that echoed across the water, shattering the stillness she had observed.

Grinning, Beth, turned and unfastened the line holding the swim ladder to the transom. She pushed it into the water, then went below to get him a towel.

Of course she was in the azure water with him a few minutes later, unable to resist his beckoning calls as he splashed around the boat.

"We've entered the nation of the Bahamas illegally," Beth observed a while later, holding up her plastic cup of white wine by the stem to look at the sun through it. Terry fitted the lid back on the barbeque and set his fork on the cutting board next to him on the seat. The aroma of grilling steaks was making her mouth water.

He looked out at the sun that was approaching the western horizon.

"Is there an entry port on this island?"

"Not that I noticed."

Terry picked up his wine and shrugged. "Then we'll say we're on our way to the nearest one, if anyone asks. It shouldn't be a big deal."

Beth sighed, scooting her behind down the long lazarette bench to lie down, cup resting on her stomach. The swim followed by the wine had softened her perspective. She felt completely relaxed, for the first time in more than a week – sometime between their departure from Miami and the leak. "I hope not. Can they insist? Say we can't stay here until we've gone somewhere and checked in?"

"I guess so. But I really doubt they'd be that demanding. If we sat here for a week maybe, or if there's an immigration office here in this bay. But if there were we'd be silly not to just go do the paperwork."

"And pay the fees."

He smiled. It always came to money with Beth. But she was right. He'd hate to pay entry and departure fees for such a short stay.

The bay appeared to be deserted, but that turned out not to be the case: when the sun's lower edge was an inch from the horizon the high pitched buzz of an outboard motor carried to them on the light breeze. They had finished their steaks and the bottle of wine and Terry had rigged the ship's hammock up on the bow. Beth had finished rinsing the food off the dishes with seawater and was stacking them into the bucket to take below when the sound reached her.

It was difficult to pinpoint the direction at first, and it was not the boat itself, but its frothy wake that pointed to it as it ran along the shoreline coming from the west as they had earlier in the day. It's current heading would take it between them and the beach.

"It's a local," Terry called out from his position on the bow.

Beth hefted the bucket and carried below to get it out of the way of whatever might happen. She had read and heard many stories of yachtsmen dealing with the locals in the islands. Most interactions were positive for all parties. Most.

She set the bucket on the galley floor and went to her cabin for her wallet, then reconsidered. Instead she pulled on a pair of shorts over her swimsuit and stuck twenty dollars in small bills into the pocket before returning to the cockpit.

The boat's origins was obvious now that it was closer: its low hull and deck was covered with splashes of bright color. The driver was a black man in his forties, or possibly his thirties, with braided hair wearing a grey t-shirt and black shorts – remarkably subdued compared to his vessel. Behind him there was a passenger seated on the floor of the boat, but Beth could not figure out its age or gender.

She was unsurprised when the boat altered course toward *Trouble*. She would have been disappointed if it had not. This was to be her first encounter with a "boat boy."

"Hello! Hello!" the man called out as he idled his craft ten feet off their port side. "Welcome to Great Iguana Island!"

Beth heard a thump on the bow as Terry rolled out of the hammock. It was not easy to get out of it gracefully. She knelt on the lazarette closest to the boat and leaned on the combing.

"Hi. Thank you."

"Have you come a long way? Dis is a good boat you got here. Solid."

"From Florida. Thank you, she is." Beth replied. They had discussed the answer to that question and agreed to simply forget their unplanned stop.

"Goin' up de islands?"

"No, going down the islands," Beth replied, struggling not to imitate his lilting accent.

"Why you want to leave us? Don you know de Bahamas is paradise?" his toothy grin was infectious. Beth returned it.

"We've got an appointment in the Virgin Islands," Terry replied from the side deck where he'd sat down on the cabin top, elbows on knees.

"Ah, maybe you come back here later den. I am Smokey, dis is my mama," the man gestured open palmed toward the figure in his boat, who Beth could now see was indeed an elderly woman sitting cross-legged on the floorboards. She nodded, her smile revealing several gaps in her teeth. Her hair was a salt and pepper brush, cropped close and framing a round face and merry eyes.

"Smokey, I'm Beth and this is Terry."

She waited, certain that he had something to sell. She wasn't disappointed.

"What can I bring you? I can get ice, fresh bread, you want some fresh fish for your supper? There's no store near this bay, but I can get you whatever you need."

"Okay, well, we already had supper. But some fresh fish tomorrow would be delicious, what do you think Terry?"

"Great idea."

They mentioned a few more items, including a block of ice, and Smokey quoted a price that seemed exorbitant. But Beth nodded and they settled on the time of Smokey's delivery tomorrow.

"Is there anything we should know about anchoring here?" she asked, business settled.

"You lucky to be alone. Another month and this bay be crowded most the time. De boats do what you doin' – stop here before crossing to Dominica or Cuba or Puerto Rico. Sometimes dey go north to Andros, too."

"You must do good business."

"In de winter I do okay." Smokey glanced to the west where the sun was about to disappear. "You be watchin' for de green flash. I see you tomorrow." He shifted his boat into gear and drove away in what felt like an abrupt departure.

"Seems like I shouldn't have mentioned his business," Beth observed as Terry joined her in the cockpit.

"I don't know. He did seem to suddenly decide to get going, but who knows, maybe mama has an appointment or something."

He drew her across the cockpit to where they had an unobstructed view of the setting sun.

"Now don't blink. I don't think we'll see it because of the clouds out there."

"It has to be perfectly clear, doesn't it?"

"Yes. But it's always good to watch the sunset." His mouth was so hear her ear his breath tickled. She was aware of his body pressed against hers, his arms locked around her. Her eyes were on the orange orb in the distance, but her thoughts were consumed by his presence. They had hardly touched since leaving Cuba.

As the sun slid below the distant waves, never showing any color but orange, and she turned in his arms and gave voice to the moan of pleasure that welled in her throat. He silenced it with his lips, hands stroking her back.

"I've missed you," she sighed after a while.
"Let's get reacquainted."

TWENTY-NINE: ST. THOMAS

Their stay in Man of War Bay was idyllic, if short. The morning after their second night at anchor they set the sails while still inside the bay motoring west. For a little while *Trouble* glided downwind on the still water in the protection of the island.

The swells grew as they came around Devil's Point and hauled in the sails to a close reach. *Trouble* rose to the new point of sail, riding up the rolling swells and slicing through their tops, then sliding easily down the other side.

"This isn't bad," Terry observed from behind the helm as he shifted the wheel slightly to compensate for a swell. The breeze ruffled his hair as he glanced upward. Three seagulls circled them, eyes cocked downward looking for signs that the boat was leaving anything tasty in its trail. With raucous cries they swooped down to get a closer look at *Trouble's* wake before arrowing away toward shore.

Beth watched them circle over the surf and then let her eyes wander along the shore of the island until they shut of their own accord. She was unaccountably sleepy after yesterday's vigorous sunning, sleeping, and swimming. But there was no reason not to indulge the urge for a nap in the sun.

Four hours later she was dreaming of sailing in Long Island Sound with her father when Terry nudged her shoulder with a cold bottle of beer.

"It's noon sweetheart, your watch."

The dream evaporated. In an instant all that was left was the sensation of being a child proudly showing off for daddy. And then that was gone too and she was left with a non-specific sense of loss and a clearer sense of guilt: She had not talked to Trish or her parents since they left Miami. Clearly she had not been able to, but that didn't matter.

She opened her eyes just in time to watch Terry take a long sip of the beer. There was a sandwich wrapped in a paper towel on the cockpit table and a can of diet Coke in one of the cup holders.

"You made lunch," she observed. More guilt.

"You looked too comfortable to rouse."

"Thanks, I guess I was." She dropped her feet to the deck and looked around. The boat was heeling more now and the island was much further away. The tropical breeze and sunshine washed away the residual sorrow of the lost dream and tempered the guilt. After all, there was no cellular service here.

"We rounded the southern end of the island. I pulled in the sails and we're heading southeast. More south than east, actually, but it's the best we can do and maintain any kind of speed. Late this evening we'll want to tack before we hit Dominica. Unless you want to go through the Windward passage."

"Uh, no," Beth pictured the chart. They could pass between Cuba and Dominica into the Caribbean Sea, but they'd have to go west to get around Haiti's western headlands before they could turn east again. And the Windward passage was notoriously rough. Instead they would cruise along the northern shores of Dominica, passing Haiti and the Dominican Republic and the island of Puerto Rico before passing into the Caribbean via the Virgin Passage between Puerto Rico and the US Virgin Islands. That passage was studded with the Spanish Virgin Islands that broke up the winds and currents. Terry knew that was the plan, so his question has been rhetorical.

Beth rose and stretched her arms high, crooking her fingers over the top of the boom and pulling her feet an inch off the deck. Dropping her arms she wiggled her shoulders and filled her lungs with salty air.

"Okay. Let me just grab my sweatshirt and I'm on."

And so the routine began again: seven hours on watch with an hour of overlap, five hours off. Each morning when he came on watch Terry pulled the ship's calendar – a free one with a photograph of an endangered animal for each month – out of the navigation desk and drew a line through the previous day. They did not speak about it, but their voyage had become something of a race against the date. Would they spend Christmas in the Virgin Islands or at sea?

At midnight on the fourth day Beth came on deck into the crystalline darkness and picked up both jib sheets.

"Let's tack," she said to Terry, who was sitting in the back corner of the cockpit watching the instruments while the autopilot steered.

Without a word he rose and poised his fingers over the instrument's buttons, then nodded.

"Go."

He pushed two buttons and the boat began to turn. Beth unwrapped the working sheet from the winch and waited for a moment until the bow swung around. The jib flapped wildly, then slapped over to the other side. Beth released the line and hauled in on the other sheet as fast as she could. The jib fell into place along the starboard bow and *Trouble*'s speed began to increase once more. She finished trimming with the winch handle, then pulled it out of the winch and stowed it.

"No stops on Dominica?" Terry's voice was low and even. They had just tacked away from the island. More specifically they had just tacked away from Bahia Del Rincon in the Dominical Republic, a deep, secure bay.

"It's December eighteenth and we have at least three more days, maybe four, of sailing. And we've got plenty of water and food, even if it is in cans, or freezer burned. Are you okay with keeping on?" Her expression showed clear uncertainty about her decision, her hands shoved deep into the pockets of her jacket reinforced it.

"I love a woman who knows her mind," he replied, and seeing that she still looked concerned he added, "I'm good with another few tacks in open water. When we get to the Virgin Passage it's going to seem crowded. We're going to laugh at how short the distances between islands are."

Beth smiled. "Need some coffee?"

"No sir, I'm going to bed in an hour. I'll hold out for an end of watch beer."

Beth pressed the parallel rulers against the chart and made a dot with her mechanical pencil to mark their position four nautical miles due east of little Savana Island. It was December twenty-second and they were in the middle of the Virgin Passage, with Culebra to their west and St. Thomas to the east beyond Savana. She stared at the chart for a long moment, not quite able to believe that they were there.

I've sailed Double Trouble *from New York to the Virgin Islands. Just like I said I would. And not at all like I said I would, too.* She giggled, then glanced out the companionway to see if Terry might have heard her. But he was at the helm enjoying steering on a screaming reach. The wind was a steady fifteen knots and *Trouble* was making the best of it.

Beth did a few more calculations on the chart, marking her predicted route, then stowed her pencil and climbed out into the cockpit.

"Well?" Terry asked, glancing to the east at the islands. They shimmered lush and green between the cobalt sky and aquamarine water. It was breathtaking.

"It's less than ten miles to Brewer's Bay. Let's head up as much as we can. We'll be at anchor by late afternoon.

And they were.

Trouble's anchor was dug in to a sandy bottom ten feet beneath her keel and her main sail was covered for the first time since they'd left Miami. The six other boats in the bay were all well spaced with plenty of privacy for all.

When they were secure Beth bent into the depths of the refrigerator and wrapped her hand around the neck of a bottle that had been waiting there since City Island: the bottle of Dom Perignon from Susan. Behind her Terry was at the navigation station slipping a CD into the stereo. Jimmy Buffett's soothing voice filled the salon.

"What 'cha got there?" Terry asked, then pulled his shirt off over his head. Beth held up the bottle of champagne. "Oh ho, nice!" he said taking the bottle to inspect the label. "Very nice," he added.

"Swim first?"

"Sorry, yeah, it's gotta happen."

"I'm with you. This will keep a few minutes longer."

It kept more than a few minutes, as the swim transitioned to damp caresses in the cockpit and ultimately more intimate caresses on a settee in the salon.

Eventually they brought the champagne along with a can of smoked oysters and the last package of saltines to the cockpit.

They were half way through the bottle, giggling together about everything and nothing, when they noticed a dinghy leave the nearest anchored boat and head in their direction.

"Uh oh, company," Beth crammed the last oyster and cracker in her mouth, then giggled again, crumbs spraying the cockpit table.

"Are we decent?" Terry wondered, oblivious to her mess. He looked down at himself and noted that he was wearing swim trunks. Beth was wrapped in a sarong that kept coming loose.

She realized this at the same moment he did and stood up. Of course it slipped off, which sent them both into gales of laughter as she hastily washed the oyster and cracker down with a gulp of champagne, then picked up the sarong and took it below.

"Ahoy there," there was a pause, then the voice went on, "*Double Trouble* – that sounds dangerous."

Terry stood on a lazarette with one foot on the gunwale and one hand on the bimini support, offering a welcoming smile to the couple in the dinghy.

"We like to think of it more as mischief," he said. "I'm Terry."

"Terry, I'm Al and this is Nancy."

"Hi Terry," Nancy put in.

Al looked along *Trouble*'s side deck at the lashed fuel cans. "Where you coming from? A long way I'll bet."

"The stern says New York," Nancy pointed out.

Terry nodded. "Beth, my girlfriend, brought her from New York. I've been aboard since Miami. That's where we came from – not counting a rest stop at Great Iguana Island."

Nancy's eyes widened and Al gave a soft whistle. "Long haul," he said, sounding impressed. We just hopped over from Puerto Rico, and the Turks and Caicos before that."

"Want to come aboard?" Terry asked, mostly because it was the polite thing to do.

"No, we know how it is when you first get in. We wanted to invite you over for a drink if you're up for it. In an hour or so?" Nancy replied.

Al and Nancy offered a multitude of useful advice about St. Thomas, starting with the simple fact that even though it was a US possession, they needed to check in. Fortunately, they were able to do so at the airport, which was a short walk from a dock where they could leave their dinghy.

In the morning they did just that, enjoying a quick check in process wholly unlike that in Cuba. From there, they caught a taxi to Charlotte Amalia and stopped at a cafe with free wireless internet. Beth guiltily skimmed the items in her mailbox, noting five messages from Trish with increasingly concerned subject lines. She typed out a hasty apology, then thought better of it and pulled her cell phone from her bag.

It had a strong signal, sure sign that they were back in civilization. She held the phone up and nodded at Terry as she stood up and headed toward the door. He nodded back and refocused his attention on his laptop.

"You made it? Oh my God we've been so worried!" was Trish's response when Beth announced first thing that they were safe on St. Thomas. "Why didn't you call or email along the way? Geez, did you get my messages?"

"I'm sorry Trish. We were never anywhere where we had a signal. Honestly. It didn't occur to me that we would be so completely out of touch for so long. I don't know what I was thinking, or I would have been clearer about it."

Beth had no intention of mentioning their Cuban stop over the phone. Eventually, when she visited, she would tell her family all about it in person.

Trish updated her on their father's condition, which had not changed either for the better or the worse. And then she asked inevitably nosey questions about Terry. Beth found herself unable to hold back honest answers. Yes they had. Yes she was. Yes, he said he was too...

"You're living a fairy tale Sis."

"I know. It's a little hard to believe. It's not going to last long, but for the moment, it's pretty amazing."

"Why won't it last?"

"Terry has to go home after Christmas. And I have to find work. I'm still getting the hang of the cruising budget."

"Well, I want you to get it. Crazy huh? After I was against it? But you sound so happy for the first time in I can't remember how long."

"I guess I am. And I'm more determined than ever to make a go of it. Your approval means a lot to me, though."

Beth's next call was to her parents, who were equally glad to hear of her safe arrival in the islands, although she could tell the place was an abstract concept to them. Her father sounded quite lucid and they talked briefly about the beauty of the stars over the open ocean before ringing off with wishes of a merry Christmas.

With email downloaded they went next to a supermarket where they restocked *Trouble*'s depleted pantry and refrigerator. When Terry insisted on paying for half the provisions Beth gave up arguing and accepted his contribution.

On Christmas Eve they took every scrap of cloth they could find ashore to a coin laundry and had lunch at the restaurant next door while it washed. It was the sort of day Beth had been imagining for months. That night they made love on *Trouble*'s foredeck under millions of pinpoints of light and then the eerie silvery glow of the rising moon.

"So, Beth, is this the Christmas dinner you imagined?"

They were seated side by side on a towel, feet in the sand, paper plates with the remains of grilled grouper and vegetables piled on the sand to the side.

Nearby a half dozen sailors were dancing to steel band Christmas carols coming from the speakers of a portable stereo. Beyond the rock that held the stereo the cooking fire still smoldered. Three pre-teens were toasting marshmallows. A few adults stood around the fire as well drinking from cups and bottles, and occasionally refilling their drinks from coolers on the ground near the stereo.

A half dozen dinghys – *Trouble*'s among them – were pulled up on the beach just above the surf. Out past them the sun was a glowing orange ball half an inch above the sea.

"This is the best Christmas ever – beyond anything I could possibly have imagined."

Terry was silent for a minute, then lifted his arm and put it around her shoulders. "Me too," he murmured against the side of her head. "I wouldn't want to be anywhere else in the world tonight."

Beth leaned into him and basked in his warmth, both of his body against hers and of the love growing between them.

In a couple days she would take him to the airport and then it would be time to begin the next chapter of her life. She wasn't quite sure what it would be, but she did know it included re-reading the cryptic email from Ori that she'd downloaded to her computer, and figuring out where her friend was, and why.

SNEAK PEAK:
TROUBLE IN PARADISE
THE NEXT *DOUBLE TROUBLE* ADVENTURE

Chapter One: St. Thomas

"Beth, I hate to do this, but things aren't going well for us."

Beth straightened up to look at Rufus, co-owner of Sunset Charters, where he stood on the dock. She was kneeling on the cockpit seat of a forty-five foot French-built sailboat holding a bleach-soaked scrub brush that she was using to scour red wine stains from the white fiberglass.

"I'm sorry?"

"We're closing down, Beth," Rufus said, his round, chocolate colored features glistening with sweat. He perspired a great deal for a native of the tropics. She wondered whether it was a symptom of a medical problem, but had not grown close enough to him to ask in the month that she'd been working for him.

"In the middle of the season?" she asked, because in that month she had come to understand quite a bit about the Caribbean boat charter business. A mid-season closure meant canceling bookings, which meant returning deposits, or running out on them. She was very glad that she was "off the books" – no creditor of Sunset Charters would know she was ever an employee.

Rufus snorted a dry, sarcastic laugh. "What season? This boat going out tomorrow is the only thing we have booked." He nodded at the boat she was cleaning. "By the time it gets back next week we'll have sold off the office computers. I'm sorry Beth. I know you need the money. I can pay you through this week."

Which ends today, she silently pointed out.

"Thanks Rufus," she said for lack of a better response. She did not have it in her to be angry with him, even though she knew that the business's failure was due, in some part to his lackadaisical management. "I'm sorry about this. I'll come up to the office when I finish here."

"You do that honey. Just stop by and I'll give you this week's pay."

That evening she stretched out in the cockpit of her sailboat, *Double Trouble*, watching the stars and listening to the sounds of the tropical harbor. Strains of steel drum music carried on the seasonal trade wind told her without having to look that there was at least one enormous cruise ship at the dock across the harbor. Closer by the gentle rattle of halyards against masts provided a counterpoint, augmented occasionally by bits of conversation coming from nearby boats in the anchorage. Beneath it all was the susurrus of the shore, the water lapping against coral sand and rocks.

There were worse places to be unemployed in.

She took a gulp of beer and looked at the cell phone in her hand, pressing buttons to find and dial her sister Trish's number.

How many times have I made this call to her? She wondered as she listened to the distant phone ring. She had been let go twice when she lived in New York, until she'd taken the upper hand and quit in order to sail her boat – her floating home – down the coast to the tropics.

"Hello?"

"Trish? It's Beth," she said, knowing her sister refused to get caller ID on the house phone.

"Bethy! It's so good to hear your voice. Is everything all right?"

Beth smiled and took another gulp of beer. That was always the first thing Trish asked her, as if she lived in constant expectation of her sister calling to report disaster. And yet, in the four months that she'd been living the vagabond life of a sailor Beth had never called her sister to report disaster. Not that there hadn't been a few, but Trish was not Beth's confidant in those situations. That would be her next call.

Meanwhile, she filled Trish in on her day, punctuated by her sister's laughs and groans at appropriate moments. Rufus had been nowhere to be found when Beth had entered the small office at the top of the dock, and Inez, the receptionist, had suddenly lost her minimal English language skills. Beth soon had Trish howling at her very politically incorrect imitation of Inez's Spanglish.

Undeterred, Beth had planted herself outside of the office door and waited. Rufus and Albert had finally come along and made up an excuse about being detained at the lawyer's office. Albert reluctantly took out his billfold and counted out Beth's pay, in cash as usual. Then he turned to Inez and did the same.

Despite her own difficult financial position, Beth had felt a pang of sorrow for Inez, whose husband was a known drunk and whose son was in jail for disturbing the peace. Trish scolded her for worrying about others when she herself needed to find another job.

Beth knew her sister wasn't really that heartless, she was just realistic and thought her sister was a bit frivolous.

She eventually managed to assure Trish that she was optimistic about finding work, although she sounded much more positive than she felt at that moment. The conversation then turned to the other requisite topic: their father. He'd been diagnosed with Alzheimer's disease last fall. Their mother had achieved a Thanksgiving miracle by convincing him to take the medications his doctor prescribed, and according to Trish his deterioration had slowed. But that was not the same as recovery, and Beth was still trying to face the fact that he would never be the same man again. She had spent the holidays sailing from Florida to the Caribbean, guiltily skipping the family gathering in California. She knew that she had to go, and soon. But the prospect of her wise, gentle father confused and angry, of having to become an adult in his presence instead of his little girl, was terrifying.

She ended the call with a promise to Trish to try and visit in February. Then she finished her beer and got another from the refrigerator in the galley. Across the harbor the cruise ship's horn blasted, startling sleeping seagulls into a surprise nocturnal flight.

"All ashore what's goin' ashore," Beth muttered. She could swear she could feel the vibration as the ship's monstrous propellers started to turn.

She settled back into the cockpit and returned to her phone's directory, seeking the number of the person she most wanted to speak to. She loved Trish, but she was in love with the man who in a moment would answer his phone while walking home from his office on the streets of Washington, DC.

In fact, Terry Faughnan was sitting on a bar stool in the bar down the block from his office where he and his partner Jeff had brought most of their team of six for Friday happy hour. He was finishing his second beer and trying to decide whether to order a burger for dinner or decline Jeff's invitation to stay and opt for an hour at the gym. The gym was winning. He'd done more than a few bachelor dinners with Jeff – who was married – lately. Before the last of the team could get away and leave him to make excuses to Jeff he slipped off the bar stool and said his good byes. He shot an apologetic shrug at his partner's disappointed look, then made his escape.

Damn, it's cold here, he thought for the millionth time since leaving Beth in the islands a month ago. The fact that it was the end of January hardly made it more comfortable. He buttoned his coat, pulled his scarf up around his chin, and summoned the memory of his last few days aboard *Trouble* to carry him home.

They had been living in the moment for more than a month and it had been a romantic, adventurous idle. No one could blame either of them for wanting it to go on and on. But such idles required financing, and aside from that Terry knew that he needed the challenges of his chosen work, if for no other reason than to provide contrast and make him appreciate the time off even more. He thought Beth shared this philosophy – after all she'd put up with that awful job in Miami to earn enough pennies for this leg of the trip when she'd surely known he'd cover the expenses. But here they were on the eve of his departure back to "the real world" and they had not yet discussed the future. Their future.

"Keep an eye on the alternator belt. You can adjust the tensioner maybe once more, then you'll have to replace it."

"I will. I'll pick up a replacement for ship's stores."

He shook his head and smiled ruefully, "I already did."

"Thanks." Thankfully Beth had given up telling him he didn't have to buy things for her boat. He had kept doing it, and the truth was she had needed his help. After he left he knew she was going to face the grim truth: she had grossly underestimated the expense of maintaining a sailboat. He was confident that she would devise a new income plan, and knew that it might include leaving *Trouble* here and flying to the states to find a job. He also knew that the idea terrified her because it was like giving up. He couldn't leave without having some idea of what she was thinking of doing, and getting a chance to reassure her.

As if knowing his thoughts, she'd stopped picking at her dinner and looked up into his eyes. She looked desperately sad.

"The question is, what are you going to do now?" Terry held his breath for a moment, fearful of Beth's response. They couldn't avoid the topic any longer. Unless, he considered as he watched her wary expression, she did not want to tell him. She was like that sometimes, or had been at first: shutting him out of things that troubled her, letting her concerns build up until she lashed out at him for no apparent reason. He feared that she was about to do that now. And that hurt him, just a little bit. What was the future of their relationship if she couldn't even share her plans, let alone include him in any of the decision making? He had no right, really, to expect her to since he was leaving her here. But if she did discuss it with him, well, that would be a sign that she considered him part of her life even if he wasn't physically present. He needed that sign to take back with him. Otherwise, why continue this long distance?

"Well, first thing is moving out to the anchorage to stop paying for the slip," she said tentatively.

"You'll need to patch that scrape on the dinghy," he said without thinking.

"I know!" she snapped.

"Sorry. I just hate to think of it deflating while you're in it, and you'll need it like a commuter needs a car if you're at anchor."

She grimaced and picked at her fish with her fork.

"That's the truth. I need to find some work."

He watched her, recognizing the familiar avoidance techniques. She really didn't want to talk about it with him. He wasn't sure whether he was more hurt or frustrated, and at moments like this he wondered whether to just let it go. Except that he was in love with this difficult, private, stubborn woman and he wasn't ready to break his own heart just yet. So he persevered despite her obvious reticence.

"You could put *Trouble* in dry storage here. I'll front you the initial payment," he shook his head slightly to silence the protest she was about to make. "You could – you should – go see your parents. Then go back to New York and work for a while. Or –," he paused, considered his next words for a split second, and then plunged on, "or come to DC."

Her head popped up, her eyes wide with surprise.

"To DC?" she repeated as if the thought had never crossed her mind. As he watched her he realized that it probably had not. He had never been involved with a woman who hadn't started hinting at cohabitation – in his habitat – after a few weeks. But then, Beth knew nothing about his home.

"Well, what's in New York to make you go back there? Some stuff in storage? But no family, right?"

"No. Just friends."

His level gaze was penetrating, his message clear: *Am I a more important friend than them?* She peered back at him, trying to find words to express her heart.

"Just to be clear, you mean come stay with you," she finally said with a teasing smirk.

"Of course I mean stay with me! What would be the point of you coming to DC and paying rent?" He allowed his frustration with her obtuseness to flare and immediately regretted it when she cringed.

"Sometimes things can seem too good to be true," she said timidly. "I didn't want to assume."

He set down his fork and reached across the table, taking her left hand in his and drawing it part way back so that their hands met in the middle of the space between them.

"This is more than just a sailing fling to you, isn't it Beth?"

"Yes. Oh yes it is Terry."

"It is to me too. So when I ask you to come to DC, you can safely assume that I mean to stay with me, in my house. And in my bed, for that matter, although I do have guest rooms."

She squeezed his hand, the tension in her face fading as her genuine smile spread over it. "Thank you Terry. I may take you up on it. But I'm not ready yet. I'm not ready to give up on sailing."

Disappointing as her decision was, he respected it.

"My girlfriend lives on St. Thomas," he said thoughtfully, at once conveying his acceptance of her choice and making himself smile. "I like the sound of that."

"So do I – except technically it's 'off of' St. Thomas, not on it."

He smirked at her. "Okay. So if you can find some work around here, what do you think you'll do? How long will it take you to replenish the bankroll? And where do you want to go next?"

He knew that she had set out from New York a few months ago with a vague plan to get here. She'd plotted her course down the East Coast, but left open the details of getting from Florida to the Caribbean, including whether she was going it alone or with help. Fortunately she'd taken him aboard in Miami, because the trouble they'd had with the boat off of Florida would have been almost impossible for her to get through single handed. He did not want to suggest that she should not sail her own boat by herself. She had heard that advice before, so he did not need to nag her. The better choice was to find out what she was thinking and try to fit into her plans.

"I guess I'd like to work my way down the islands," she said thoughtfully. "I've heard so many stories, it seems like each one has its own personality. I'd like to meet them all."

His enthusiastic smile encouraged her to fantasize further.

"And then, what about the Panama Canal? Cross through to the Pacific. Maybe I'll visit my parents by boat!"

"Show up at their house like the end of *Romancing the Stone*?"

They both chuckled at the mental image. He saw *Trouble* on a trailer on Third Avenue, but she saw her boat parked in the driveway of her parents' suburban house, the nosey next door neighbor looking out between the slats of the Venetian blind on her living room window.

"So you'll come back and join me for the Canal?" she asked.

"I'd love to. But I was hoping you'd invite me for the entire cruise."

"It'll take months," she shrugged, shooting him an apologetic smile. "How could you do it?"

"I could arrange a six month leave starting around the end of March."

"Really?"

"It's still top secret, but Jeff and I are selling the company. He's such a workaholic he wants to stay on during the transition, but given my current situation I don't. That's how we're negotiating the deal."

"Wow. What will you do afterwards?"

"You mean, after sailing around the world with you?"

"You're really negotiating yourself out of a job so you can sail with me?"

"I'm negotiating the very profitable sale of a business that will leave me with free time. I'd like to use that time to sail with you, if you'll have me."

Beth looked down at the half-eaten snapper filet on her plate. She picked up her fork, clearly buying time to absorb his offer. He knew that it flew in the face of her basic plan to do this on her own. But what was the point of that, really? When she could do it with a man she loved? Life didn't offer chances like this very often.

"So I have until the end of March to pad the bankroll and plan the next leg," she said, afraid to come out and accept his offer. But he wasn't going to let her off the hook.

"You'll have me, then?"

"Yes! Of course I'll have you. God, I'm going to miss you while you're gone. Maybe I'll go visit my parents for a few days after all."

The wave of pleasure that surged over Terry took him completely by surprise. He had not realized how much he wanted to hear her express regret for his departure. What he'd feared was ambivalence had been Beth playing it cool, probably not wanting to make him feel guilty for having to go.

"I'm going to miss you too Bethy," he sighed, reaching for her hand to squeeze it once more.

Later that night they'd moved the boat out to the anchorage and made love under the stars in the cockpit, a pleasure that they had experienced several times during the month of their cruise. At dawn they'd brought her back to the slip so that he could offload his luggage. As they stood together outside of the marina office waiting for the airport van he studied his calendar in his Palm Pilot, looking for an opportunity to return for a visit. But the van had come before they had firmed up a plan. They'd kissed goodbye and Beth had stood waving until the van rounded a on the waterfront road and he lost sight of her.

As planned, she'd moved *Trouble* out to the anchorage, singlehandedly dropping the anchors and digging them in with the boat's engine. It was a skill he'd helped her to perfect, making her do it on her own until she had both failed and succeeded enough times to know how to respond to any situation. He realized as he walked along the hard sidewalks that he'd never asked whether she'd patched the worn spot on the inflatable dinghy. He knew the reason she was reluctant was because of how hard it was to take off the outboard engine, and then put it back on. But she had practiced each of these tasks too, and he knew she could do it.

He'd been thrilled and a little surprised when they spoke two days after he got back to Washington and she was excited about finding a job. come upon the notice from Sunset Charters on a bulletin board in the local grocery store. It wasn't her first choice, cleaning charter boats and helping the over-excited customers get settled aboard at the start of their holidays. But she'd said that the charter company owners, Rufus and Albert, had offered it to her on the spot when she came to inquire and she'd thought that must be a sign. To Terry it sounded like to small a business to compete against the sailing charter dynasties that served most of the Caribbean. But he hadn't told her that.

She'd told him that she found it amusing the way the charter customers, mostly Americans, consistently latched on to her as an authority figure as they were checking out their rented boats. Her ego prevented her from telling them that she was just the boat cleaner. He wasn't at all surprised that soon she'd started acting in a liaison role, fetching missing supplies, explaining policies, and even offering restaurant suggestions. Her deep tan, carefully built up through constant application of sunscreen, suggested that she was a local and the customers simply assumed she knew the island. Terry wasn't sure why, but she'd tried to tell most guests that she was almost as new there as the he was. Rufust had overheard and pulled her aside, telling her not to disillusion them, just answer their questions. She'd said felt used, knowing that he was getting a lot more from her than just the boat washing he was paying for. Terry agreed, but he didn't urge her to push for a promotion. He was sure that Rufus didn't have the resources – if he did he would have hired someone for customer service.

He looked forward to talking to her, and expected that she'd call before he made it home. The prospect of hearing her voice made him fizz with excitement and he caught himself feeling for his cell phone in his pocket to make sure it wasn't ringing.

"Bethy my love, how are de islands, mon?"

She smiled despite his lame Rasta accent. "Paradise, mon. Just another shitty day in paradise." She allowed her voice to convey that her description was real, not just a joke.

"Uh-oh, that doesn't sound so good." He picked up on her meaning. "Something wrong Sweetheart?"

"Sunset Charters is no longer in business. I hope you hadn't booked a vacation with them."

"Damn! I was just about to write the check. So you're out of work?"

"That would be the bottom line. I had to practically pick Albert's pocket to get my last pay, too."

"I'm sorry honey, that sucks."

"I know. It really does. Another two weeks and I'd have saved enough to fill the fuel tank." She was joking, but her savings were not all that much more extensive.

"But hey, it's the high season. I bet you'll find something else pretty easily."

To his credit, he did not offer to send her money. She was especially glad because after a couple beers, and loosing her job, she might not have been able to say no.

"How's your father? Have you told him and your mom yet?" This was his unsubtle way of reminding her that she should go visit. She could not blame him for taking advantage of the timing.

"I talked to Trish. They're doing okay – he's taking his meds."

"That's good. Are they helping?"

"Some. I guess. She says so anyway."

"Good. You know there is a lot of study of that disease going on. Who knows, they may cure it any day."

"I know. Anything's possible. How's the wheeling and dealing going?" This was her unsubtle question about his possibly visiting.

"I feel like a hamster – on a treadmill, you know? I've reviewed the same contracts and agreements six times. They keep going back and forth from our lawyer to us to their lawyer to them, each of us making little changes. And at the same time we've got five training programs going at once in three different countries."

"Crazy."

"And I'm crazy to let it keep me here away from you."

"Don't be silly. You need to close this deal. I'll muddle along here."

"It's so frigging cold here though. What's the temperature there? Eighty?"

"Eighty three."

"Don't say another word. I – hold on." There was a scream of tires on asphalt and Beth waited for the concluding thunk, but none came. "It's okay," Terry went on. "Taxi thinking it could make the yellow light nearly hit a pedestrian. Not me, though."

"I can't even remember what it's like to walk on city streets."

"I know how to refresh your memory."

"Yeah, yeah. I know."

"Okay," she could hear the grin in his voice. He accepted her decision, but he wasn't going to give up. "Listen, I'm almost home and I really want to hit the gym. It's been days. Can I call you back later?"

"You know that you can."

"Good. I'll call when I get home later."

"Love you."

"Yeah, that too."

Beth was grinning when she stood up to stretch and look around the dark anchorage. The cruise ship was a white blob on the horizon now, a horizontal plume of smoke leading west from its stacks lit eerily by the half moon. There were warm yellow lights in the cabins of some of the boats anchored nearby. Her neighbors in this strange water-borne community. After she'd set her anchors a month ago two residents had come by in their dinghys to welcome her. One had brought two mangos and a papaya, the other had brought a bottle of wine. The next day a third sailor came by with a snapper he'd caught that morning. Beth had taken their cue and when a new boat anchored a couple days later she puttered over in her patched dingy to welcome them and offer a half dozen muffins she'd baked.

In this way she'd become a part of the sailing community, exchanging cell phone numbers, hailing frequencies and collecting boat calling cards from the experienced cruisers. As soon as she had a positive balance in her savings account she wanted to get cards made with her name and S/V *Double Trouble*.

Speaking to the neighbors, as well as the sailors hanging around the marina and even some of the customers at Sunset Charters she had begun to amass their collected wisdom about her planned cruise. Even today, knowing that it was her last one at Sunset, she had enjoyed a chat with the arriving charterers and added to her notes about the anchorages around the British Virgin Islands. Today's sailor had strongly recommended a stop to snorkel the Dogs near Virgin Gorda.

Beth took her beer below and fired up the laptop. She smiled to herself at the gauge on *Trouble's* switch panel that told her the batteries were completely charged. She had successfully installed a solar panel over the bimini after scrounging it from the boatyard where Sunset had some of their repair work done. She'd had to invest in the wires and converter, but she'd found them used along with a lot of free advice at one of the parts shops in town.

Two hours later she had captured her day's experiences in a dozen or so pages and consumed yet another beer. She had come to realize months ago when she first undertook this voyage just how much time watching television robbed from her. Living without one she could easily spend two hours writing and not think anything of it. She had always been a good writer – she had made a living writing marketing copy for publishers and corporations before giving it all up and setting sail. She knew that her evenings documenting experiences that were entirely new to her were refining and altering her style. For the moment she was doing it for herself, but the notion of using what she had written somehow was bobbing around at the back of her mind. Still, whenever it forced its way to the fore she squelched it, noting to herself that there were dozens – hundreds – of literate sailors out cruising the world and plenty of them submitted their stories to magazines. Why would hers be selected over all the others? She had nothing special to say.

ABOUT THE AUTHOR

A Southern California native, S. Mia McCroskey started writing when she was in ninth grade. She took up sailing when she was in her twenties as an antidote to an unpleasant job. It was a toss up between sailing lessons and pottery classes. She flipped a coin; the quarter was a lucky one. She moved from California to New York for a better job a couple years later and continued sailing in Long Island Sound and the Chesapeake Bay. Since stepping aboard that first soling in Marina del Rey she has become qualified to charter large, valuable sailboats in fascinating locales all over the world, and has gotten used to being called "the lady captain" by the locals. In her professional career she transitioned from a magazine and book editor to managing software development. She attributes most of her professional leadership skills to her experience handling crews of friends and acquaintances aboard sailboats. She has never owned her own boat, but she did eventually take pottery classes.